Fairywing

D. H. Torkavian

ISBN: 978-1-7352273-0-6

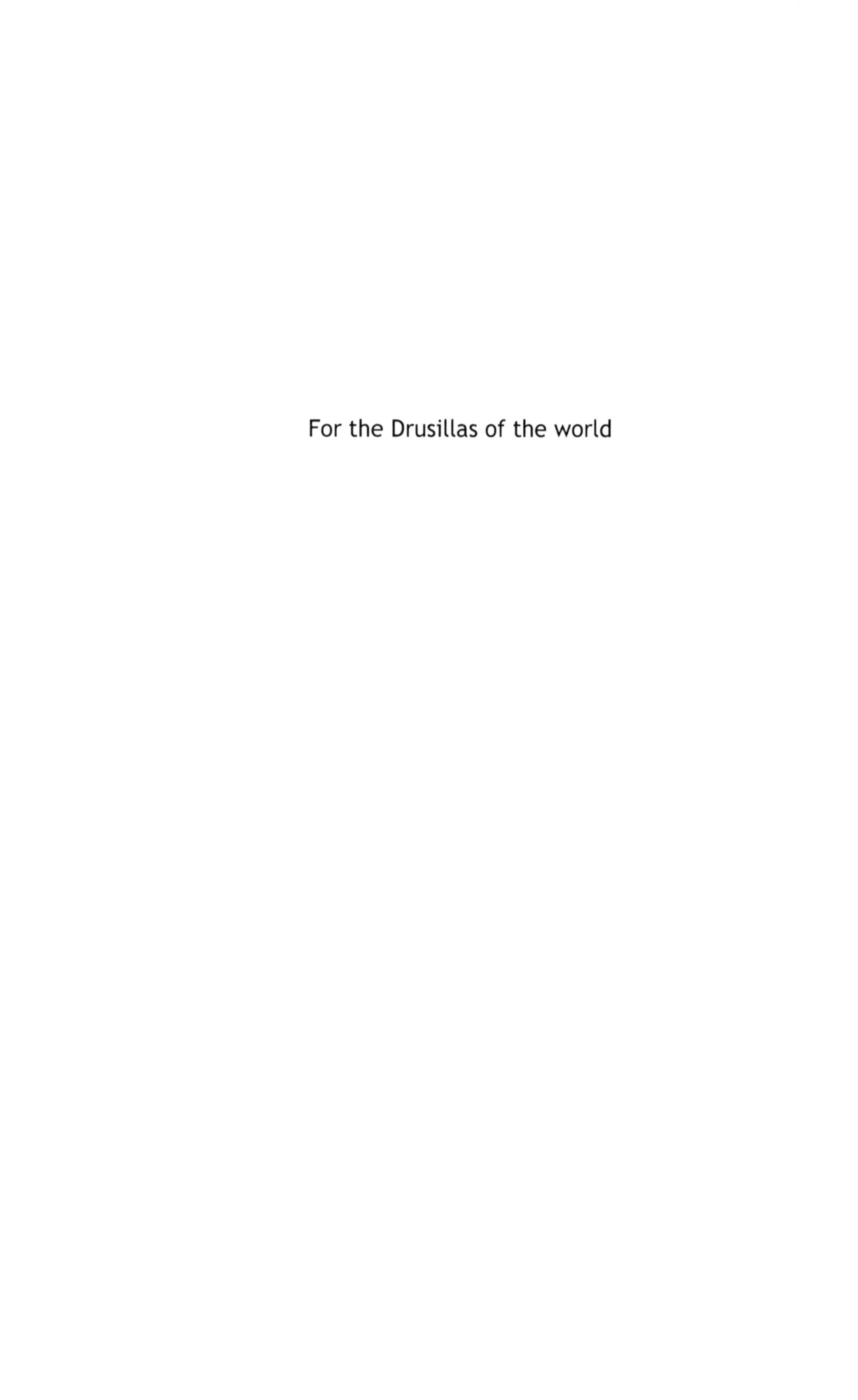

For the Drusillas of the world

ACKNOWLEDGMENTS

Thank you to my sister Jessica for being there every step of the way. To Brett for being Brett when I needed a Brett. To all my beta readers, you know who you are. To Dawn for her amazing editing skills. To Kelly and Paul of Velveteen Lounge Kitsch-en, Cindy and Stacy of the Creepy Kitch Podcast, and the music of the Birthday Massacre for helping me through the tough times, And to Jodie, Kriss, and Zarazaiel for final touches. Without you this would not be possible. Thank you.

CONTENTS

Trigger warning:

This narrative includes themes of violence, sexual abuse, snark, ugly moments, and at times even uglier fashion choices. If you find you are too sensitive to these themes I would recommend against reading Fairywing.

Prologue

Jack was nimble. Jack was quick. Jack was Elderberry High's track star. Not many people could hold a candlestick to Jack. Everybody wanted a piece of Jack. His father wanted Jack to go into the family business, and he had been accepted to Brown in the fall. Girls always found time to let Jack have his way with them. Every guy wanted Jack as a buddy. He really did have it all, but most importantly, Jack ran. Jack ran so fast. It was what he really cared about. He was happiest when he ran. Every night after dinner, Jack would go for a run through the woods. It was his time away from it all. No pressure. Just running.

Jack laced his running shoes and kissed his mother goodbye as he left through the side door. Jack checked his watch, and then he ran through the brisk air along the sidewalk. The woods lay beyond. He slipped between two trees and booked it through the woods, zig-zagging to avoid trees and bushes. He was testing himself, timing his runs every night. Pulling his time tighter and tighter together. Keep moving, Jack. Always room to improve.

Jack ran so fast that it felt like he wasn't even touching the ground. Everything whizzed past Jack as he ran. The perfect blue-eyed, blond haired track star flew through the woods at speeds that defied human capability. He felt free. It felt like he accomplished everything. Intoxication flooded his veins as Jack howled with delight. This was everything.

The branch whipped out of nowhere. It was too fast for Jack

to react. It collided with his Adam's apple, and the force of the tree branch knocked him flat. His head lay at an awkward angle. Then with a dull snapping sound, the whole tree came crashing down on Jack. No one heard a thing. The trunk splintered over his broken body and then, silence. Jack was nimble, Jack was quick, and now? Jack was dead.

Chapter 1

Mary Bonnet had locked herself in the bathroom. It was six o'clock in the morning, and her father and sister were fighting... again. She did her best to shut them out as she got ready for school. Mary smeared cover-up over the bags under her eyes and wished her mother was- Mary stopped that dirty thought. She shook her head like it was an Etch A Sketch; she wanted to erase any image that remained of her mother. Don't think about her; not her purple eyes, not her long black hair, not the coldness. The yelling between her father and older sibling became louder, derailing Mary's train of thought. She hated it when they fought. Mary added mascara and eyeliner. Her goal was to make herself look nothing like herself.

"This is not the time for your bullshit! I have to get Mary to school!" she heard Drusilla screech.

"You sound just like your mother, you filthy faggot!" their father roared.

"Oh yeah that's nice. You're dad of the fucking year!"

"Well, maybe if you weren't such a freak she'd – I wouldn't have to do this alone!"

Smack! Mary wasn't sure if Drusilla had slapped her father, or the other way around, but she could make her guesses.

"Shut your fucking mouth. Mary can hear you, Dumbass." Drusilla's voice was angry, but hushed. Mary could still hear.

Tears mingled with Mary's makeup and streaked down her face. Taking a powder puff, Mary patted over her tears with setting powder. It only worked if she looked perfect. Then, Mary covered everything around her eyes with setting spray. There, that should-

A sharp knock against the door startled Mary into a jump. "Mary, we have to go," came Drusilla's husky voice. "You almost done?"

Mary opened the door to the bathroom. Drusilla looked wild. Her violet eyes were bloodshot, rimmed in heavy black eyeliner and shadow, and the pale concealer she used to cover up her stubble was thick like pancake batter. Mary didn't understand why Drusilla wanted to be a girl, but then shoot herself in the foot by hacking off all of her hair and wearing frumpy black clothes. Back when Drusilla was still Mary's brother, she had long, thick black hair like... that wasn't important. What was important was that Drusilla get out of that black hoodie and weird ass legging-miniskirt combo. She needed to let that hair grow to help soften that jawline. It was almost absurd how easy she would be to fix.

"I'm not being seen in public with you like that. Go put on a nice dress," Mary said.

"Mary, you have five minutes to get in Tank, or you can walk to school," Drusilla growled, and then stomped off.

Drusilla's van was just as frumpy and just as black as Drusilla. There were no back windows so everyone at school thought Drusilla kept missing kids in the back. Like she was snacking on them, or something. Mary and Drusilla loved the van. Tank, they named her. Mary decided a long time ago that if Tank were a person, she would be the biggest, butchest, most sexiest lesbian on the block. Drusilla went along with it, but she drew the line when Mary wanted to add chubby mud-flap maidens to Tank's back tires.

Mary darted out of the bathroom like a cat and followed. Her father - a chunky man with a crooked back, balding scalp, bristly mustache, and thick-ass glasses - sat in his beat-up comfy chair in the corner of a grubby living room. Mary gave a quick wave and darted out to the van. Drusilla probably wouldn't have really left her, but being late for the first day of school was not going to happen.

*

Drusilla looked up at the old, dingy house. It was leaning a little more than it was yesterday. Drusilla groaned. Mary hopped into her seat. Drusilla cranked Tank to life. She gave a side-glance to Mary to see if she was alright. Mary sat in the passenger seat looking perfect and scrolling through her phone. Her blond hair was in soft waves with a pink headband in it, neat makeup in natural tones, and baggy clothes that hid her suggestive outfit from their father. Mary's green eyes caught Drusilla's. Drusilla drove.

"You could be such a pretty girl if you wanted," Mary said.

"Mary, not today." Drusilla groaned. "We've been over this every day, and-"

"And I'm right!" Mary declared dramatically.

"Yes, well, I don't want to be a 'pretty girl'. It's not who I am."

"But-"

"But, nothing. I can't just start wearing pink and twirling my hair."

"Well, yeah. You keep chopping it the fuck off," Mary fired. "I am just trying to help you."

"I know Mary, but-"

"It's not who you are, got it." Mary rolled her eyes and went back to her phone. "But maybe if you tried to be cute, you'd get laid, and then you'd walk around with a big smile on your face instead of being a big, old bitch to everybody. Maybe Paul would-"

Drusilla slammed on the brakes at a red light. Mary's rib cage collided with the seat belt and flung her back against the seat. Frightened children cringed in the middle of the crosswalk. An elderly crossing guard blew his whistle and pushed the red stop sign in Tank's direction. Drusilla glared at the old man, wishing she had mowed him and the children down. She shot a glance to Mary, who was breathing heavily.

"Paul would what, Mary?" Drusilla had to fight to keep from yelling.

"Oh, come on, so him and his friends didn't get it at first. I'm sure-"

"He and his friends," Drusilla corrected. "And Paul Hunt and the other traitors jumped me. I think that's way beyond 'didn't get it'. What are you, crazy?"

"It's not like you didn't get them back for it. I'm sure Paul is still carrying scars," Mary replied.

Drusilla thought on that. "Emotional or physical?"

"Well, I'm sure he still has teeth marks," Mary said

Drusilla laughed and hoped it was both. "The scumbag."

"You'd look cuter with a red lip. That black on black on black is so bland," Mary said, quickly switching back to her main point.

"I'll think about it." Drusilla said it more to shut her up than anything. Mary always tried to dress her up. It was sweet really, but it was too bad Drusilla hated sweet.

Elderberry was a small, bland little slice of East Coast suburbia. Most of the town's money came from the wineries. Drusilla sneered at the boring, neat homes, shopping center, mall, and finally Elderberry high school. Drusilla's heart sank to her stomach as it did every weekday morning. Mary went into the back of the van to strip out of her sweater and baggy jeans. Drusilla parked. Mary slid open the side door to hop out in her pink halter-top and white miniskirt. She kicked her sneakers into the van and slipped her pink-socked feet into white pumps. Mary walked as if she were on a catwalk to the driver's side for Drusilla's approval.

"Well?" Mary said.

Drusilla took one look at her sister. She was way passed mortification and now was just mildly guilty. "You look like you're ready to break dress codes."

Mary smiled. "Perfect!"

Drusilla rolled her eyes at that. "You have condoms, right?"

"How else do you touch all the boys?" Mary smiled.

"Not every boy plays nice, Mary," Drusilla warned. "Maybe I should try to teach you how to kick box again. What do you-?"

"Can we stop at the garden supply place after school today?" asked Mary.

"I have work today," Drusilla said as she played with her hair in the side mirror. Her bangs weren't keeping in the triangle point she wanted them to. She would need to cut them again. It was annoying how fast her hair grew. "Tomorrow I'm off, though. We can go then."

"Awesome – love you, bye," Mary said as she made her way towards the school.

"But what about... never mind," Drusilla sighed. There she goes, Drusilla thought as she watched Mary's back. Off to break hearts, or penises, or whatever she thinks she's doing. Drusilla shook off her worry and gave herself one final look over before locking up Tank. Her makeup was already smudging; of course it was. Fuck! If she wanted to look beautiful, she'd let Mary dress her. Drusilla moved past the van towards the building. Another fucking day. If she was lucky, nothing interesting would happen. Or did she mean unfortunate? Whatever. Drusilla rolled her eyes at that thought and moved in the direction of school.

The car came out of nowhere. It was a sleek, fast, silvery blue. Loud, crappy music blared at her from within the vehicle. It was like a large techno spewing land-shark, and it was darting for her. Drusilla's stomach lurched. She could feel her body start to lock up on her. The car was going to hit her. She forced her body into action and jumped back, hoping that she wouldn't end up a bloody smear. Drusilla fell back out of the driver's path. The car skidded to a stop and reversed. Drusilla crinkled her nose against the burnt rubber smell and lifted her hurting body off the asphalt. Someone was going to die for this.

The driver rolled down the window with the click of a button and swallowed hard. Drusilla didn't recognize him. The new guy stuck his shaggy head out of the window. His crystal eyes and brown skin paled as panic set in. He would have been cute if not for the fact that his brains were located in his ass, Drusilla thought. She picked herself off the pavement and dusted grit off her. She shot a glare at the guy. He had on a blue and white flannel over a baggy gray shirt.

"Shit, are you okay?" he asked in what must have been half a panic attack. "I am so sorry."

"Hey, man, what's that? Techno?" Drusilla asked in a friendly voice.

"Um..." The new guy looked confused a little. "No, dub-step."

"Who the fuck listens to dub-step?" Drusilla yelled as she kicked the driver side tire. Heat clotted in her face and warmed her rage. "Learn to drive, Asshole!"

"Hey!"

Drusilla walked in front of his shiny car. Her black-polished middle finger held firmly up at him the whole way around. Welcome to Elderberry High, you big bag of dicks, Drusilla thought as she sneaked a peek at his shocked face. His large eyes blinked at her with disbelief. Drusilla wished she could flip his car with him in it. The fuckhead. Speeding through a busy parking lot with her in it. He should have had the good sense to do that shit when Paul was in the parking lot, or Pan. It would be awesome if Pan got mowed over by that fuckhead. Drusilla looked at the new guy again. There were enough assholes to go around at this school.

*

Michael Prince made his way through the cramped traffic jam that was Elderberry High's hallways, and he was lost. He had a map in one hand, a class schedule in the other, and with the welcome he got, there was no way in hell he was asking for directions. Michael looked around. The faceless student body bustled past him clumsily. Michael sighed and rubbed his eyes. This was all giving him a headache. He should go take out his contacts and plop on his glasses. Maybe once he found out where he was going, Michael told himself.

"Michael Prince?" Michael thought he heard. He looked around. It sounded like an echo. There was no one. Michael went back to his map. "Michael Prince?" Again, Michael looked around and no one was calling his name. What was this? "Michael Prince?" Michael turned to look. Nothing. Okay then. He turned back to walk away.

The hand clapped down on his shoulder, and Michael jumped. A scrawny beanpole of a guy stood there as if he had popped out of the ground. He was mahogany skinned, with closely clipped hair and a green and white shirt that hung off of his shoulders. His jeans had holes in them.

“Where did you come from?” Michael said.

“Hey, didn't mean to startle you. I was calling your name. You are Michael Prince, right?” he said. “I'm George Geppetto.”

“Oh, cool,” Michael said. “Are you supposed to show me around?”

“I like to help out the new people.” George shrugged and held out his hand. “Let me look at your schedule,” then he yanked it out of Michael's hands. “Okay, cool. Your classes aren’t too out of the way from each other.”

George showed Michael where the cafeteria, gym and the nurse's office were. Everyone around Michael seemed to melt into a blur. A half-dazed looking girl in a red hoodie walked past with her hairy boyfriend who had on shades and a gray blazer. Three really fat, blond guys that had pig-like turned up noses sneered at Michael as they passed. A tall, broad guy with a full black beard, a red flannel, and trucker hat flipped through a hunting magazine with a pretty blond standing triumphantly over a dead elephant on the cover. He was surrounded by worshiping guys.

Michael and George passed a row of lockers, and Michael spotted the goth girl struggling with her locker. She yanked on it violently, spun the combination lock around a few times, and tried again. She threw her fist into the already dented metal, and then yanked a couple more times. In frustration, she raked her nails along the locker. The screech of the metal made Michael want to tear out his ears. A few passers-by moved out of her way and gave her a wide birth.

“Who's that?” Michael asked George.

George's eyes widened. “Stay away from *that*,” George warned

“What do you mean, *that*?” Michael asked.

“It's a witch, don't touch it!”

"What do you mean, it's a witch?" Michael asked.

"Yo, I am not even joking. That's a witch; don't mess with it unless you want something bad to happen to you. Look at Jack Horner. He pissed her off for something or other, and he died a few days ago. Coincidence? I think not. He's not the only one, too."

"Holy shit!" Michael exclaimed. "Someone died?"

"Yeah. Jack Horner was the school's track star, but not after *that* got done with him. They found him in the woods. I heard his neck was snapped. Everyone that pisses the witch off gets it." George wasn't joking. There was real fear in his eyes.

"But why did you call her an it?" Michael asked.

"Yo, man. If Drusilla Bonnet's around, I want nothing to do with the situation, and trust me, you don't either." George said that, and like a flash, was gone.

Michael didn't know what was with George, but Michael walked over to Drusilla. She had gone back to scratching and pounding on the locker. Drusilla breathed heavily and little patches of pink were on her cheeks like little blush butterflies. Wow, Michael thought. He liked that. He liked the short, jagged hair too. It was different. He had seen goth girls before, yeah, but they always seemed so frilly. There was something feral about her, like if you weren't careful...

"Hey," Michael said. "You need help with that?"

She turned to glare at him. "You know everything your friend said over there? It's true."

"Not all of it. You're not an it," Michael said.

Drusilla froze for a second. Then, she rolled her violet eyes and went back to spinning the combo lock. "What is this, some peace offering? Well, don't worry, you didn't make my list. You can go now." She made a shooing motion at him with her wicked claws.

"I'm really good with locks. I'll have you out of here in two seconds."

"Fine." Drusilla gave a big sigh and moved out of the way. "The combo is 2-10-22."

"Cool, I'm Michael Prince," he said as he shifted in front of the locker.

"Somebody has to be," Drusilla said, more to herself than him.

The maroon paint was flaked off from years of deep scratches. He fiddled with the locker. With ease, Michael unlocked and opened it. Drusilla shoved him away as she moved in to grab her stuff. She was strong, Michael noted. It excited him. Then, she turned to Michael. Her stubble peeked through the heavy makeup. She wasn't very pretty, but there was something about those eyes. Purple eyes. Michael had never seen purple eyes before, and never had he seen eyes as on fire with repressed rage. His blood rushed from one head to another in an instant.

"Thanks, now fuck off." Drusilla growled as she slammed her locker shut.

Michael watched as Drusilla turned and faded away like a ghost in the crowd. Impressed, he lifted his chin, stood on the tips of his toes, and tried to spot her, but she was gone. Perhaps she really was a witch. Nice. Michael kind of liked the thought of that. Witches were cool. Drusilla Bonnet. "How interesting."

*

Mary sat with her friends, Anne and Sarah, in homeroom. They weren't really her friends. She didn't hang out with them outside of school, but they did make her look good. They gossiped, flipped their hair, and checked their makeup. Mary fell in suit. It was easy. Everyone was abuzz about Jack Horner's death. Mary didn't want to think about it, so she steered her friends away from that topic as best she could. Not like it was working or anything. What she needed was a distraction.

The door opened and Mary flipped her long blond hair as she looked, in case it was a boy. She was so glad she did. He was new, a Latino guy, and *oh so* very sexy! He was tall, with dark messy hair and a muscular build. At least she hoped that's what was under those horrible clothes. He didn't dress well, but it was a good thing you didn't need clothes in bed, she thought. Yummy, Mary mouthed in hopes that he would see. He didn't seem to, but the only empty desk was next to her. This just kept getting better and better for Mary. The new guy made his apologies for being late and sat next to her.

“Hi, I'm Mary Bonnet,” Mary said before anyone could get a word in. Mary decorated herself with a wide smile and her hand outstretched.

“Oh, so you must be related to Drusilla Bonnet,” he replied. “I'm Michael Prince.”

Of course. Mary felt her insides curdle. Her friends snickered behind her. Michael’s perfect blue eyes shifted to them, and his eyebrows furrowed. Mary tried to wilt. Maybe looking sad could get the attention back on her. Michael Prince was unmoved. Shit! She was losing him. Work fast, Bitch. She hiked her smile back up and did her best to grab his attention. Michael's eyes flicked back on her, but not in the way she wanted.

“Yeah, I'm her sister,” Mary answered, feeling *mortified*.

“Oh my god, she actually admitted that!” Anne said to Sarah.

“I know! I wouldn't have.” Sarah cackled and Anne joined in. They laughed like hyenas.

Mary felt awful, but she didn't say anything. Michael shook his head, pulled out a notebook, and began writing something down. He didn't seem to be in the mood to talk anymore. Mary could feel the heat from her chest reach her ears. She quickly primped her hair to hide any redness. It didn't matter anyway. Michael didn't look up for the rest of homeroom. Fucking awesome, Mary grumbled to herself. Her friends went back to the topic of Jack. Mary half wished that she'd be next.

*

Drusilla sat in the corner of the art room, away from everyone else. It was how she liked it. No one bothered her. They didn't even bother to look at her. It was awesome. She could almost be herself here... almost. Drusilla's hands rested on the lump of clay, and she closed her eyes. She molded the clay in her mind into the shape of a functional teapot and opened her eyes.

The clay was that perfect teapot. Just as she imagined it. She almost let herself smile, but she remembered where she was and closed her eyes. She imagined the teapot was a woman holding a basket and opened her eyes. The sculpture was perfect. It was exactly what she wanted it to be. The woman's long clay hair fell smoothly against the folds of her clay dress. A familiar, cold smile on her clay face. Drusilla smashed it down savagely and started sculpting with her hands. She wondered how closely she could match it to the lady. Maybe this time her sculpture would be closer than last time.

After the bell, Drusilla packed up her sculpture, but she didn't bother to wash the wet clay from her hand. It was clear to her that the lady would look nothing like what she sculpted with her mind. Still, it would probably land her a solid B. Not too bad. She yawned hard and grabbed her stuff before she made for the door. Michael Prince was in it, of course. Drusilla nearly kicked the fucker in the shin. Instead, she settled for glaring at him as he smugly leaned an elbow on the door frame. The bastard.

"We meet again," he said.

"Awesome, now my life gets harder." Drusilla shut her mouth. She didn't mean to be that honest out loud. Fuck!

Things were uncomfortable suddenly. Michael's eyes filled with pity under his furrowed brows. Drusilla didn't have time for this. She wiped her wet clay hand on his flannel and moved past him to make her way down the stupid halls. Michael Prince called after her, but she couldn't hear what he was saying over the blood pumping in her ears. That was a close one. Her heart thumped in her chest. She would have to pack up a little earlier from now on, but right now she wanted to get as far away from Michael Prince as she could. She didn't get very far before Mary hooked arms with her.

"What-"

"We need to talk." Mary dragged Drusilla off to the girl's bathroom.

"Damn it, Mary -" Drusilla started, but...

"What did you do to the new guy?" Mary asked.

"What?" Drusilla felt oddly hollow all of a sudden. "I don't -"

“I really, really like him, Drusilla.”

“You *really, really* like everybody, Mary. You keep going through these guys, and it's always the same. You 'really, really' like them, but once you've had them, you’re over it. You move on to the next guy. That's not very safe. You could...” Drusilla stopped. She had to fight hard to swallow down the crushing emptiness that was consuming her.

“This one’s different. I do *really, really* like him, and it's not my fault that once I’ve slept with them, they get all boring. I'm not going to be with some boring guy, I have standards.”

Mary leaned against a pink tiled wall in exactly the same way Michael Prince had. The bathroom was filthy. Drusilla really hoped that Mary intended to wash that arm after this. Drusilla knew she wasn't going to, but she really, really wished she would. All kinds of germs lived in a school bathroom. Who knows when the last time someone got around to cleaning it. It was a one-way ticket to... Dysentery land, or... whatever. Drusilla shook herself. She was getting off topic.

“I wasn't trying to make it seem like your fault.” Drusilla sighed. “I just think you should slow down with this guy, is all. He gives me the shivers.”

“Whatever, *Mom*!” Mary giggled, then gasped and clamped her hand over her mouth. Drusilla didn't say anything. For a long while she and Mary just watched each other. Drusilla couldn't move.

“*Is* this about Mom?” Drusilla said, finally. “Is that why-”

“Fuck Mom, and fuck you for bringing her up!” Mary exploded. “That whore left us, and she's not coming back! Even if she did come back, I'd fucking spit in her face. *Fuck* her! I hope she's dead. I hope-”

“I'm sorry.” Drusilla sighed.

“Don't you fucking be sorry for that sack of shit. You didn't make her leave us. She decided to abandon us! That bitch gave up. She's the reason you and Dad keep-”

“No, Mary. She's not the reason Dad and I fight.”

“I heard you this morning.” Mary scraped her front tooth along the edge of her glittery pink thumbnail. “Every word.”

"Let's not talk about that, okay?" Drusilla pleaded. Mary didn't say a word. "Okay?" Drusilla pressed. Mary still didn't answer. "Damn it, Mary, you have bigger problems than Mom right now. This Michael guy..." The emptiness burned in Drusilla's gut.

Mary bit off her nail and spit it into the distance. "They were boring. I don't feel shame about my failed relationships. Michael's different. He's new and exciting. How could that turn boring?" Mary asked.

"I don't care who you do, Mary, I'm just saying that you should be more careful. Sometimes people wind up hurt. I don't want to see you go through... that. Okay?" "I'm a big girl," Mary replied.

"Are you, Mary?" Drusilla asked. "You're a sixteen year old girl."

The bell rang. Mary sighed angrily. "Look, just don't mess with him, okay? For me."

"I'm not interested in him." So, why this feeling?

"No, I mean, don't fuck him up. I know how you do, Dru."

"You're late for class, Mary."

"Promise me," Mary said.

"I don't want to mess him up," Drusilla said. "You hate being late, Mary. You're going to get in trouble."

"I'll be fine," Mary replied. "That's what tits are for."

Drusilla watched with a heavy heart as Mary ran off. Then, Drusilla faded into her next class. Math class. She appeared seated in the back corner as if she had always been there. The spell took a lot out of her. Math was something Drusilla was good at, so the class went by easily enough. There wasn't much she could screw up on, and people generally left her alone, so it was okay. Drusilla worked in peace until the bell rang. She packed up and left for her next class, English.

In the hallway, she passed Paul Hunt and his gang of meathead jerkoffs. Paul was tall, meaty, with broad shoulders and a full, dark beard. He was captain of the wrestling team and President of the wilderness club, which was an excuse of a club to go hunting. That day, he had on a red flannel with his dirty jeans and brown boots. Redneck chic, Drusilla thought.

"Freak alert!" one of Paul's friends shouted. Pan. Always fucking Pan!

Drusilla smiled to herself. At least the day wasn't a total suck fest. With one look, Pan was on his knees in pain. Drusilla felt the power drain from her in one long rush. Everyone around Drusilla panicked. The smell of feces began to permeate the air. What a shame he wore light colored shorts, Drusilla thought. She pulled back and let nature do the rest. She was tickled pink.

"Well, Pan, at least I'm potty trained!" Drusilla called back. The rest of Paul's lackeys ran off in the direction of the nurse's office. Paul wasn't laughing. Drusilla walked right up to him. He had a nasty expression on his face.

"That was amusing," Drusilla said. Her eyes flashed dangerously.

"You're dead," Paul growled.

"Aw, like your buddy, Jack?" Drusilla said wickedly. The sticky sweetness of it made her smile.

Paul wasn't so tough all of a sudden. Drusilla lifted a brow and walked away. That felt good. Drusilla hadn't actually killed Jack. She didn't quite care that he was dead, but she hadn't killed him. That didn't mean she wouldn't take advantage of the fact that he was dead. That little stunt would get everyone off her back for a while. At least Drusilla hoped it would. She walked like a supermodel down the halls. Passing a few of Mary's friends, Drusilla flipped them the middle finger and laughed as they flinched.

*

Drusilla slipped into the lunchroom after English. She sat at her table alone and pulled out her sketchbook and a brown paper bag. Drusilla ate her butter, honey, and sprout sandwich on whole wheat bread as she flipped open the book. The red hoodie girl and her hairy boyfriend entered the lunchroom and gave Drusilla a wide birth. Drusilla looked up, and her eyes locked with the boyfriend's yellow ones. Drusilla knew a wolf when she saw one. She tried to remember the girl's name. Maybe Ramona, or

Ronda.... whatever, Drusilla thought. She rolled her eyes and began to sketch.

She barely had time to get the jester drawing down before she heard the heavy lunchroom doors creak open. Drusilla could feel every footstep Michael Prince made toward her. Her eyes flitted up to stare at him angrily. She watched his eyes linger on the open page of her sketchbook. He quirked a brow and started open his mouth, but...

"Yo, Prince!" called George. "Over here!"

Drusilla was grateful. She locked eyes with George for a dangerously brief moment. Then, she tucked into her food. Food was an easy distraction from the bullshit. Drusilla sketched and ate. Every once in a while, she felt eyes on her and she looked up. Michael's back was to her. A slight hollow feeling stirred in her stomach. Her eyes flicked to Paul. Paul looked away. Drusilla sighed and looked away.

After the lunch bell rang, Drusilla packed up her stuff and put her book back in her bag. She stood and threw her trash away, and then off to study hall. Her study hall was in a cramped, crowded classroom. She hated it. There was no way she could get a seat that was any farther away from the others. The best she could do was to position herself behind the only other empty desk. That way it was between her and *them*. The rest was a matter of ignoring their chatter.

She pulled out her book and continued to sketch. As the other students filled the seats, someone sat in Drusilla's empty seat. Her eyes flicked up, and of course, Michael Prince. Taking a deep, cleansing breath, Drusilla tried her best to look back at her book. Michael Prince lifted a brow. Drusilla was very confident that it hadn't worked and resolved to scratch his face if he tried to talk to her.

"Do you want a cookie?" Michael offered. Drusilla flicked her eyes up to see that yes, he did actually have a cookie.

"No, thank you," Drusilla said before turning back to her sketchbook.

"Are you sure?" Michael pressed. "You seem a little hangry?"

Drusilla dropped her pencil on the page and looked at him.

"Michael, what does that even mean?"

"Nothing, don't worry about it," Michael said, and plopped the cookie onto her desk.

"Listen up, you nuisance. I will-" Drusilla began, but then she remembered her promise. "You're very lucky someone at this school likes you or else I'd crush you like that!" Drusilla snapped her fingers and a spark zapped Michael Prince behind his left ear with a crackle. Michael grabbed his ear and hissed in pain.

"Ouch!" Michael's eyebrows crinkled together as he rubbed his ear.

"I don't often break promises, Michael. Don't make me."

"What are you so afraid of, Drusilla?" Michael asked.

Drusilla shook her head and went back to her sketch. She could feel Michael's eyes on her, but she wasn't giving him the satisfaction of an answer. She just let him stare, sketched on the page, and waited for the bell to ring. It took forever. Drusilla was half ready to snap and shove her pencil up Michael's nose. She chanced a look at him. He was reading a very old paperback, the cover was cracked and faded. His large, blue eyes slid in her direction, and Drusilla felt her face grow very hot. She snapped her attention back to her sketchbook and waited for the damn bell.

*

After the last bell rang, Mary got her things and headed for the parking lot. Drusilla was in the back of Tank, digging for something when she got there. Drusilla's too short skirt was not covering a thing while bent over, and her leggings were stretched to the brink. Mary almost giggled at the pink and white polka dot panties showing through.

"What are you looking for?" Mary asked.

Drusilla stood upright and yanked the hem of her skirt down. "My stupid button up for work."

"Oh," Mary said. "What time's work?"

"In a half hour. Enough time to hit the market to get you some dinner. I didn't have time to shop last night," Drusilla said. "We'll go shopping for real when we go to the garden supply store."

"Sure, whatever you want," Mary said as she pulled a diet grape soda out of her bag and cracked the top open.

Drusilla slid the door shut. "Did you have a good day?" Drusilla's eyes lingered on the soda can, and Mary knew Drusilla was calculating how many chemicals were in each sip. Drusilla shook her head and opened the passenger door for Mary.

Mary shrugged and got in. "Not really," Mary said with a burp. She sipped from the can, then tilted it towards Drusilla. "Want some?"

Drusilla's face fell. "No, thank you."

Mary shrugged, "It's not your fault," and downed the can before crushing it and tossing it in the messy back, "in case you're wondering."

"What's not?" Drusilla put an arm around her sister and gave her a little squeeze.

"The way today turned out."

"Did nothing good happen?" Drusilla asked.

"I heard you made Pan shit his pants. That was pretty awesome," Mary answered.

"I thought you liked Pan? You dated him for a few weeks, at least."

"Yeah, he was alright, but he wanted to get high all the time and drag race his pinto, Tinker. Plus, he was a lousy fuck. I mean, like he just laid there and waited for me to do all the work *and* whined at me when I wouldn't. He's a fucking man-child. It's *so* grody. Plus, he treats you like shit, so none for him."

"That sucks," Drusilla said as she hopped into the driver's seat and buckled in.

"Yeah, ugh," Mary said.

Then, they both stopped. Michael Prince was walking through the parking lot. Drusilla took a deep breath and rolled her eyes. Mary felt that. She shot Drusilla a quick glare, then went back to watching him. He was *so* perfect, Mary thought. He waved at them. Mary beamed and waved back. Drusilla sighed heavily next to her. Mary glared at her sister.

"Don't do that. He'll come over here," Drusilla growled.

"Oh, stop. He's nice."

"He is a buffet of dicks!" Drusilla half shrieked as she and Mary watched him.

Michael stopped for a second. He looked at them. Mary shrank in her seat. She was pretty sure that he heard Drusilla. Drusilla looked as if she could care less. She revved the engine and shot off. Tank nearly hit Michael on the way out of the parking lot, Drusilla's middle finger up at him. Mary groaned into her hands as Drusilla giggled to herself.

"You're a buttface," Mary grumbled.

"Oh relax," Drusilla sighed, "it's not like I killed him."

Chapter 2

The black van sped off. Michael felt the heat in his body rise. Drusilla had almost run him over. Yeah, he had almost done the same that morning, but he didn't mean to. She flipped him off as she gunned for him. Michael went to his car, unlocked it, and slid into the driver's seat. He didn't feel like going home, and he didn't know where anything was yet. Michael just drove around the town. He passed neat little homes, the hospital, the post office, which was also the police and fire station for some reason, a shopping center with a supermarket and cafe, and a perfect, little park. Michael stopped. He parked, went to his trunk, and pulled out his basketball. Then, he moved to the black top and started to shoot hoops.

After an hour of this, Michael felt bored and hungry. He got back in his car and turned the key in the ignition. It revved to life, and Michael's cell went off. He sighed heavily and pulled it out of his pants pocket. His mother's pretty, smiling face flashed on the screen. Damn it, Michael thought.

Michael answered, “Hey, Madre.”

“Where are you?” his mother asked in easy Spanish.

“Um... I'm exploring the town. You know, trying to get my bearings. Did you know there is a cafe here? Maybe I can get a job there,” Michael replied in English.

“Maybe, we’ll have to see what your grades look like first.

Maybe after your first report card. Now, what time are you coming home?" his mother asked switching to English.

"I'm not sure. Before dark, for sure," Michael said.

"Okay, don't get too lost. I'm cooking dinner for you and your father. I have a late shift at the hospital tonight. Make sure you eat the dinner, Michael. Don't let your father talk you into ordering pizza again."

"Promise. I'll see you soon," Michael said, and then he hung up.

He drove back to the cafe. It was a small hole-in-the-wall in between a sports store and a pharmacy. A wooden sign with a Canadian goose painted on it read Goose's Café. Michael opened the door and jingly bells chimed at him. The walls were a mural of green grass and geese flying in front of a perfect cyan backdrop. The counters, tables, and chairs were laminated wood. Drusilla stood behind the counter. Her stubby hair pulled back by a thick, black headband. Hardly any makeup graced her round face. She was prettier without the makeup mask. Michael did not miss that detail. Drusilla was dressed in a white shirt and a quilted apron in the shape of a red rooster. She looked up and sighed heavily. Michael didn't know what to do. Should he leave and just go home? He watched Drusilla standing there, looking awkwardly in his direction. Michael wasn't sure.

"Did you need something?" Drusilla asked in a 'I'm at work' voice that clearly told Michael to shit or get off the pot.

Michael walked up to the counter. Drusilla looked impatient, which made Michael feel less uncomfortable oddly. "Um... I like your cock." Drusilla's eyes widened. She looked supremely uncomfortable. It bounced off her and slammed into Michael. "I was... you have a rooster thing... apron going on... I was trying to make you laugh."

"Coffee... tea... something?" she pressed.

"I hate coffee," he said. "Not that you make bad coffee!" Michael added quickly.

Little pink patches bloomed on Drusilla's cheeks. Michael hoped he could salvage this, though the pink butterfly patches were nice. Her purple eyes looked down for a moment and then up to meet his again, nervously. Michael couldn't tell if it was a good nervous or bad nervous. Drusilla's tiny, pink lip went into her mouth and then came back out as her upper teeth dragged along it. The last bit of lower lip flicked out. “I know. I'm crashing and burning faster than the Hindenburg.”

“Tea?” Drusilla asked. A desperate edge crept into her voice. “You'd have to yank that foot out of your mouth to drink it, but...”

“Yeah,” Michael agreed. “I really-”

“Green, black, Earl Gray, jasmine, or English breakfast?” she rattled quickly.

“Green, please,” Michael answered.

“Okay,” Drusilla sighed.

Michael watched Drusilla fill a tea bag with leaves and fill a paper cup with hot water from a spigot. She tied a knot in the tea bag and dropped it in the hot water. Then, pushed it over to him in a way that told Michael that she'd done this for forever. He reached for the cup and his fingertips brushed against her knuckles. Drusilla pulled the hand back as if his touch burned. The look she gave him was a mixture of fear and fury.

“So, you work at a coffee shop?” Michael asked, trying to make conversation.

“Someone has to pay for the hormones and electrolysis,” she replied as she dug her hands in her apron pockets.

“Oh,” Michael said as he began to notice light gray stubble under her chin. He fished in his wallet for the money. “Is that stuff expensive?”

“No, just take it. Call it a peace offering, or I don't fucking know. A bribe? Whatever helps you sleep at night.” Drusilla looked suddenly uncomfortable.

“Do you wanna grab a bite sometime?” Michael put a dollar in the tip jar. Drusilla's eyes flicked to his, and Michael was pinned by her purple irises. He couldn't tell if they looked fearful or angry.

“What are you doing?” Drusilla asked.

“Uh?” Michael couldn't think of a way to answer that wouldn't lead to Drusilla being pissed at him.

“I'm trans,” Drusilla said, as if she had said she was busy.

"I know that," Michael said.

Drusilla shook her head and reached into the tip jar. "I can't take this."

"The tip or the food?" Michael asked

Drusilla pulled the dollar out and held it for him to take. "Both. It's too weird."

"Why?"

"It just is, Michael. Now take it back." Drusilla held out the dollar. "Just take it all back."

"Alright," Michael said as he took the dollar back. "You know, you don't have to be afraid of me."

"You know what? You're right, but it's a personal choice." Drusilla's breathing was heavy.

"Okay, then." That pierced Michael in his chest like a jolt. "Well... see you at school tomorrow."

"What?"

"School," Michael replied. "We go there.... together."

"What?" Drusilla looked flustered.

"You know... never mind." Michael didn't know how else to turn this around, so he took his cup and held it up to her briefly before turning to leave.

"Michael..." Drusilla called after him. Then, he heard her cuss under her breath.

Michael turned to look at her. His eyebrow lifted in what he hoped was a comical way. "Yes, Drusilla?"

"Have a good night," she said, though it almost looked painful.

Michael's smile faltered. Drusilla winced at that, too. Why was she so afraid? He made his way to the door. Her eyes practically burned holes into his back. He turned to look at her. She wasn't quick enough. Michael watched her eyes fall and her hand purposefully wipe down the table with a dirty rag. It was time to go. There was nothing left to say. Michael knew it, but he wanted to talk to her more. Drusilla's eyes flicked up, and Michael smiled again.

"Hey," Michael said, as softly as he could. Drusilla stopped and looked at him. "Have a good night, too."

*

The moment Drusilla walked in the door, she knew her father was pissed. He sat in his comfy chair with the newspaper close to his face. His fat knuckles were white as he gripped the trembling newspaper way too hard. A baseball game blared from the entertainment system. The only nice thing in their shitty little house. Drusilla didn't even try to talk to him. She just wasn't in the mood. Instead, Drusilla walked down the hallway to Mary's room. Drusilla knocked on the door. There was no answer. She opened the door and found that Mary wasn't in her room. Drusilla looked at all the plants growing out of pots for the winter and the sprouts under a heat lamp. Drusilla pulled out her cell and called Mary. No answer. She sent Mary a text. Drusilla went back into the living room to her father.

"Did Mary go out?" she asked.

"No," her father said abrasively.

"*Okay...*" Drusilla said, "except she's not in her room."

"Then, *she* went out."

"And you don't know where she went?" Drusilla wasn't surprised. Just aggravated. "It's a school night. Are you kidding me? She's out on a school night, and you have no idea where she is or even when the fuck she's supposed to be home? Do you even care about her grades at all? What if she has homework to do?"

Her father flicked the paper and refused to answer. Drusilla rolled her eyes in frustration and pulled her keys out of her pocket. "Fine. I'm going out to look for her, you filthy deadbeat."

Drusilla's father began to bellow, but she was already slamming the front door. Drusilla walked across the lawn towards Tank. Her father opened the door and continued to yell, but Drusilla didn't care. She had to find Mary. What if she was dead in the woods, or something? The irresponsible idiot. If she really was dead in the woods, Drusilla would kill her! She hopped back into Tank and drove off. Her eyes scanning every visible space of road and sidewalk, as if Mary would just be there. Of course she wasn't. Drusilla did her best to breathe deeply and evenly. She looked at the clock. It was a little after eight. Awesome, Mary. Just awesome.

*

Mary stood with the others. They held candles and flowers for Jack. Mary watched and cried with the others as Jack's parents spoke. Mary remembered how he was in bed, not very good. Then, she remembered it was bad to think ill of the dead, so she stopped thinking. A hand gripped her arm and Mary's eyes snapped in the direction of the offender. It was Drusilla. She didn't look mad or upset. She just stood there with her. Even after people started whispering about her. Mary knew everyone blamed it on Drusilla. Jack had pissed her off for some reason or another. It still bothered Mary. They stood there a while after everyone left. Mary stared at the picture of Jack smiling, blissfully unaware that he would die at seventeen. Drusilla's hand squeezed hers.

"Are you mad?" Mary asked.

"No," Drusilla replied. "Do you want to get some ice cream or dinner, or something?"

"No."

"Alright. Ready to go home?" Drusilla asked.

"No." Mary looked at the front of the darkened school. It was going to get a lot harder, she thought.

"Okay," Drusilla replied.

They stood there until Mary could think of no other reason to stay. Then, she let Drusilla lead her to Tank, and for a while they just drove with the windows open. Drusilla glanced over at Mary. Mary knew she put up a good front, but Drusilla always had a way of seeing through the bullshit. It was so unfair. Mary hoped Drusilla would teach that trick to her sometime, but she knew better than to hope. The town rushed by in a gust of chilly air.

"Mary, are you okay? I mean, for real. You didn't even like Jack all that much."

Drusilla saw the yellow light and slowed down.

Mary deflated in her seat. Drusilla never slowed for the yellows. It felt like Mary had bugs crawling around in her stomach, or worms. Worms would be more appropriate. More real or something. Mary didn't know. She just liked worms. The van stopped, and the red light glowed softly against the dash. What now? Mary didn't have an answer for herself, let alone Drusilla.

"I don't see the point anymore," Mary said. "Everyone leaves. They die or they quit."

Mary's face flushed. She didn't mean to say that out loud. The light turned green. Drusilla drove and Mary clammed up. Drusilla didn't say anything.

"Where are we going?" Mary asked.

"Ice cream," Drusilla said.

"It's nine fifty eight on a school night," Mary said.

"You take tomorrow off, if you want," Drusilla said. "No one will be mad at you."

"I can't do that," Mary replied, "but ice cream sounds nice."

"Okay," Drusilla said. "Ice cream it is."

*

The next morning, Drusilla didn't bother dressing up. She was in sweat pants and a gray shirt. Not a stitch of makeup on her face. She almost looked like a boy again. Mary raked her eyes over Drusilla. She needed to burn that stretched out shirt like nobody's business. Mary got into Tank, and they drove. Drusilla dropped Mary – who was wearing a blue mini-dress and black pumps – off at the front of the school building. Well, at least it looked like nobody would see her in that. Mary wrinkled her nose as she gave it another once over. Whoever said hobo was the new trend in goth culture needed a swift kick to the fucking face!

"I'll pick you up after school and we will go to the garden store, okay?"

"Sure," Mary said, "but you better put your real clothes on when you come to pick me up. I can't be seen with you looking like some dumpster woman."

"Yeah, whatever." And Drusilla sped off.

"Yeah, whatever," Mary mocked and walked towards the doors.

Mary turned back to watch Drusilla nearly plow somebody

over, and then made her way to homeroom. On the way, she saw Michael wandering the halls. A rose was in his hand. Mary's insides squealed. He was bringing her flowers already. Mary raced as fast as her heels could allow to homeroom. She wanted to look perfect while she awaited her prince with his rose. She imagined what she would do when he gave her the rose. Mary would bat her eyelashes and make herself blush. Michael is mine, she thought. All mine. Fuck off, bitches!

Michael came into class empty handed. Mary's heart smashed. Who the fuck did he give it to? Michael sat next to her with an easy smile and a wave. Mary waved back, weakly. This was going to suck. Mary just felt it. Felt it right down to her asshole. Mary took a deep, casual breath, or at least what she hoped looked casual. Michael pursed his lips. Yep, crashing and burning. Mary swallowed raw emotion and hoped the bell would ring soon. She looked back at Michael. Please shut up, Michael, Mary thought at him with all her might. Please just...

"Hi, Mary," he said. "Is your sister here today? I didn't see her."

Oh, god dammit. "She's sick."

"Oh, well, that's too bad. Tell her I hope she feels better." Michael's smile widened.

Oh, go fuck yourself! "Will do."

*

Drusilla was dressed up again. Tank putt putted as she idled in front of the school. Mary hopped in with a mighty roar. They were stuck in a massive line of cars. Mary looked ready to explode. Her scrunched up face was tomato red. Drusilla's relaxed muscles tensed. Now what? Drusilla sat there and waited for Mary's red face to subside. It showed no signs of going anywhere. Drusilla sighed. Neither were these cars. Drusilla did not have it in her to shift her, her sister, and Tank out at the moment.

"Bad day?" Drusilla asked.

"I want my ice cream, now!"

"Okay," Drusilla replied.

“Hey,” Michael said, cheerily. He was knocking on Drusilla's driver’s side window. Both she and Mary took deep calming breaths.

Drusilla rolled down her window. “Stop assaulting my car! She's elderly.”

“A classic,” Michael said. His eyebrow lifted. “I just wanted to say I hope you feel better.”

Drusilla mouthed *later* at him. “Eat shit and die, Prince!” Drusilla growled.

Michael popped a smile. Drusilla closed her eyes in frustration. She could feel Mary's anger build up. Why did Drusilla have to be in the middle of this? This was going to get a lot uglier before it got better. He was looking at her. Drusilla hated the way the look in Michael's eyes made her insides wobble. The cars weren’t budging and heat seemed to radiate off of Mary. Soon, she would open her mouth and fuck! Michael wasn't leaving. Drusilla mouthed for him to go away. The cars began to move slightly. Finally! Drusilla moved with them, and so did Michael. Why me? Drusilla wanted to scream.

“See you tomorrow?” asked Michael.

Drusilla and Mary didn't say anything. Mary sat there with her arms crossed. Drusilla wanted to scream even harder. Instead, she just glared at Michael, making him as uncomfortable as she could. Michael stared back, unflinchingly. He was infuriating. It felt like forever, but finally the cars began to drive. Yes, Drusilla thought. She would drive him off. Take that! Let him be the one caught in an uncomfortable situation. The ass.

“The cars are moving,” Mary said, flatly.

Drusilla put her eyes back to the road and started to drive. She felt Michael open his mouth, but she silenced him with a look. He winked at her instead. Something wriggled its way up from her stomach, and Drusilla had to fight hard to keep it down. A car rumbled out, and Drusilla found her opening. She drove, cutting off a nice family wagon in the process. They were out of the pickup zone. Mary was stone. She wouldn't move. Her arms were crossed, and her mouth was a very thin line.

“I hate him,” Drusilla said.

"I know," Mary said.

"All I wanted to do today was hang out with you. I got extra money out so we could eat out after the garden store. We haven't done that in a long time. Fuck! I hope he dies next."

"I don't think you should let him mess up our day," Mary said. "We can still do these things. I'm just -."

"Pissed," Drusilla finished for her.

"Frustrated," Mary corrected.

*

George sat across from Michael at the mall's burger place. George liked his new friend. Michael was pretty cool, but his weird fascination with Drusilla Bonnet was getting annoying. Every moment Michael spent staring off into space, George knew was spent thinking about Drusilla. What was the point? George should have just got up and left Michael to his musings. Not that it mattered that he was probably the best chance at a friend in a long time. What did Michael care if George spent most of his time alone? Yeah, people were cool with him, and George was cool back, but man. Michael was one of the only other dudes of color in this white ass town. Couldn't that count for something? Nope. He had to keep dwelling on Drusilla Bonnet. That was problematic as it was.

"Why do you think she's like that?" Michael asked over the echo of the crowded voices and bad, old people music.

George rolled his eyes and spotted her. Mary Bonnet. She was so perfect. Her smile warmed his bones like brandy. Why wasn't her name Brandy, he thought. She was the most beautiful girl at Elderberry high. George's eyes lingered on the way her blond hair bounced when she walked. Drusilla stomped behind her, carrying big plastic shopping bags. She looked miserable. God, what did Michael see in her that he couldn't stop talking about Drusilla for ten minutes?

"Drusilla's right over there. Why don't you ask?" George said.

"Nah, she's pissed at me."

"It's always pissed," George mused.

"Stop calling her that," Michael growled. "She's not an it."

"I have my reasons." This was getting harder and harder, George thought, as the pangs of guilt ripped him hollow. Almost not worth it.

"Well, you're pissing me off," Michael replied.

"Look, man. Drusilla just wants to be left alone." As much as it sucks, George added privately.

"Did she tell you that?" Michael's eyes narrowed.

"Not in those words," George said, "but the last few people that messed with her got a case of the hurt really bad."

"That doesn't mean she wants to be left alone," Michael said. "How do you know?"

"Because, Drusilla wants everyone to leave her alone. Maybe you should just respect that." George shut his mouth. He had almost said too much. Maybe he already had. He went back to staring at Mary Bonnet. She was so lovely.

"So," Michael said in a tone that clearly said let's change the subject. "Mary Bonnet, huh?"

"Dude, really?" George wanted to leave.

"Does she know?"

George felt like his chest was caving in. Michael looked like he wanted to say something, but he let it go. They both went back to staring at the pair. Drusilla was the first to notice, and her face turned red when she did. Mary half waved. George and Michael waved back. Drusilla's head snapped back in Mary's direction, and they exchanged quick, heated words. Then, they sat and ignored Michael and George for the rest of their meals. Michael looked at Drusilla for a little bit longer than anyone would have liked. George certainly didn't.

"You have to let that go. Whatever you got going on between the two of you. Drop it. Before you get dropped." George was trying to be understanding.

Michael didn't look at George. "Nah, not yet. There's something up with that one."

*

"What are you growing this summer?" Drusilla asked as she and Mary walked with a cart through the garden supply store.

"Everything!" Mary said, dramatically. "Maybe beets instead of turnips, though. I didn't like the way they came out last year. Did you?"

"They were alright," Drusilla said. "Do you have homework?"

"Nope," Mary said. "I did it in study hall."

"Good girl."

Drusilla was glad that Mary was in a better mood since Michael had apparently stared at her in the mall, at least in her mind. Drusilla was worried for Mary. It looked like Mary was headed for a brick wall, and quick. Try telling her that though, Drusilla thought. No way she'd listen. No way to help her sister. Drusilla sighed and helped Mary pick out tomato seeds. Since when did tomatoes come in black? That's awesome! Drusilla pulled a couple envelopes of black tomato seeds and dropped them into the cart. Maybe she would start her own little garden this summer.

"I'm already growing you Black Beauties under the lamps," Mary said as she considered two types of carrot seed packs in her hands.

Drusilla put the seeds back. "Oh."

*

The next morning, Drusilla was fighting with her locker again. The filthy thing never seemed to want to open for her. Drusilla got frustrated and raked it with her nails. She spun the dial again and again, and after the fiftieth try, it unlocked. The door quivered as it creaked open. A single slightly wilted red rose in a murky water bottle rested atop her books. Oh, no! Drusilla's breath caught in her throat, and she spluttered. What was he doing? Fire broiled her insides as she snatched it - flower petals and murky water bottle falling to the floor - and marched down the hall.

She spotted Michael Prince talking to George in front of some lockers. Drusilla was tempted to grab Michael by his smug looking football shirt and slam him against the metal. Instead, she settled for screeching. She attempted a swipe at his face with her jagged nails, but Michael slapped her hand away, lightly. Like she was some bad, little kitten, or something equally perverse. George jumped. Drusilla had expected Michael to do the jumping, but instead he just looked at her with exasperation.

"What the *fuck* is this shit?" Drusilla growled. She held up the rose.

Michael Prince's concerned eyes locked with hers. He pushed his slipping glasses back up his nose with his fingers. It oddly reminded Drusilla of the doddering school librarian. Drusilla had taken to calling the old man Mr. Peepers, but only to herself. Michael's demeanor was infuriatingly patient, and Drusilla hated him for it. She wanted to scratch out his pretty eyes.

"It's a flower," Michael replied, calmly.

"What is it doing in my locker?"

"I found a flower on the way to school. It made me think of you, so I picked it for you. Except, you didn't show up to school, so I put it there for you. I didn't know what else to do with it," Michael explained with irritating calm. "I'm sorry if I upset you."

Drusilla saw the look on George's face. Damn it. "Why would you do that, Michael?"

"It was a gift?" Michael sounded unsure. "Don't girls like flowers?"

"Do I fucking look like I like flowers?" Drusilla demanded.

"Well, not now that you're yelling at me for it, no," Michael answered.

"Well, take it back," Drusilla demanded.

"Wow. Okay." Michael's eyebrows crunched together. "I tried to do something nice for you. I'm sorry it upset you."

Drusilla took a deep, cleansing breath and the head of the rose burst into purple flame. The sweet burning smell permeated the air. Michael looked at the ash in Drusilla's hands and shook his head. Drusilla sighed. She hadn't meant to do that. She looked past Michael to George's frozen expression. They locked eyes, and without a word, he slipped into the crowd and went the way of the current. Drusilla swallowed the hardness in her throat.

"I am done playing games, Michael," Drusilla said to her feet.

"You think I'm impressed?" he replied, flatly. "I'm not."

"Well..." She knew she should tell him to fuck off. Tell him she didn't want to see him, and that he better stay away. Instead, Drusilla turned and stormed off. Pushing her way past the flood of the student body. She shoved one of the three jock brothers into the lockers with a loud clang. Drusilla ignored his squeals as she made her way out of the building. It didn't make her feel any better. In fact it made her feel worse, but she had a reputation to uphold. No matter how hollow it made her insides feel. She grumbled and stomped on her way.

Chapter 3

Instead of getting in her car, Drusilla made her way through the thick cluster of old oaks and maples that claimed so many lives. It was hauntingly beautiful, with all the green, like a better world slowly giving way to the deathly orange of fall. Just her and the trees. She didn't have to worry here. The trees didn't want her. No eyes on her here in nature. No Michael, either. She took a deep breath and sucked in the last dregs of summer. Yes. This was right. Everything was-

"Hey," Michael Prince called after her.

Drusilla kept walking. She could hear him running up behind her. Drusilla pulled at her power and gathered it up in her hand. The spark ignited in her and there was heat there. She spun to face him, but he was too close. His arm came up easily to block her glowing fist. Her spell went wide. Purple fire erupted from her hand in a ball and slammed into the trunk of a wide tree. The tree splintered. Michael let go of her arm and made to back away. Dammit! Drusilla wasn't trying to set him on fire, just push him back.

Michael's sparkling blue-gray eyes hardened. Drusilla felt her own face slip into a hard stare. Two could play, Prince. They glared at each other for what felt like forever. Drusilla lunged, her hands out to grab Michael by the hair, but he dodged easily. Drusilla spun into a feinting kick. Michael dodged again, but

Drusilla was ready for him. She pulled her knee in and kicked out at him. Michael easily hooked the leg and pushed it out of his way. Drusilla stumbled slightly, but recovered herself nicely.

"What is your damn problem?" Michael demanded.

"You! You're my damn problem!" Drusilla yelled as she shoved at Michael.

"Well, get used to me," Michael said as he blocked the shove and trapped her wrists with his hands. "You're not scaring me off."

Drusilla twisted her hands in towards herself and then out to clamp down on Michael's wrists. She pushed down to free herself from his grip. Michael watched her, and Drusilla watched him. She was waiting for his next move. Michael just stood there watching for hers. He was just going to stand there looking at her, Drusilla decided. Fine then! She turned to walk deeper into the woods.

*

Michael didn't let her get far. He followed after her in the stillness of the green forest. "I'm not afraid of you, you know."

Drusilla stopped and turned around. The rustle of her little, black velvet dress caught his eye. Her purple and black striped stockings hugged tightly around her shapely legs. Nice, Michael thought. Drusilla glowered at him. Michael was certain that he could see heat streaks radiating from her. Michael's face softened as his anger ebbed. He took a step towards her, but Drusilla backed away a pace. Michael took another step and again Drusilla backed away. Michael made to take another step, but...

Crack! Drusilla opened her mouth in a snarl, but the tree next to her was falling. Michael rushed her, tackling her out of the way. They hit the ground with a hard thud. The ground rumbled as the heavy oak fell, a little too close for Michael's comfort. Drusilla's breathing verged on hyperventilation. Her eyes were wild and distant as if she was seeing something that Michael could not. Tears ran down the sides of her face as her body quaked, long after the ground had stopped.

"Hey? Drusilla?" Michael asked. Drusilla's chest was heaving with each breath. Her breathing became faster and faster. "Drusilla, relax."

"I...am...trying...to!" she gasped between sharp intakes of breath.

"We're safe," Michael said. He sat up, pulling Drusilla up with him. Then, he crushed her to him. "We're safe, Drusilla. Breathe. You're okay."

He had to repeat it over and over again before she finally seemed to calm down. She pushed him away. Michael fell back. Looking up at her, Michael couldn't help notice how her purple eyes sparkled in the sun. The pink butterfly patches were back on her face, and Michael could feel his pulse jump. This feels right, thought Michael, as he sat back up. Michael scooted closer to her. He was very close to her now. Closer than he had ever been before. Their noses touched.

"What are we doing?" Drusilla's breath hit him in the face.

"Going with it, I think," Michael replied.

"Michael!" she breathed, and then pushed him away again. "This isn't supposed to happen."

Michael looked at her. Her eyes were alert and staring at him intently, though her body was shaking like a leaf. "Anything is possible in the woods, Drusilla."

"Michael!" Drusilla's arms wound around him, and before Michael had time to react, Drusilla pushed. They fell over together. The earth thundered as another tree carcass came smashing down right beside them. Michael's heart was playing a drum solo on his rib cage as he looked up and saw yet another tree crashing down on them. Michael tried to push Drusilla off and away from the impending crash, but she held fast. Drusilla pulled him with her to relative safety. Michael rolled – pulling Drusilla with him – again, for safe measure. Drusilla flopped on top of him, and Michael could feel their two hearts beating against each other. Boom! The tree crashed a few inches away from their feet.

"I think we're safe now," Michael gasped.

The sudden cracking of wood, and Michael knew in that moment that they weren't getting out of this. Drusilla didn't pull him in. She just hugged him in fear as she screamed, and the mossy trunk fell towards them. A sudden whiplash feeling, and blackness. No pain. Only a dull throbbing remained. So this was what death felt like, Michael thought. They seemed to float through nothingness. Drusilla still clung to him. Her screams had stopped. How nice to at least have her in the end. He opened his mouth to tell her it was alright. That it was all over. There would be no more pain from now on. Just the two of them in this nothingness of peace, but all that came out was more of the rushing sound that seemed to clog his ears.

The woods came back around him in a rush. Michael smacked his head painfully against the cold hard ground. Then, he sat up. They had moved a few yards away from the spot where the trees were falling. Three trees came crashing down to crunch the ghost of them. Michael almost felt the timber crush into his body. They looked at the clearing of downed trees. The feeling in Michael's gut made him want the throw up or cry. He looked over to Drusilla, she was holding herself next to him. Her whole body shivered. Michael scooted even closer to her, but Drusilla tried to push him away again.

"Don't," she said, her eyes darting from tree to tree. "I can't save us again, Michael. I'm too weak. I did too much magic."

"It's okay now," Michael said. "We're safe."

"No! Damn it. Michael, don't get too close to me when the next one comes."

"There won't be a next one."

"When the next one comes down!" Drusilla growled. "It'll get both of us if we are too close."

Michael couldn't beat that logic, but he wasn't going to let anything happen to her. This, he knew. "Come on, then. We need to rush back in."

"Are you nuts?" Drusilla demanded. Her eyes, still wildly scanning the forest.

"No, look. Those trees already fell. It's a clearing now. If we can get there before the next tree falls, we'll be safe. The trees can't get us there."

He grabbed Drusilla's hand and stood before she could argue. Drusilla rushed to her feet almost right after and began to run before Michael knew what was happening. Michael ran with her. He expected more trees to come crashing down in their wake, but to his surprise, the trees stayed put. They reached the clearing safely, and Drusilla's hand slipped from his. Michael's heart sank a little. Drusilla leaned against a fallen oak and gasped for air. Michael was there, rubbing her back. Half worried and half glad for an excuse to be touching her again.

"Are you okay?" Michael asked.

"Panic..." Drusilla managed to get out between breaths. "Panic attack... just let me... just let me."

"Okay," Michael said as he continued to rub her back rhythmically. Drusilla fell to her knees and buried her face in her arms. "Do you get a lot of these?"

Drusilla didn't say anything. She just shrugged into her folded arms. Michael knelt beside her and kept rubbing, unsure of what else to do. After a while, Drusilla came up for air. Tears streaked her dark makeup. She took a deep breath and slouched. Her hands came up and wiped beneath her raw looking eyes, leaving black makeup smudges on her face. Michael was half tempted to clean them, but it was yet another excuse to touch her. And he knew it. So instead, he pulled himself up and help out his hand to her. She looked up at it, the red rings around her eyes making the violet irises more vibrant.

"Why can't you just be afraid of me like everyone else?" She didn't wait for an answer. Instead, she took his hand and pulled herself upright.

"Because I'm not a bigot?" Michael half asked, half offered.

Drusilla cackled at that. "Touché."

Michael didn't let go of her hot, clammy hand. Nor did Drusilla try to pull it back. They just stood there watching each other for a small moment. A fresh wave of tiny tears ran down Drusilla's red, hot cheeks. Then, before he knew it, she was crashing against him. Her mouth, nearly biting his off in her ferocity. Then, as quickly as she came, she pulled back, but before their lips were apart for long, Michael grabbed her and pulled her back onto him with matching ferociousness. Drusilla's kiss was more of a head-butt than an actual kiss, but Michael didn't care. He liked her fury and the pain.

"Damn it!" Drusilla shoved Michael away. "Fuck! What am I doing?"

"What?" Michael asked. "What's wrong?"

"This is," Drusilla answered. "This is *so* wrong."

"What do you mean?"

Drusilla's words were like sharp shards of glass to the gut. She began dusting dead leaves and dirt from her clothing. "You have to stop, Michael."

"What? Why?"

"You just have to stop." Drusilla took a deep breath. "I can't-"

"Damn it-" Michael began to say, more to himself than to her.

"I just can't!" Drusilla roared.

Crack! A branch from another tree crash-landed between them. It happened so fast that Michael missed his chance to save her again. Drusilla's eyes were fixed on it. She wouldn't look at him anymore. Misery clung to Michael's throat like the promise of an asthma attack, yet his lips still burned with the memory of Drusilla's assault on them. He knew he couldn't stop. Drusilla's wet, hamburger eyes looked up at him and Michael knew she knew it, too. It was the distress that gave her away.

"Drusilla..."

Drusilla just shook her head and closed her eyes. Her arms wound around herself. "This isn't how this story goes."

"I believe we write our own stories," Michael said, then automatically regretted it. It was a cliché, and not a sexy one at that.

"It's not how this is supposed to go," Drusilla repeated. "There will be consequences, and I'm the one who has to pay for your curiosity."

"This isn't..." He stopped. Lying was something that never sat well with him. "I'm not trying to use you."

"Michael, this is too weird for me, okay. I can't deal with this on top of..." her words exploded from her mouth, only to die quietly away.

She was looking at her feet. One arm crossed her middle. Michael stepped over the thick branch. Drusilla shrank back, to a place Michael could not follow. In that moment, Michael could see through Drusilla's bullshit. The big, bad Drusilla everybody was so afraid of. She was just some wounded chick. Now she was here, and she was afraid. Drusilla took a deep breath and opened her mouth to say something, but Michael cut her off.

"On top of what?" he asked.

She opened her eyes and it was amazing how dazzling they were when she was glaring at him like that. "Michael we have to go. We have class."

"So what? We probably already missed first period. We could just blow off the rest. Let me take you-"

"No!" she said, sharply. "Michael... look. I am trying to do the right thing here, okay? Besides, I have to get into a good school, so I can get out of this hole. I can't just fuck off."

"You didn't seem to care about that when you were skipping school to avoid me."

"Yeah, well, you overwhelm me," Drusilla growled.

"I have that effect on women," Michael teased, in an attempt to lighten the mood.

Drusilla rolled her eyes. "We really should get back to class. Well, school... whatever."

A breeze came across Drusilla, and she shivered against it. Michael moved closer to her. His hands rubbed Drusilla's arms to warm her. She didn't push him away. She only rested her forehead against his. Michael watched her as her eyes closed. Her small frown faltered. More tears slipped from beneath her lashes. Michael slid his hands up to cradle her head, his thumbs brushing away her tears.

"School..." Michael said in a half interested voice. "Maybe we could stay here for a little longer. It's cozy."

"Falling trees, yeah, real fucking cozy." Drusilla looked at him. "This isn't how this is supposed to go."

"Why not?" Michael asked.

"Because," Drusilla said as she wrenched herself free.

"No, really, why?" Michael said, though he felt he knew

already.

“Because,” Drusilla repeated, sounding a little more aggravated.

“Hmm...” Michael mused.

Drusilla closed her eyes on a sigh of annoyance. “What?”

“I didn't say anything,” Michael said, but he could tell he wasn't going to get away with anything.

“I hate you.” Drusilla sighed.

“Do you really?” Michael asked.

“What?” Drusilla asked in returned.

“Hate me?”

*

Mary sat in homeroom. Michael was nowhere to be found. She didn't feel like giggling with her stupid friends. Something felt very wrong. The bell rang, and Mary bolted for the door. Something very bad was happening. Her gut cramped up. In the hallways, she couldn't find Drusilla anywhere. Mary dipped into the girl’s bathroom. She looked for Drusilla's boots and purple stockings, and found them.

“There you are,” Mary said, letting out the deep breath she was holding.

“What’s up, Mary?” Drusilla said in a weird voice.

“Have you seen, Michael?”

There was a long enough pause that Mary felt uncomfortable. “Um.... yes. I yelled at him before homeroom. Why?”

“Why did you yell at him? And why are still in the stall?”

“Mary, it's kind of personal.”

“Oh? Why?”

“You’re not going to like it.”

Just then, two giggling girls walked into the bathroom. Mary turned on them. “Get out! This is a private conversation!” To Mary's satisfaction, the girls fled in a hurry. “Now, what are you talking about?”

“Mary-”

"What were you talking about?" Mary insisted.

"I caught him snooping around in my locker," Drusilla said, quickly.

Mary's heart dropped. "What? He didn't put anything in there, did he?"

"Nope. I yelled at him. Then, he got all mad and ran away," Drusilla said in a matter of fact, yet nervous, tone of voice.

Mary was sure Michael was a lot stronger than that. "Are you sure?"

"Why would I lie?"

Mary wasn't sure anymore.

*

The ride home was very uncomfortable for Drusilla. Mary seemed to scrutinize every little thing that Drusilla did. There was very little cheer in her and that was worrisome. The last thing she wanted was-. Drusilla stopped herself. She couldn't think about that. It just would never happen. Everything's fine. Just fine. Michael Prince, Drusilla thought. He could wreck all- No! It's fine. It's fine! Damn it! It's fine!

"It's fine!" Drusilla blurted out.

"What are you thinking about?" Mary asked in an accusatory way.

"I'm thinking that Michael Prince kind of scares me," she said honestly.

"What?"

"I mean it, Mary. I don't think that you should go after him. It feels like a bad idea."

"What, like he's going to hurt me?"

More like I might. "He just scared me today."

"What did he do?"

Drusilla slammed on the brakes. The silvery blue car darted across the intersection. Horn blaring as it did. Drusilla's eyes fixed on the red light she almost ran. Drusilla's eyes lingered on Michael's taillights, and a shiver went up her back. Why did she do it? What was wrong with her? She needed a shower, or some ice cream. Something. She didn't know what she needed, but she needed it now. Michael-

"No!" Drusilla half shouted.

"What the fuck is going on with you, Lady?" Mary looked at her, and Drusilla could detect shock in Mary's forest bright eyes.

"I can't, Mary. I don't want to go through this again. Just find someone else, please." She tapped her thumb impatiently against the steering wheel as the red light dragged on.

"Did he hurt you? I'll bust his face!" Mary suddenly thrashed against the seat belt.

"Mary, no. Please. Just stop for a second."

Tears welled up in Mary's eyes. "What am I supposed to do?"

"Stop!" Drusilla said. "Just breathe for a second, okay. He didn't hurt me. I'm just scared."

The car behind them honked loudly. Mary rolled down her window. Oh crap, Drusilla thought. Mary stuck her head out of the window and yelled something very unladylike. Drusilla looked at the green light and floored it. They spent the rest of the drive in silence. Terrifyingly uncomfortable silence. Drusilla didn't know what she was going to do. She just drove. When they got to the house, their father's car wasn't there, to Drusilla's relief. They went inside, and Drusilla went to the answering machine. She hit play and listened to the message that would have informed her father of the absences Drusilla now had that week. Drusilla hit delete and turned to Mary.

"That never happened." Drusilla didn't wait to see Mary nod. Instead, she went for her father's liquor cabinet. "Want a drink?"

"Oh, that's nice," Mary said. "You're drinking, now? Really?"

"Mary, shut up. I know you drink at parties. Do you want some, or not?"

"Don't you have work today?"

"Nope. My day off," Drusilla said as she made her way to their tiny, badly lit kitchen and poured herself some wine in a tall drinking glass. She then filled the wine bottle with grape juice. Drusilla reached into her pocket and pulled out a twenty.

"Go crazy. Get two pizzas. I'm off to bed." And with that, Drusilla moved past Mary to her bedroom and locked herself in for the night.

Drusilla's room was bubble gum pink, but she did her best to make do with the nightmarish choices of her youth. A few dark posters of her favorite bands, plastic skulls, dead flowers from Mary's garden, and the newest addition - a few dozen construction paper butterflies strung across the ceiling - made it livable. Drusilla slumped into her bed and looked at her latest glittering purple creations. The wine burned as she gulped. It didn't burn as much as Michael's mouth. A heat was there, suddenly. Drusilla wasn't sure if it was from the wine or Michael's... She shuddered.

"What a weird day," Drusilla said on a sigh.

She kicked off her boots and got up to light some candles with the point of her finger. Cursing herself for not thinking of it before getting comfortable. Still, the lavender scent the purple candles gave off was soothing and well worth getting back up to light. Drusilla downed the last of her wine and fell back into bed. Her eyes unfocused and the crisscross lines of glittering purple began to dance. It was a fairy's dance, just for her. Maybe it would take her away.

*

Mary ordered pizza with everything on it. When the pizza came, Mary skipped flirting with the delivery boy. Even though she knew she could get free pizza if she tried her hardest. She had pulled it off twice before just because she could. She paid him and politely shut the door in pizza boy's face. The tip was his eyes plunging down her top and Mary not ripping him for it. You're welcome, Mary thought. By the time her father came home, she was halfway through the pizza. Mary didn't offer her father any. She didn't feel in a sharing mood.

"Hi, Princess," he said, and then cracked his crooked back. "How was your day?"

"Fine, Daddy. Did you sell any cars today?"

"Not a damn one, Princess," her father said. "Where is the thing?"

"Drew's not feeling well and went to bed." Mary was very

careful not to address Drusilla in female pronouns around their father.

"The freak's a freeloader, and he's getting fat. Do you hear that?" their father yelled in the direction of Drusilla's door. "You're getting fat!"

Mary hid her disapproval. She continued eating her pizza and privately disagreed. Mary had done all her own research when she found out Drusilla was taking hormones. You gained weight like crazy if you weren't careful. Drusilla was only a little bit chubby compared to the whale she could have been if she really let herself go. Drusilla was not letting herself go. She was letting herself develop. Not that her father would understand that.

"As soon as the school year's out, that thing's out. The fucking freak."

Mary was happy that it was September. It gave her plenty of time to help change his mind. For now, she could do her best to steer him away from the subject. "When can I have a car, Daddy?"

*

Michael couldn't get Drusilla out of his head. He had the feeling that Drusilla was a puzzle he was going to enjoy solving. His lips stung where she kissed him, and a quick check in the mirror confirmed for him that his lips were bruised. He smiled to himself and pulled his car into the driveway of the little blue and white house that was now his house. His mother was standing in her scrubs at the door with a very disapproving look. Shit, Michael thought.

"Hey, Madre," he said, cheerfully, as he got out of the car.

"You better have a good reason for missing school today, Michael," she said in Spanish. She was a head shorter than Michael, with large, tawny eyes and thick, dark hair, and she was terrifying when angered.

"I only missed homeroom," Michael replied. "I had stomach problems, and I wound up spending too much time in the bathroom today."

Her eyes narrowed. "Are you telling me the truth?" she

demanded.

"Si, Madre."

"Why didn't you go to the nurse?" she asked, switching back to English.

"It was only a little diarrhea. They would have sent me home, and I didn't want to miss school over that."

Michael's mother put her hand on his forehead. "You don't have a fever. Did you stop somewhere for breakfast this morning?"

"I got a breakfast sandwich when I got gas, yeah," Michael offered. He thought he might have a sandwich wrapper in the back of his car somewhere. Hopefully.

"Hmm. Maybe don't eat there anymore, okay," she said.

"Not after today," Michael said. "My stomach's still messed up."

"Okay. I have a graveyard shift at the hospital, but dinner's in the fridge. All your father has to do is throw the casserole dish in the oven. Make sure you eat it. I mean it, Michael. Don't let your father order a pizza again."

"Okay," Michael replied.

His mother cradled his cheek in her hand. "Good boy. I'll see you in the morning, before school."

"Have a good night." Michael smiled.

*

Drusilla walked into the cafeteria with her lunch, and a knot in her stomach. She sat at her table and ate her tomato and sprout sandwich in silence. She was waiting for something, but she didn't know what. What she did know was that she wasn't going to like it. When she was done, she took her trash to the trashcan. As she turned, a scrawny boy with an egg shaped head pointed at her. Drusilla recognized him from study hall. The guy stood up. Drusilla rolled her eyes. Here we go, she thought.

"You're a bitch!" he yelled.

Drusilla nearly lost herself in a giggle fit. Was that the best he had? Wow! She was about to demolish him when Drusilla caught Michael's face. He was looking at the boy, and he did not look pleased. All the guys around Michael laughed and high fived each other stupidly, but Michael just glared. Paul Hunt was glaring, too, only it was directed at Drusilla. Drusilla returned the glare and ran her pointer finger delicately across her throat before walking away.

Drusilla walked calmly up to the teacher on lunchroom duty. “I need to go to the bathroom.”

The teacher wrote her a pass as if he was on autopilot. She snatched it up and left for the girl’s room. Drusilla sat there until the bell rang. Then, she gathered her stuff and fazed into her study hall. A girl from her art class was already sitting in a chair and weaving a tapestry. She had long, dark hair that fell down her back like an oil spill against her aqua blue dress. Drusilla sat in her normal seat. The boy with an egghead came in and walked right up to Drusilla. This ought to be good, Drusilla thought.

“Um... I'm Edgar,” he said.

What an unfortunate name, Drusilla thought, as she regarded the shape of his head. “What do you want?”

“I just wanted to say I'm sorry for calling you a bitch in the lunchroom. I feel really guilty about it. I was just wondering if you would shake my hand and accept my apology.” He held out his hand.

“Um....” Drusilla blinked at that. She was frozen in her seat. Her eyes fixed on the outstretched hand. Her gaze flicked to the girl from art. The girl's eyes flitted from Drusilla to the boy, and back again.

“That is so nice!” the girl from art class said, loudly and pointedly.

Drusilla snapped out of it. She shook his hand with a quiet “Sure, whatever.”

Edgar looked very relieved. Just then, Michael Prince walked in. Convenient, Drusilla thought, darkly. Michael got right up in Edgar's face for a moment. The boy looked afraid, and Michael looked menacing. Then, Michael moved past him to his seat next to Drusilla. Drusilla's lunch traveled to her throat and sat there. Swallow it, she told herself. The lump was hard, but she managed. Michael regarded her for a long moment. Now what? Drusilla sighed, internally. Michael watched her for another long moment.

"Hi," Michael finally said.

Butterflies nibbled at Drusilla's innards. "Hi."

She quickly pulled something out of her bag at random. Her plan was to pretend to read her math book for the rest of the period. She could feel Michael's smirk, and Drusilla wanted nothing more than to slap his smart, little mouth. Sadly, she was too afraid. A pity, since Michael was now watching her read a stupid math book. Michael ran a finger along her knuckle. I'm pathetic, Drusilla thought, and looked up at him.

"Are you enjoying your algebra?" Michael teased.

"I hate you," Drusilla grumbled, and went back to her book.

*

Drusilla was stocking up paper cups. Work was empty. A dead night, and Drusilla welcomed it. The chiming bells made Drusilla look up, but she already knew. It was Michael. Of course it was Michael. As if she hadn't had enough Michael in her life. Drusilla was half tempted to throw hot coffee in his face. Then, she remembered he hated coffee, so she began to make a green tea, extra hot. Michael reached the counter. A squirming desire began to assert itself in her gut, and emotion reverberated through her bones. It was like the stomach faeries decided to mosh pit. Little shits.

"What do you want?" Drusilla sighed without turning to face him.

"You know what I want," Michael answered, seductively. Drusilla's body jumped at that, and she looked at him. Michael pointed at the tea steeping in Drusilla's hand.

"Michael," Drusilla groaned.

"Bad day?"

"Ever since you came to town," Drusilla teased, but Michael's face fell. He looked about to cry.

"I'm not a bad guy," Michael said.

"I know," Drusilla said, a little softer. If this kept up, she would barely be speaking at all.

Michael leaned closer. Drusilla was shivering in her nonslip shoes. She wanted to back away, but she was stuck behind the damn counter. Michael reached over and touched her cheek. It felt like being turned to stone, Drusilla decided. She half hoped the intensity of his crystal, clear eyes would shatter her, but Drusilla knew better. This would linger long into the night. A deep-rooted feeling that would, and did, keep her up most nights. She wanted to reach up and hold his hand firmly there, but she knew better.

"Please, my boss is in today," Drusilla mumbled.

"What time do you get off?"

"Soon, but I-"

"I can wait," he murmured, as he pulled the hand away. "Will you let me pay for it this time?"

"Yeah," Drusilla said, dumbly. She rung him up and gave him the screaming hot cup. When she handed back Michael's change, he grasped her hand. Drusilla hated herself for the way her heart fluttered. He moved her hand to hover over the tip jar. "Michael."

"Don't give it back," he murmured.

"Michael, what are we doing?"

But he took his tea and sat at a table. Drusilla watched him as he took out his contact lenses and put on his birth control glasses. She liked him better with glasses. For some reason, Drusilla was comforted by that weakness. Michael sipped from the paper cup and yanked his mouth away with a sharp intake of breath. Drusilla did her best not to laugh. Michael gave her an accusatory look. Drusilla shrugged as if that meant anything.

Michael was still there when Drusilla's boss - Mrs. Gooseberry - came out of her office to count the till. She was a beautiful black woman with synthetic, butterscotch curls and a pleasantly plump body. Her feather patterned caftan swished as she moved. Mrs. Gooseberry took Drusilla back with her to count the till. Drusilla felt her heart slide from her throat back down to its proper place. Then, Mrs. Gooseberry gave her a sly look, and Drusilla's heart shot right back up to nest in her throat again.

"He's cute," Mrs. Gooseberry said as she nodded her head at the image of Michael on the security monitor. She put the till in the safe and closed the door.

“Aren’t you going to count my till?” Drusilla asked.

“Baby, have you ever been short on a till?”

“No, but-” Drusilla replied.

“It's a damn shame you’re almost out of here. I'll hate to lose you, babe.”

“Well, they’re going to build that community college soon, and Mary -“

“No! You got to get your butt out this town, Drusilla,” Mrs. Gooseberry said. “This isn't the place for you.”

“I know, but Mary -“

“Your sister is going to have to be fine on her own. You give that girl everything. You have to start thinking about yourself, Fairy Queen.”

“I know – wait, what did you call me?”

Mrs. Gooseberry gave a confused tilt of her head. “I called you baby. I always call you baby.”

“Oh.” Drusilla could have sworn, “I thought -“

“Mind getting all cloudy? I don't blame you. That boy is gorgeous, and he's looking at you, baby. Better snatch that before someone else does.”

“I am not snatching anybody,” Drusilla pointed out.

“Okay,” Mrs. Gooseberry gave a knowing smile, “if you say so.”

*

Michael sloshed the last bit of cold tea around in his paper cup and waited for Drusilla. She was taking a really long time, he thought. Not that he needed to worry about things like that. It's not like Drusilla would- no, she would totally skip out the back door. He swirled his cold tea around the cup a few more times. The teabag flopped around impudently. Michael's boredom was taking on a sharpness. He took deep breaths and hoped for a quick passing of this new misery living in his chest.

Drusilla's boss came back out. “Can I refill your cup?” she asked.

Michael got up to walk over to the woman. “No, thanks. I'm

just waiting for Drusilla."

"She's changing out of her uniform. She told me to keep you company until she's back out."

"Okay-"

"What are you two love birds up to tonight? A romantic evening on Kissing Hill? Maybe split some fries over at the diner?" She put one hand on her hip and leaned an elbow on the counter.

"I just wanted to talk to her about –"

"Just-"

"Stuff." Michael was getting sick of everyone cutting him off. "I don't know. I didn't plan anything out, and we aren't..."

Drusilla's boss had a scarier glare then Drusilla and his mother combined. "You better not be messing with her."

Michael almost laughed, but he didn't want to get on her bad side. Still, it was nice knowing at least someone else cared. "No, ma'am."

"She has it hard enough. She don't need another Paul Hunt in her life."

"No, ma' - wait, what?"

Mrs. Gooseberry turned to grab a tin canister. She was clearly not going to say any more on the subject. Drusilla came out from the back room in sweatpants and a shirt with a stretched out collar. Both were black. Michael couldn't help noticing the pale shoulder that peeked out from the stretched top. Drusilla looked at the two of them awkwardly. The little butterfly patches were back on her face. She walked cautiously over to Michael.

"I'll see you tomorrow," Drusilla said to her boss.

"Have fun, you two," Mrs. Gooseberry replied, and she winked at Michael.

Michael walked Drusilla over to her van. Drusilla wouldn't look at him. Michael wasn't sure if that was a good thing or not. The wind rustled past them. Autumn was coming. Drusilla shivered against it, and then, tried to hide it. Michael attempted to put his arm around her, but she pushed it away.

"Dammit, Michael," she said as she looked around, desperately.

"What? I'm just trying to keep you from catching a cold."

"Trying to cop a feel, more likely." Drusilla turned to look at him. Her eyes were pleading. "We both know this isn't going to go anywhere, and..."

Drusilla shifted where she stood. Discomfort plain on her pallid face. Her eyes flicked up to meet Michael's, and the purple orbs swam with regret. This was not going the way Michael had hoped it would. Drusilla's arms hugged around herself. Autumn winds blustered past them again. There was a fragility to her, like she was in several pieces and trying desperately to not let anything slip away. This was a rare glimpse into the Drusilla within, Michael thought. Better not waste it.

"I am the perfect gentleman." Michael half meant it, or at least he could be when it counted, he thought. "Besides, I think I know what you really want."

"Michael, why?" Drusilla groaned.

"I'm just saying," Michael teased. "In the woods you-"

"I only hold malice in my heart, Michael," Drusilla said, sharply.

She narrowed her eyes at him, and Michael was a little pleased at how afraid she was. That had to mean something right? Like maybe she did like him? He crept closer to her. Drusilla trembled and looked away. Michael extended his hand and ran his fingertip along the rough, dry skin of her lower lip. Drusilla trapped his finger in her teeth, but she didn't bite down. What a weird response, Michael thought. Lightly – as if she were made of glass – he caressed Drusilla's chin with his remaining fingers. The skin was a little stubbly. She released the finger and continued to look at the side of her van.

"I know that's not true. You told me so in the woods," Michael said.

"I wish that never happened," Drusilla said, flatly. Her gaze stubbornly fixed on him.

"I don't think you do. Sure, you're freaking out over this, but deep down..."

"Yeah, because you have the magical snowflake penis that's going to solve all of my problems, right?" Drusilla asked, sarcastically. She glared at him. "How dare you?"

Michael felt a tightness in his chest and heat in his ears. He took a deep breath. “That was a messed up thing to say.”

“Well, it's true. Why else is all of this going on here?” Drusilla's hands gestured wildly. “You can't save me, Michael.”

“What's there to save?”

“What's that supposed to mean?” Drusilla spat.

“I'm not trying to fuck your life better with my 'magical snowflake dick’.” Michael made air quotes with his fingers. “I happen to like you the way you are.”

“Ew, what's wrong with you?” Drusilla replied.

All fire flooded out of Michael. “I like you. Why is that so hard to believe?”

“Because!” Drusilla exploded. “We literally just met a few days ago, and now you’re like in love with me, or something. Who does that?”

Michael's face fell. “No. It's more *like at first sight*.”

“Ugh,” Drusilla said with her arms crossed. “You would believe in that crap, wouldn't you?”

“Yeah, I do, actually.” Michael was fighting to keep the sinking feeling from his voice. “I'm sorry I'm not edgy and jaded like you.”

“Yeah, then you could be all 'like at first sight' with yourself,” Drusilla said in air quotes, mocking his.

“Screw you,” Michael growled as fresh fury erupted in him.

“No, thanks. If I was in the mood for four minutes on my back with nothing to do, it'd be with anyone but you.”

“Yeah, well, I'm sure I have Paul Hunt to thank for that gripping description,” Michael shot back, without thinking.

Drusilla's hand flew across his face before he knew what hit him. Michael stood there with a stinging feeling that penetrated deeper than his face. He looked at Drusilla, and angry tears welled up in her eyes. Regret hit him harder than even Drusilla could. Michael watched as she walked around to the driver’s side and hopped in. She slammed the door. The engine whined as Drusilla cranked it to life, and without another moment wasted, she peeled off. Michael watched as her taillights disappeared in the distance. He could feel eyes on his back. He was sure that

Drusilla's boss was watching him. Michael looked back at the coffee shop, but there was no one in the window.

*

Mary sat in her room. She flipped through a few magazines. After that got old, she went to check on her plants. A small tomato plant wasn't doing so well under the heat lamp. The poor thing was all limp and yellowing. Mary stuck her finger in the plant's soil and reached for her power. She watched the slightly yellowing, wilting plant spring back with a lush green. The leaves stood strong. A wave of gratification warmed Mary through.

"That's better, my love," she said to the tomato plant.

After that, Mary flopped back on her bed and began putting an outfit together in her head. Friday was the most important day for her. She had to wow in order to make them think about her the two days they didn't see her, but not Michael. She would probably have to try harder than a Friday outfit to reach his mind. He would be a challenge to get, and Drusilla was afraid of him. That made him doubly appealing to Mary. The thrill of the hunt. Mary's pulse jumped at the thought of the moment when Michael would be wrapped around her little finger.

*

Drusilla walked in the door as quietly as she could. The last thing she needed after today was a run in with her father. There was no chance that he would be waiting up for Drusilla. Her father didn't care about her enough to be worried that she was running late. Drusilla slipped into the bathroom. She looked in the mirror. Dark streaks of makeup ran down her face. She rubbed at them with her grubby fingertips. Then, she yanked off her clothes and curled up into a ball in the bathtub. She closed her eyes as the hot water beat against her and tried to forget. A sob wrenched through her lungs. She failed to swallow the flood. After she showered, she slipped into her room and found Mary sitting straight up in her bed, arms crossed.

"Whoa-"

"Where the hell have you been?" Mary hissed in quiet anger.

"I'm sorry I worried-"

"Don't change the subject. You should have been home an hour ago. Where were you? Answer me!"

"Mary, you're acting like it's-"

"I'm going to bed!" Mary got up from Drusilla's bed and stormed dramatically out. "I don't have to listen to this."

"What else?" Drusilla asked herself.

She shut the door behind her and flopped onto her large, squishy bed. Drusilla looked up at the purple construction paper butterflies. Then, Drusilla lit a few candles and turned out the lights. It made the ugly, pink walls she had wanted so much as a child more bearable. Michael's face danced through her thoughts. Smashing her face against a pillow, Drusilla screamed into it. She knew she shouldn't let herself get involved. What little semblance of normal she had was slipping away from her. There was, of course, no way Michael Prince was done with her. She should have let the tree crush Michael; she knew it. Her moment of weakness was going to cost her. It was all too exhausting. The last thing she saw before she drifted off to sleep was gentle glinting of the butterflies' wings.

Chapter 4

Michael whistled as he made his way through the crowded halls. The box in his pocket was burning a hole right through, but he played it cool. He heard the sound of nails against metal, and his heart sank. He stopped whistling and made his way over to her. She was in her everyday black leggings and hoodie that probably used to be as black as her mood. A little, pleated skirt peeked out from underneath that. She shot a glare at him. Then, she yanked on the locker a couple of times with a frustrated growl. After that, Drusilla punched the thing leaving a new dent.

"Please, just let me open it," Michael offered.

"Do what you want. You always do," she said as she slammed the next locker over to her and moved out of the way.

"About yesterday," Michael said as he opened the locker with ease.

"Mary's acting like a psycho because you held me up last night with your bullshit."

"I'm sorry," Michael said. "For that, and the other thing. I shouldn't have said that to you."

Drusilla rolled her large, purple eyes. "Whatever, like I care."

"You hit me pretty hard."

"Well, maybe you shouldn't comment on things you know nothing about." Drusilla didn't bother waiting for him to move away to get into her locker. She just shoved him and pulled out her books.

"I know. I'm trying to apologize. I got you this... to say sorry." He reached into his pocket and pulled out the box.

"Put that away, people can see you. That's all you need."

"I don't give a shit what other people think. You should try it sometime."

"Michael!" The bell rang. "Go to class," Drusilla said, then vanished.

Michael looked at the spot where Drusilla had been standing for a little. Then, he slipped the box into Drusilla's open locker, shut it, and hauled ass to homeroom.

Michael slipped into the classroom and to his seat next to Mary, who glared at him briefly, then looked away dramatically. Whatever, Michael thought. He opened his science book and started reviewing for a test he had later that day. He could feel Mary's eyes on him, but he didn't care. If she was going act like a child, she would have to do it to someone who was willing to put up with it. Michael took out his neon highlighter and began marking information he thought might be important.

*

Drusilla was glad it was Friday. She had an awesome weekend of work ahead of her, and she was super excited about not having to be home much. Drusilla went into the art class' backroom to get her lady sculpture, only to discover that it had been squished. Her heart lurched. She had worked so hard on it. Drusilla had to flutter her eyelashes and swallow hard, twice, to keep from crying. Remember where you are, she told herself. She took a couple deep breaths and assessed the damage like she didn't already know it was wrecked.

"Why did you do that to your piece?" asked a soft voice. "It was so pretty."

"What?" Drusilla looked. It was Shelly Lots, from study hall. Her tapestry hung from a belt around her jeans. "I didn't," Drusilla replied, flatly, but she stopped herself. Now she was talking to people? Ugh. “Never mind.”

“That's horrible. Just because you are dating the new guy.”

“Um... come again?” Drusilla felt a hard sharpness plunge through her chest.

Shelly stopped. “Aren’t you dating that new guy? Michael, right? From study hall?”

“Who told you that?” Drusilla demanded. “Did you tell anyone that?”

“I didn't, but everyone's talking about it. I'm sorry. Is it not true? I heard it from Peter Piper, and then yesterday... you know. In study hall.” The girl’s face looked flushed. “So, I assumed...”

“It's fine. Whatever.” Drusilla felt sick. “People can say what they want. It's not like I care.”

And with that she stormed out of the backroom. Everyone was looking at her. The room was so quiet that Drusilla could hear the buzz of the florescent lights, or was that the sound of everything everyone wasn't saying. Drusilla went to the chalkboard and grabbed the rainbow painted block of wood that was the art teacher's hall pass. She made up some lie about feeling ill and left.

*

Principal Peep's office was clean and tidy, with boring blue walls and a little sheep plushy on her tan painted metal desk. She was Mrs. Gooseberry's sister, so they looked a lot alike, only Principal Peep was slim and preferred her hair in a simple bun as opposed to the extravagant hair that Mrs. Gooseberry loved to rock. Principal Peep liked business suits, and Mrs. Gooseberry loved more colorful flowing fabrics. Both sisters were beautiful, Drusilla thought, in their own ways, and Drusilla was very fond of each. Principal Peep’s smile was wide and welcoming.

“Come in, Drusilla. I thought I'd be seeing you soon,” she greeted Drusilla. “You look like you need a cup of Gooseberry tea.”

“Yes, please,” Drusilla said, dropping the Little Miss Badass act.

She sat in the little plastic chair in front of Principal Peep's desk. Principal Peep poured water from an electric kettle into a dainty china teacup. "Are we going to be talking about Jack Horner, Miss Bonnet?"

"No, why?" Drusilla took the cup from Principal Peep.

"Now, let me see," Principal Peep said, more to herself. "Ah ha!"

Drusilla watched as Principal Peep grabbed a tin out of a wicker basket filled to the brim with tea. She opened it and began scooping herbs into a little metal tea ball. Then, she turned to plunk the ball into Drusilla's cup. Red like blood leached into the hot water. Drusilla put the cup on Principal Peep's desk to steep.

"I was worried I had run out of Gooseberry tea. Now, what's got you all bothered and cutting art class?"

"Not Jack," Drusilla replied.

"Not Jack," Principal Peep echoed. "Everyone's real shook up over that poor boy. I've been seeing five - six students a day upset over him. Mary, even."

"Yeah, I think she's pretty messed up over him. She won't admit it, but I mean..." Drusilla looked down at her clasped hands.

"What's got you down here?" Principal Peep asked. She was sitting behind her desk. Peep pulled a tin of tea biscuits out of a squeaky desk drawer and offered them to Drusilla wordlessly. Drusilla declined. Principal Peep left them on the desk.

"I'm having a really hard time with..." Drusilla paused. She didn't want to call out Michael directly. "Just this week has been... chaotic."

"Ah, I see. Well, it's the first week of your senior year. How was your summer, by the way?"

"What?" Drusilla asked, stupidly. "Oh, fine. I guess."

"That's good," Principal Peep said. "Well, like I said, it's the first week of school, and with the death of that poor boy the weekend before school started... there are bound to be a lot of... emotions happening. Give it some time. Things will calm down. Did you go to the student memorial?"

"Yeah," Drusilla said. "Mary wanted to go, so..."

Principal Peep nodded. “She seems to have really been fond of Jack.”

“Everyone was very fond of Jack,” Drusilla said. “He always seemed so nice.”

“You didn't seem too fond of him,” Principal Peep replied.

“I used to be.” Drusilla pulled the tea ball out of the cup by the chain and began to dunk it. “You know until... you know.”

“Still, after what happened with him and Paul, I don't blame you,” said Principal Peep. “Still, there is college next year to look forward to. Have you thought about schools, yet?”

“No. I know I want to get into a good school,” Drusilla answered with the same lame lie. In reality, she didn't know what she wanted to do. “A part of me is worried about Mary.”

“Well, that new community college will be opening up soon. I'm sure you could get a full scholarship, easily.”

“Yeah, but it'll mostly be the same people all over again.”

“That's true,” Principal Peep said, “but college has a way of maturing people. Give it some thought.”

“Okay,” Drusilla relented.

“Alright.” Principal Peep smiled.

“I should probably get going to class, or something,” Drusilla said.

“Well, thank you for coming in.” Principal Peep stood to see Drusilla out. “I love having you kids around. You keep me young.”

*

George sat across from Michael in the lunchroom. Michael seemed to be eating in thought. George didn't even want to know. Drusilla Bonnet was a no show for lunch today, which was good, but every time Paul Hunt said anything, Michael would shoot him a quick, dirty look. What was going on now, George thought. He knew the rumors going around, and he knew what went down between Bonnet and Prince in the woods. George had a very bad feeling in his gut. Something he couldn't shake. You don't kiss a witch like that and expect it to be just a kiss. Was Michael in trouble?

"Hey, man?" George asked Michael. "Want to hang after school today?"

"Nah, I can't. Maybe Saturday, though. Give me a call Saturday," Michael said before he retreated back to his brain.

George looked at Michael. "Everything okay?"

"Huh?" Michael said as he looked up from his mashed potatoes. "I'm sorry, man, what happened?"

"I asked if you were okay. You're acting weird, man."

"Yeah, just thinking." Michael scooped up some mashed potatoes with his plastic spoon and let it plop back down on his tray.

"Yo, your friend okay over there, George?" came Paul's voice.

"Yeah, man," Michael replied. George didn't like the flat edge to Michael's voice or the blank look in his eyes as he watched the food on his tray. Michael looked up at Paul, and George's bad gut feeling intensified. "I'm good. You?"

"What?" asked Paul.

"You good, man?" Michael asked in that same flat voice.

"Um... yeah," Paul said, a little unsure of what just happened.

"Yeah, we'll see about that," Michael said under his breath as he went back to playing with his food.

"Man, what is your problem?" George asked.

"Nothing," Michael said as he took a drink from his tiny milk carton.

*

Drusilla stomped her way down the hallway. Everyone made plenty of room for her, but they were looking at her and whispering. Her whole day was like that. Drusilla was losing control. She could feel it slipping through her fingers. She wanted to snatch it back, but she couldn't see how. Her mind spun. How was she going to get everything under control? Drusilla knew better. Everything was crumbling into the sea, and if she wasn't careful-

Hands too strong to be Mary's grabbed her and pulled her into a bathroom. Drusilla was thrown hard into a wall. Her body bounced off the blue tile. The boys' room. A meaty fist collided with her gut, so hard she nearly vomited. The other hand pulled her upright by the hair. Drusilla struggled to be free, but it was no use. The grip was too strong. She looked up at her attacker. Paul Hunt, of course. He was too strong. Too hard to beat. It was happening all over again. No! Drusilla reached for her power and felt it wash over her body. It seeped into her muscles making them strong and hard.

"Hair pulling?" Kick. Drusilla punctuated her words with a stiff thrust of her boot into Paul's abdomen. "Really, Paul?" Kick. Paul fell back and landed on his butt. Drusilla – not missing a beat – walked right over to where he sat, and with the same boot, kicked him across the face. Blood exploded from his nose as Drusilla knocked him over.

"Get up, Paul. You're making a mess," Drusilla said as she cracked her neck.

Drusilla watched him. She noticed every muscle and movement as she let Paul struggle to his feet. Paul wiped the blood from his face. Then, he lunged, grabbing her by the shoulders. Drusilla slipped her arms up between Paul's and grabbed his rock hard biceps. She pulled down and kneed Paul Hunt in the face, twice, before he got his grip on her again. Paul lifted her off of the ground and slammed her hard against the large, plate glass mirror. Drusilla felt the mirror break beneath her skull. She shut her eyes against any shards of glass. All her power began to seep out of her muscles. She was running out of time. Balling her hand into a fist, Drusilla clocked Paul once, twice, three times in the face before he dropped her.

Drusilla landed in a crouch and swept Paul off his feet with a kick. Paul came crashing down on his side. Drusilla leaped over Paul, intending to run out of the bathroom, but Paul snatched her by the ankle. It was Drusilla's turn to come crashing to the dirty, tiled floor. Drusilla brought up her arms in an attempt to buffer the fall. She collided with a hard slap! The wind was knocked out of her for the second time.

She felt Paul's hands at her side. He flipped her on her back. Drusilla struggled, and Paul gave her a hook to the ribs for it. More pain exploded in her, and Drusilla cried out. Paul grabbed her by the waist of her leggings and yanked her under him. Drusilla felt a bare butt cheek touch cold tile, and panic set in. Drusilla flailed like a bag of squirrels. Her fingers bent into claws, and she tore at him. At the same time, she kicked wildly, but she could not seem to buck him. Paul struggled for control, and Drusilla received another shot in the mouth.

Drusilla struggled harder. With a frustrated roar, Paul grabbed her by the shoulders, lifted Drusilla a little, and slammed her down. All fight drained out of her. It felt like Drusilla's brain was swelling to twice its size. Her ears were ringing. Paul yanked her leggings down and was fiddling with his pants. Drusilla could hear the jingle of his belt buckle. It was happening again, and she promised herself she wouldn't let him. She blinked several times to get her eyes to focus. Paul's face contorted in beet red frustration. Never again, she told herself. Drusilla gritted her teeth and head-butted Paul. He grunted, and Drusilla kneed him between the legs. Paul howled. She shoved at Paul. She didn't really have it in her to push him off, but she could slide free from underneath him.

Drusilla struggled to her feet. Paul lay on his side, clutching his tender parts. Drusilla scowled and kicked him. Paul cried out and rolled over. Drusilla kicked him again, and again, and again. Paul lay there, like the crumpled, pitiful thing he was. Only, Drusilla had no pity for him. Relentlessly, she stomped him. A guttural roar escaping her as she did. Until finally, Drusilla watched Paul writhe in pain for a little. It gave her time to catch her breath. Then, she turned to leave. Paul grunted something out. Drusilla stopped.

"What did you just say?" Drusilla growled. She marched over to him and kicked him across the face. "You really don't know when to stop, do you, Paul? Fine. Have it your way." And she raised her boot again.

When she was finished, Drusilla hobbled out into the hall. She had to get to Tank. The bell rang. Of course, Drusilla thought, and she found that thinking hurt. She hobbled faster. Get to Tank. She pulled at her personal power and tried her best to shift. She felt herself blink out. She was in the cool, dark rush of nothingness, but as suddenly as she was plunged in, she was ripped out.

*

Michael walked out of his science class, feeling more confused than anything. It's not like he wanted to be a scientist anyway. He slung his backpack over his shoulder and went to head for his locker. He stopped. Drusilla looked up at him, and for the second that she was there, he could see fear in her eyes. Then, she faded away. A pang hit Michael in his chest. It happened so fast, but Michael couldn't help feeling responsible. He really messed up. He should never have kissed her. Michael tried, and failed, to swallow his guilt over that. Trying to make it up to her blew up in his face the last time.

Michael walked down the hall towards the bathroom. He was so deep in thought, he didn't notice Paul staggering away. Michael stepped in, walked past the stalls towards the urinals, and stopped. The mirror had been smashed, and Michael spotted blood speckles, despite someone doing their best to wipe it away. His brows furrowed. The damage made him think of Drusilla instantly. He turned on his heel and ran out of the bathroom.

*

Mary got into Tank. Drusilla was already there, waiting. She was wearing sunglasses, and her hood was up. Mary hopped in the back to change. She wondered who Drusilla was fighting with. Mary pulled on her jeans and oversized shirt. Drusilla cranked the engine and sped off. Mary was knocked off her feet as Drusilla drove. An old soda can crunched against her side, painfully. Cranky, Drusilla was the crankiest after fights with Paul Hunt.

"Hey," Mary roared. "I'm not even dressed yet."

"I saw Michael coming," Drusilla explained, flatly. "You don't want him to see you changing into those frumpy ass clothes, do you?"

"Yeah," Mary said, sarcastically, "he might actually notice me then."

Drusilla slammed on the brakes, throwing Mary forward. Mary was over it. Drusilla twisted in her seat to look at Mary. "What is that supposed to mean?"

"Oh, please," Mary said as she slumped into the front seat to strap herself in. "Everyone's talking about you and Michael."

"Yuck, Mary."

"I know. If you were getting laid, it would calm you the fuck down, so clearly what they're saying is a bunch of bullshit."

"Yep," Drusilla answered. Then, she sped off.

"Just like you getting into a fight with Paul Hunt is bullshit," Mary said under her breath.

"Hmm?" Drusilla pondered, pointedly. "You have something you want to say, Mary?"

Mary looked out of her window. She was pretending to watch the boring town roll by. Same houses, same fucked up shopping center, and same bumpy cracks in the fucked up road. Just the same old, same old. Mary was sick of it all. Her mind wandered to Jack Horner. Such privilege, that boy, she thought to herself. He got unstuck. Of course, he had to die to do it, but he went out in a blaze of glory. Well, probably anyway. Knowing Jack...

"I wish we didn't have to do this anymore," Mary mumbled to herself.

"Ice cream for dinner?" Drusilla offered.

"No..." Mary sulked.

"Okay," Drusilla said as she merged onto the interstate.

"What are you doing?" Mary asked.

"It's Friday. We don't have to be home in time for bed. Wanna do whatever?" Drusilla was smiling.

"Doesn't that hurt your face?" Mary asked.

"Only a little," Drusilla replied.

"Dad's going to be pissed."

"Dad doesn't give a shit, Mary."

Mary looked out of her window again. Trees whizzed past.

They were taller and lusher on the interstate. Which was nice. "Fine, but I don't want you and Dad getting into a huge fight on my weekend."

"Text him," Drusilla offered. "Just tell him we're grabbing dinner out, or whatever. It'll probably be the truth anyway."

"Fine," Mary said as she swiped her phone and began to text.

"Okay, Princess," Mary read the reply. Predictable. Mary rolled her eyes.

"Okay, parental unit informed," Mary sighed. "Now, my turn."

Drusilla groaned. "It was just a scuffle."

"No shit, Drusilla," Mary spat. "With Paul?"

"Just let it go," Drusilla demanded.

"Fine, whatever." Mary crossed her arms. "It's not like I don't already know anyway."

"That's a redundant sentence, Mary," Drusilla said as she pulled off the interstate.

"You're a redundant sentence," Mary retorted.

"Sass, Mary," Drusilla accused.

"Your bruised face is sass!" Mary spat back.

"Burn," Drusilla said in an approving, deadpan voice.

They drove in silence. Mary scowled at the mansions and wine vineyards. More boring stuff. They passed the Geppetto estate. How bland, Mary thought. It was getting darker out. What were they doing? She looked over at Drusilla and sighed. Drusilla had taken off her sunglasses, and Mary could see some of the bruising. Hopefully it wasn't that bad. Knowing Drusilla, it would probably be ten times worse. They drove a little further, and they found a quiet spot. Mary knew the spot well. Guys took her here to get fresh.

"Come on," Mary said, opening her door. "I'll show you the best spot to look at the stars."

Chapter 5

Drusilla opened her eyes, and a smile played on her face. Saturday, Drusilla remembered, as she took a deep, stinging breath of morning air. She was swaddled in freedom, and everything was perfect. Her stress melted away like butter. The door to her bedroom opened slowly, and a groggy Mary in an over-sized shirt stepped in. Mary closed the door behind her. She crawled into bed with Drusilla and snuggled up close. Her hair smelled of strawberries and honey.

"Good morning," Mary whispered. "Dad's gone. I heard him leave early this morning."

"Awesome!" Drusilla said as she stretched her injured body, gingerly. "What do you want for breakfast?"

Mary's eyes wandered in thought. "Pizza?"

"Pizza it is, then." Drusilla struggled to sit up, but she managed. Her body was tense and sore.

"Oh my god," Mary screamed. "Look at you!"

"Huh?" Drusilla yawned, and then winced.

Mary grabbed Drusilla's bruised face. Drusilla yelped and smacked her hand away. "Damn it, Drusilla! I didn't know it was this bad."

"Oh, Mary, relax. It's not like-"

"It's not like what?" Mary cried. The tears streaming down her face. "You look like-"

"I know what I look like, Mary. Dammit. It's Saturday. You know the rules."

"Nothing to do with school on weekends," Mary and Drusilla both said.

"Well, I'm ordering a pizza, and I want sausage," Mary whined.

"I'll suffer through it," Drusilla playacted.

"Damn right, you will," Mary mumbled to herself as she got off the bed and stomped to the door. "You..."

The rest of Mary's tantrum left with her. Drusilla rolled her sore shoulders. Her fight with Paul did more damage than she thought. Drusilla dragged herself out of bed and went to her mirror. Her face was busted. Dry blood crusted the inside of her nose, her left eye looked like an eggplant, and the right side of her cheek was bruised and tender. The metallic taste of blood still lingered in her mouth. A tooth felt loose. She wiggled it with her tongue. Fabulous. Drusilla pulled her black t-shirt over her head to examine the rest of her blotchy body. More skin was bruised than not. There was no way this was going away before Monday. Drusilla groaned and got back into bed. She slept until Mary came into her room with a large pizza box, the scent of meat assaulting Drusilla's nostrils. It was nauseating.

*

It was mid-afternoon when Michael finally rolled off of the mattress on the floor. His room looked as if a bomb had exploded in it. The floor was completely covered by clothes, books, half unpacked boxes, and boxes that he hadn't bothered to unpack yet. Michael's bed frame rested against one wall, while the box spring rested against another. His closet door was slid open, and more stuff was piled up in a small mountain almost as tall as he was. Michael slid on his boxers and his glasses. Now he could see the mess in clearer detail. A tickle in his throat made him clear it.

Michael pulled a long sleeve, green shirt and a faded pair of jeans off of the floor at random. Then, threw them on. After struggling to open his door, Michael made his way through the hallway and into the living room, which was now blue for some reason. The scent of wet paint was in the air. Michael's father - a tall blond man - was untwisting a dirty paint roller off of a broom length wooden pole. Blue paint splattered Michael's father's clothes, skin, and wild mane of hair.

"Morning," greeted Michael's father with a booming, cheerful voice.

"Mom know you did this?" Michael said as he looked at the uncovered, cream color carpet. Michael spotted a patch of rug that looked like it had been scrubbed and was now a washed out, almost blue-gray smudge.

"No. I'm going to surprise her. She was thinking about painting, but she works so hard."

"Well, she does like blue..." Considering the outside of the house was also blue. Michael's insides were cringing. "Where's Mom now?"

"She should be home from work momentarily." Michael's father looked so proud of himself.

Michael was not going to be there for that fight. "Okay, I'm going to go get a carpet cleaner for the rug, Dad."

Michael watched his father survey the rug with his hands on his hips. "Good man."

Michael grabbed his keys and reached into his pocket as he left the house. He scanned his phone for his mother, and then tapped her name with his thumb. Putting the phone to his ear, he listened to the ringing. She was going to be so pissed, Michael thought, as he slid his key into the driver's side door. More ringing. Please pick up, Michael thought at his mother. He hopped into his car. More ringing, then voicemail. Michael hung up and started to text. He explained to her about going out to get a carpet cleaner and to not be mad.

Then, Michael drove. Originally he had planned on going to the coffee shop, but he remembered that Drusilla worked there. Michael needed a break from whatever was going on there, so he made his way to the park. Michael was going to shoot hoops until his mother called him back. Michael's phone was ringing. He felt as though his stomach was a bottomless hole that he was falling down like some Salvador Dali bullshit. Michael pulled over and answered.

"What did your father do, Michael?" Her voice was restrained rage.

"It's actually kind of sweet. I'm going to clean the mess," Michael rushed to say. "No need to freak."

"Oh no, you're not," his mother said. "I'll pick up the carpet cleaner on the way home, and your father can clean up his *own* mess!"

Michael felt pins and needles in his heart. This was going to be a long and loud argument. Suddenly, Michael wished he hadn't... Michael stopped. That wouldn't have been right. "He just wanted to help you out."

"What's on the carpet, Michael?"

"It's only a little paint."

"Goddamnit," Michael heard his mother say to herself. "That carpet was new! I made the Realtor put in all new carpeting and flooring before we bought it."

"It's not that bad. I'm on the way to the store now. I'll have it-"

"No!" Her voice roared through the phone. Now, Michael's heart fell right out of his asshole. "Look, Honey. I know what you're trying to do, but you can't go around saving everyone. It's good that you want to help people, but now is the time for you to live your life. Let everyone else sort themselves out. You can't help others without first taking care of yourself, Michael."

Michael felt like he was the one who had worked an all night shift at the hospital. This was such bullshit, Michael thought. He wasn't trying to save the world. He was just trying to keep his parents from fighting for one day. God fucking damn it! A moistness stung at Michael's eyes, and he swallowed his thoughts before they became words.

"Yeah, maybe you're right." Michael sighed.

"I know it's hard, Michael."

Oh fuck you, and your useless sympathy, Michael thought. "Yeah."

"I'll be home soon, okay?"

No shit, and you'll only be mad at Dad for half a day since I called ahead of time instead of the whole fucking weekend. Michael's fists were clenched. "Okay. I'm going exploring some more since I'm already out."

"Okay, Honey. Have fun."

"I love you, Mom." I just have to keep remembering that.

He hung up the phone and slammed the palm of his hand against the steering wheel. Fire burned his lungs as tears shed from his crystalline eyes. He was weeping and breathing so fast that Michael wasn't sure he actually could breathe. Out of frustration more than anything else, Michael beat his fist against the steering wheel some more. Fuck everything, Michael thought. Just fuck it! Then, he took a deep cleansing breath, wiped his face, and drove.

He suddenly very much wanted to see Drusilla, but she probably didn't want to see him. He was fine with that. Well, no, he wasn't really, but he wasn't about to invade her weekend like that. Also, Michael didn't want anyone to see him like this. He pulled up to a red light. The crossing guard was escorting children across the street with their little backpacks and happy little faces. What was wrong with this scene? Michael pondered. The crossing guard followed up the rear, and the light turned green. Michael was off, speeding through this little town he was growing to hate. Same faceless people, every damn day.

Michael pulled up to the park. It was a flat, gray cement basketball court with one hoop. A stretch of very green grass and a swing set with someone sitting on one. No parking lot. Michael's eyes fell on the large, black van. Exasperation made Michael hang his head. His sweaty forehead rested against the abused steering wheel. Michael could feel the purple orbs of Drusilla upon him. How mad would she feel if he just left now? How personally would she take it? Very, and very. Damn it! Michael slammed his hand against the steering wheel once more, and the horn beeped loudly.

"Fuck!" Michael groaned into the steering wheel, and he got out of the car.

As he walked over to her sitting in the swing, Michael noted how oddly dressed she was. She had her faded black hoodie on with the hood low over her head, blue sweatpants, flip flops of all things, and large dark glasses. She sat sill in the swing and watched Michael as he got closer and closer. Her stillness put Michael even more on edge.

"And I thought that pest, George, was everywhere," Drusilla said in greeting.

"Hey, he's alright." Michael was about to add a 'give him a chance', but thought better of that statement.

"Well, at least he leaves me alone, so yes. I think you're right," Drusilla said. Her glasses were so dark that her eyes were barely visible. "Would you like to sit a while?"

"Whoa." Her invitation threw Michael for a loop. "You're acting different today."

"We're not at school, Michael," Drusilla replied as if that was supposed to mean something.

"It's like someone came and sucked all the bitchiness out of you, like some... bitch sucking... vampire... thing... I guess..." Shut your mouth, Michael.

"I'm only like that because I need to be. Plus, you look like you're having a bad day, so you get a pass," Drusilla said. She gestured to the only other swing next to her.

"You choose to act like that?" Michael said as he took the swing. "Why?"

Michael watched as Drusilla sighed. Her eyes flicked sideways at him through the sunglasses before she began staring into space. "It's my defense mechanism."

"Well, it works," Michael said, reassuringly.

"Worked," Drusilla corrected. She slowly began rocking her swing back and forth with her feet. "Why did you come here?"

"I wanted to be alone," Michael answered.

"No, that's... never mind." Drusilla went back to rocking herself.

"Hm," Michael mused. "What kind of music do you like?"

"Oh?" Drusilla sounded so smug. "Ditching love at first sight for something more substantial?"

"Like at first sight," Michael corrected. "Answer the

question."

"No," Drusilla said.

"Come on?"

"No, it's too easy," Drusilla said. "You have to guess."

"Hm. How many guesses do I get?"

"Um... three. Why not?" Drusilla replied.

"I'll think about that one, then."

"You do that, Michael."

They sat in silence for a long while. Drusilla's head lolled to one side. A small smile played on her dark lips. It was nice to see, Michael thought. She abandoned rocking the swing for twisting it slightly. Michael looked down and saw that her toenails were painted purple with black crackle.

"I bet I can guess your favorite color," Michael said, breaking the stillness.

"Damn it," Drusilla sighed. "We were just getting comfortable."

"We?" Michael asked.

"Mhmm," Drusilla hummed her affirmation. The stillness began to settle around them again. "Well, Michael?" Drusilla said shattering it again.

"Guess," Michael replied.

"What?"

"Yeah, guess what color I was going to guess."

"Ugh," Drusilla said. "This game sucks."

Drusilla gripped the swing chain with her hand, and Michael saw angry scabs bubbled on her knuckles. Suddenly, it made way too much sense. A lot of feelings bubbled up inside him. The wrecked bathroom flashed before his eyes, and he was having a hard time unseeing it. Michael took a deep breath, and Drusilla mirrored it. She let her jacked up hand drop. It hung limply at her side. Michael felt his brows knit together.

"Well, not that it's an actual color, but-"

"Why are you wearing your hood up like that?" Michael tried to keep his voice even, but every muscle in his body tightened, instantly. The tips of his ears burned as he inhaled fire.

"Hey, I thought we were still on the color-"

"No, really." Michael was fighting to keep the anger out of his voice.

Drusilla looked away. Her face was completely concealed.

"Don't hide from me!" he burst, and instantly regretted it. He took a breath. "I'm sorry."

"I have to leave," Drusilla said as she stood.

"Wait," Michael pleaded. Drusilla stopped. "You don't have to tell me. Just..."

"Just what, Michael?" her voice cracked a little.

"Just... don't leave." Michael's last word was a sigh.

Drusilla didn't turn to face him. She just stood there with her back to him for a while. Michael wasn't sure if she would stay, but before long she slumped back into the swing. She still wouldn't look at him, but at least she was there. Drusilla's chest heaved, and Michael was sure she was going to explode on him at any moment. They sat there for a long and uncomfortable silence.

"I'm sorry, Drusilla, I-"

"Why were you crying?" Drusilla asked.

"Um..." Michael's mouth ran dry.

"If you tell me," Drusilla paused to sigh, "I'll pull down my hood."

"Look at me first?" Michael asked.

Drusilla was very quiet, and very still. Then, she sighed again and looked at him. "Fine."

"Thank you," Michael said. Then, he took a deep breath. "My parents fight. Like all the time, and over the dumbest shit. I know they love each other, but I can never get a break. I'm sure that doesn't sound like a real problem to you, but-"

"No. That really sucks," Drusilla said.

"Yeah, well... that's why," Michael said. His eyes never left her.

Drusilla huffed as she yanked her hood down with one hand and looked at Michael. She had a full face of makeup on, but Michael could still see the swelling where the bruises were beneath. Involuntarily, Michael began to reach out to touch them, but Drusilla yanked her head away. Her glasses slid down her nose, and Michael could see the black panda bear eye makeup that was probably concealing a black eye or two. Now he knew why the glasses were so dark.

"Do you feel like telling me what happened?" Michael's lungs were ablaze.

Drusilla hung her head. "I didn't feel like pulling my hood down, but here we are."

"Well, it looks like you fought back at least." Michael didn't feel like bringing up the bathroom.

"It's not that I don't want to tell you, Michael," Drusilla said in a pitiful voice. "It's just, I'm a part of this thing, and we have these rules-"

"Gotcha," Michael said with a laugh. "Did you make any money?"

"What?" Drusilla asked, dumbly.

"In your 'pit fights'. Did you make any money? That's the whole point. It's all gambling." Drusilla looked confused. Michael sighed. "See my car over there?"

"Yeah," Drusilla said. "Must have cost your parents a shitload."

"No," Michael said as he cracked his knuckles. "I paid for it by myself."

"You paid for your car with winnings you got from fighting?" Drusilla rolled her eyes.

"Yeah, back in Michigan," Michael said. "My mom still thinks I broke my hand skateboarding."

"Bullshit." Drusilla laughed. "But good story, though."

"Tell me who did that to you." Michael looked deeply into her eyes. The purple was so dark, they were nearly black. "And I'll prove it."

"You're full of shit." Drusilla wasn't laughing, suddenly. Pink butterfly patches fought like hell to show through the heavy layers of white.

Michael shook his head. He sank off of his swing onto one knee before her. Drusilla had a shocked wonder about her. Their eyes locked, terror rippled through Drusilla. Michael could see it radiating off of her. Michael held out his hands for her to take. Her clammy fingers curled around his. Something between them sparked. Michael's breath caught in his chest at Drusilla's sharp gasp. Drusilla's hands clamped on his, and the thrum of power rippled through them.

"Tell me who did this, and I'll make him go away."

"Michael, you're scaring me," Drusilla breathed.

Michael rubbed along Drusilla's knuckles with his thumbs. "You don't have to be."

"Michael, I'm... I believe you. *Okay?* Just... *just stop*."

Her last word was a whisper. Tears mingled with makeup and plummeted down her face, leaving blackness in their wake. Michael took Drusilla's hand in his and stood. A breeze came, and Michael was sure it would cut across them, but instead, it seemed to encircle them. The sound of dead leaves rustled at their feet, and Michael shivered against it. Drusilla's eyes shook as she tried to maintain eye contact.

"Never fear," Michael said as he pressed his lips against her bruised knuckles. "I will right this wrong done to you." Then, he let her hand go.

"Um?" Drusilla looked dumbfounded and a little grossed out. "Michael? What does that even mean?"

"I already think I know. I just need you to say his name out loud." Michael said.

"I don't -"

"I want to," Michael said. "Let me."

Drusilla crumpled. "Fine. Paul Hunt. Are you happy now?"

"He will never hurt you again," Michael said.

"Michael."

Michael pressed her hand to his lips again, and then stood. Drusilla's face seemed to fall further. Michael turned to leave. She was calling after him. He would not be detoured from this. He fished his car keys from his pocket as he made his way to the car. Clouds rolled in, and Drusilla was still calling his name. Sorry, Michael thought. This is just something a man has to do. Michael looked up at the sky. It was black. Droplets fell slowly, but it was picking up. Michael looked back at Drusilla. She was marching over to him.

"Michael, I don't need you to do this!" she roared as she

reached him.

"I know you don't!" Michael called back. He walked back to her.

"Damn it, Michael!" Drusilla groaned. "Why can't you just... why are you smiling?"

"Because," Michael said. A different kind of heat filled him. A flame that only seemed to burn for her. It dazed him for a moment. "You have no idea what effect you have on me."

"Um..." Drusilla was wide-eyed and wordless. Then she gulped. Her small Adam's apple jumping up her throat. "Actually, I think I might."

"Not even close," Michael teased. Their mouths were dangerously close.

"Michael!" It was meant to be an angry yell, Michael knew, but Drusilla's voice was a raspy whisper. "Don't save me. Please!"

Michael's hands hugged the curves of her hips, and Drusilla winced. That bastard really did a number on her. Michael imagined how good it would feel, as Paul Hunt's jaw broke under his foot. The image was short lived, however. Someone more important garnered immediate attention. As gently as his lust would allow, Michael wrapped his arms around her chubby form and pulled her in. Drusilla winced a little and gasped, but she didn't push him away. She looked up at him, more scared bunny than ferocious witch.

"Don't kiss me," she breathed. "I don't think I could bare it."

She shivered in Michael's arms. There was no ferocious witch left. The bunny had consumed her and left her like this. Paul had left her like this. A beastly part of Michael knew he could take advantage of her state. It would be so easy. Drusilla looked up at him with her scared, purple eyes and he hated himself for even thinking it. Michael leaned in and pressed his lips against Drusilla's ear. She gasped into his, and Michael pulled away. The grimace of pain in Drusilla's beautiful eyes was too much for him. Rage flooded Michael's system.

"I'm going to kill him and dump his body in the woods with those busted trees." Michael's voice was ice.

*

Mary sat on her bed with a wooden bowl in her lap. In it was a lump of mud. The rain beat against her windows, and Mary smiled. She rubbed the mud in her fingers until it was warm. Then, she took a plastic bear filled with honey and squeezed an amber stream from its head into the bowl. It ended with a funny, little fart noise. She worked the mixture aggressively with her hand. Letting all of her frustration go in the mixing. The mixture thickened, and then thinned. A knock at the door threatened to break Mary's concentration, but she held fast to it.

"Yeah?" she called, knowing full well who it was.

"It's me, Princess."

No shit, Mary thought, as she added a handful of pink salt to the mix. "What's up, Daddy?"

"I need to go into the office for a little bit-"

"Okay," Mary called, cutting her father off.

"Alright. I'll be home later tonight."

"Okay, love you," she called, and then went back to her potion that now needed to be reworked. Damn, she thought.

Her fingernails scraped the bottom of the wooden bowl as she worked. She loved this concoction. The door opened as she mixed, and Drusilla clumped in with her muddy feet. Then, she stopped. So did Mary. Then, Mary nodded to the two sundresses laid out beside her on the bed. One was tiny and white. The other was large and black. Drusilla's eyes flicked back to Mary. Mary understood the fear Drusilla's eyes could instill in others, but what she didn't understand is how no one thought to stop and marvel at them. Lavender for luck, Mary heard the voice echo in her head. She shut it out.

"Are you okay?" Drusilla asked.

Mary looked up at her sister. "It's time."

Drusilla smiled and attempted to take off her hoodie. She winced. Mary stood to help her sister out of the garment. Their eyes met, and Mary dragged her muddy hand along the bruised side of Drusilla's face. Brown streaks were left in her wake. Then, Mary turned, and as she did, she crossed her arms to lift the oversized shirt over her head. Drusilla reached beside her for the bowl and dipped both hands in the muck. Mary felt the cool mud mixture as Drusilla's hands moved down the length of her shoulder blades. Mary stuck a finger in and traced along Drusilla's collarbone. Drusilla stepped out of her pants, and Mary added mud to Drusilla's thighs. The sisters took turns painting each other's naked flesh until the mixture was gone. After that, they slipped into the dresses and left Mary's room as painted women.

The two of them crept through the darkened house to the back door. The rain had let up only a little. Perfect. They slipped into the back yard to dance - among Mary's empty garden beds - in the rain. Mary felt the energy spin around her as they twirled and flailed their arms. Elation filled her, as if Mary were going down the first drop on a roller coaster. She almost felt her feet lift off the ground, she was so buoyant. For a long while they danced. Stomping their bare feet in the wet soil of the flower beds and howling like wild animals. The rain had long stopped, and the sound of crickets singing added to the music of their spell.

*

George sat on a very comfortable leather sofa in the den. He was shooting Nazis in the face on his flat screen. His fingers worked the buttons of his wireless controller effortlessly, as the voices of the other players on his team shrieked orders and insults to each other in his headset. All in all, a good Saturday so far, thought George. He tapped the top bumper, and his character lobbed a grenade. Boom! Yeah, good Saturday.

A vibration from his pocket caused George to find a corner to camp in for a few seconds. He pulled his phone from his pocket and looked at the screen. Michael Prince. George hoped this wasn't about Drusilla Bonnet, but he knew it was. George contemplated leaving it and going back to his game, but Michael was alright. He just didn't get how things worked yet, was all. George swiped and put the phone to his ear.

"Yo?" George answered.

"Hey, man, what's up?"

"Gaming. You?" George picked his controller back up and went back to his rampage with a tilted head.

"Nice, wanna chill today?"

"Yeah," George said in surprise. For once, this wasn't about Drusilla Bonnet.

"Cool, I have to ask you something."

Just kidding, George thought. This was going to be about nothing but Drusilla Bonnet. "Okay, fine. When do you want to meet up?"

*

Michael waited outside of the mall. An old clunker of a green car pulled up and parked. George got out of the driver's side and shut the door. Then, he locked the car with the press of a button. In one hand, he held a book. He looked annoyed, Michael noted. George walked over to him briskly. This may be awkward, Michael worried. When George reached him, the two slapped hands and bumped knuckles.

"What's going on?" Michael asked in greeting.

"You tell me," George replied, coldly.

"What's with the book?"

"Look, Michael, I get that you got this weird obsession with Drusilla Bonnet."

"It's not weird," Michael interjected.

"Everyone thinks it's weird. Including Drusilla."

Michael crossed his arms against that. "Did she say that?"

"I may have overheard a conversation to that effect."

There was a long pause between them. Michael took a deep breath. "Well, I still have questions."

"Good," George said. "I'll tell you everything I know, but after that, I want nothing more to do with this. Don't ask me about anything, and I don't want to hear any more about Drusilla. Do that stuff on your own time. Deal?" George held out his free hand.

"What?" Michael asked.

"That's my price, man," George added.

Michael looked at the hand and shook it. "Deal."

"Awesome, let's get a burger, or something."

Michael followed his friend through the mall to the burger hut, and they ordered two big burgers before taking a table. The burger hut looked decent enough, with yellow and green striped wallpaper and big brown booths. George slid the book across the table wordlessly. Michael picked it up. It was last year's Elderberry High yearbook. Michael opened the mint green and maroon cover, and flipped past the page filled with signatures. He flipped past the seniors' section to juniors. There, on the first page of the junior section, was Paul Hunt in one of his plaid shirts, with his beard looking big and stupid. He had an idiot grin and held a thumbs-up for the camera. His other arm was around the shoulder of...

"Whoa." Michael almost slammed the book shut.

"Yup," George said.

Paul had his arm around a scrawny figure with long, thick, poker straight black hair. A lavender button up shirt concealed the scarecrow thin torso and was buttoned up to the collar. A collar trimmed in lace. The pole-like arms crisscrossed over books, pressed against the ribs. Drusilla's violet eyes looked up at Michael with a complete lack of any hardness they held now.

"Michael Prince. Meet Drew Bonnet."

"Wow." Michael was stunned. "I never even pictured..."

"Well, lucky for you, the yearbook did. Keep looking," George urged.

Michael turned the page. There was a bunch of photos splayed out, with cartoon confetti and streamers in the negative spaces. Michael's crystal eyes fixed on an image of Paul and his pack of assholes. There were a few faces he didn't recognize, but the one he did was Drew Bonnet. Right next to Paul again, with arms crossed over a book against the chest. Paul looked as if he was laughing at something, and Drew looked a little embarrassed, or maybe Drew was just in a fit of nervous laughter. Paul's hand was around Drew's waist.

"This doesn't make any sense," Michael said.

"Keep looking."

Michael turned the page. A row of boys in uniform. The basketball team, and on the end, there was Drew, long hair in a braid over the shoulder. Drew Bonnet, again in the men's swim team, and again in soccer. In each photo, the eyes were the same. Eager, cheerful, soft. Michael turned the page. He was almost relieved to see the death glare. Michael took a deep breath. He knew there was a story there that he did want to hear, but at the same time...

"So, what happened?" Michael asked. "I'm guessing it wasn't good."

"Yeah," George began. "Drew Bonnet was a cool guy, once upon a time. Of course, we didn't know about the not being a guy part. She hung out with all the right people, was pretty popular, and was really sweet to everyone, to boot. She rolled with Paul and his friends for a long time, ever since preschool. Drew was just lucky like that. She would have been the weak kid everyone picked on if it weren't for Paul. High school was no different, well... I mean, not completely. I think we can all see what was going on there, but yeah, Drew was Paul Hunt's little puppy. She followed Paul everywhere, and no one crossed Paul Hunt. Not until Drew became Drusilla."

Michael thought on this, and a lot of disgusting images plagued Michael's brain. "So, what happened?"

The waitress came with their food, but Michael wasn't really feeling that hungry anymore. George bit into his big burger. Michael bit into his as well, if only to fit in, but the food was tasteless in his mouth. He took a bigger bite, and another. George took a big gulp from his soda. So did Michael. A clenching spread through him.

"Well, man. I mean, one day Drew Bonnet came to school, but you know... in a dress. They kicked the crap out of her."

Michael's soul burned. "Yeah, well, so what? Look at these pictures. Look at what she was wearing. I mean, it's not like this would have been a big shock to Paul, or anyone."

"No, I don't think it was either," George said as he took a pull from his soda. "Paul was more mad than anything. He was fuming over the whole thing for a few days after. He kept muttering to himself when he thought no one was looking. Muttering about how Drew messed everything up, and how could he, how could he. Over and over again. Crazy stuff."

"Hmm, keep going. What happened next?"

"That's the crazy part. When Drew came back, she came back, you know, as Drusilla, and completely wiped the floor with Paul and his whole gang. I mean, some of them went to the hospital. I'm not exaggerating. She went off."

"This whole time, you've been calling her a she?" Michael asked, suspiciously. "What happened to calling her it?"

George looked around. "Look, Michael. I told you everything I can."

"Okay." Michael couldn't help have more questions, but a deal was a deal.

*

Drusilla lay next to Mary in the mud, and the two of them watched the clouds roll by. The rain had long since passed. Everything was so perfect. Drusilla inhaled the cool peace deeply and listened to Mary sigh against the setting sun. They needed that. Mary's instincts were getting good. Her arm linked with Drusilla's, and Drusilla smiled despite the pain in her face.

"I'm never going to get Michael," Mary breathed.

"Yeah," Drusilla answered, honestly. She took another deep breath. She caught the scent of the mud and felt the magic coursing through her.

"He's in love with you, isn't he?" Mary asked.

"Yeah, I think he is."

"I knew it," Mary said on a sigh. "I don't think I'm going to be able to handle this well."

"I know," Drusilla added, feeling completely relaxed. "It's why I push him away."

"Just let him have you. You both want him to."

Drusilla tried to speak, but the words got caught in her throat. Leaving her feeling like a bullfrog.

"Oh, not being honest with yourself in the mud are you?" Mary accused. "Well, spit it out, or the mud will make you."

"I don't want to. Once we're out of the mud, everything will be a dumpster fire, and I can't live through another world collapse."

"What do you mean? Stop holding back. We're in the mud." Mary fixed her with a hard glare. She was getting good at that, too. Soon Mary wouldn't need her at all anymore.

"I've lost everyone, Mary. Mom left, Dad hates me, Paul..." Drusilla stopped. "You're all I have left."

Mary's arm tightened on Drusilla's as if she were afraid some unseen force would pull them apart. "I'm not going to throw you away. Things will get ugly, I mean, really ugly. I'm not sure I can help that, but Mom left me, too. I'll have to learn how to share you, or lose everything, too."

"That's true." Drusilla watched the clouds part and sunlight bleed through.

"Yeah, so go blow Michael already. Men have the attention span of a goldfish."

"What is wrong with you, Mary?"

"Mother abandonment issues. You?"

"I really thought Paul loved me, and mother abandonment issues," Drusilla answered.

"Fancy that. We should start a support group."

"Yeah," Drusilla laughed. "I can't believe we haven't already."

*

Mary sat in the shower and watched the last of the mud go down the drain. The last of the magic went with it. Fear gripped her, as she knew it would. It was exactly like putting the weight back on her chest. Mary took a deep breath. She tried to hold on to the clarity of the mud, but she never could. She washed her hair and inhaled the scent of mint and lavender. At least the day was peaceful, Mary thought, as she curled up under the steady stream of hot water.

Sudden shouting, and Mary's peace was shattered like a windshield. Her father's angry yelling mingled with Drusilla's snark.

Mary tried to smother out the sound by pressing her hands to her ears, but only the words were muffled. There was no escape for Mary. She could only stuff her ears, hum as loud as she could, and wait it out.

"It's your fault your mother left!" Her father's booming voice shattered through Mary's attempt to block it out.

Tears flooded Mary's vision, blurring her dimly yellow-lit surroundings. There would never be an end to this, Mary thought, as the screaming gave way to a thumping sound. How long before her father snapped and just threw Drusilla onto the street? Mary didn't know how to stop worrying about that, so Mary hugged her knees close to her. She had given up trying to block it out. There was no point, Mary told herself. This was just the way things were.

"Oh, yeah. That's right, Dad!" Mary could hear Drusilla yell. "Run away. Just like she did! Fucking coward."

Mary heard the front door slam, and then Drusilla's phone rang. Mary turned off the water to better hear.

"Speak," Drusilla barked, then paused. "Now's not the best... okay... fine! I understand... yeah... I'll be there soon... yeah, give me fifteen minutes... fine, bye!"

What the hell was that about? Mary stood and wrapped a towel around herself. The booming knock on the door came.

"Hey, Mary?" Drusilla's voice came through the door. "I have to go out for a little. Do you need anything?"

What the fuck was she up to? "No."

"Okay, do you want anything?"

"No, I'm fine," Mary called through the wood.

"Okay, I'll be back in an hour." And then Drusilla's footsteps stomped away.

*

George sat in the café, waiting. Drusilla said she would be fifteen minutes, but she was there in five. George's eyes widened as he caught sight of her. Drusilla was bruised and mud splattered. Her knee length dress was too skimpy for the weather. She walked up, looking annoyed. She had every right to be, George thought.

Drusilla slumped in the chair across from him and crossed her mud-streaked arms.

“Well?” she asked.

“What do you *do* during the weekend? Shit!” George asked, flabbergasted.

“Dammit, George, just tell me why I'm here.”

George took a deep breath. “He knows, Drusilla.”

“Um... excuse me?” Her dark eyes narrowed.

“I told Michael.”

“Are you *fucking* kidding me?” Drusilla buried her face in her hands. “How much does he know?”

“Everything. I gave him everything.”

George watched as Drusilla slammed her head into the metal table a few times. Then, her head popped up to look at him. Her eyes wide, and for a moment, George saw the old Drew shine through. Then, Drusilla blinked a couple of times, and Drew was gone. George reached into his pocket, pulled out a roll of money. He slid it across the table towards her, but she pushed it back.

“Keep it. I paid you to hype my scary image. Michael Prince wasn't your fault.” Drusilla's face fell into the palms of her hands. “Ugh, who could have known...? Michael Prince.”

Chapter 6

Drusilla walked down the school hallways, and it was already too early for this shit. She weaved past the masses of faceless assholes. People she hopefully would never see again, once school was over. It was the second Monday of the school year, and ugh, this year was *really* dragging. Drusilla passed the pack of guys that was normally led by Paul, but he wasn't there. A sudden nervousness tickled Drusilla's gut. She had intended to gloat over her victory in their little bathroom brawl. Instead, she had to be content with reminding Pan that she made him shit his pants, and glare in Peter Piper's direction. Paul was probably jerking off, or something. Probably to pictures of endangered animal corpses shot dead on the Serengeti, so why this gut feeling? What if? Drusilla stopped. Must all roads lead to *fucking* Michael Prince, she asked herself.

"No!" she said aloud.

"My," a lilting voice caught Drusilla's ear out of the crowd, "what big hands you have."

Drusilla rolled her eyes as she passed the red hoodie girl and her hairy boyfriend. Ruby, she wanted to say, but who can keep track. The wolfish boy-toy grabbed the girl and pulled her close to nibble at her neck. Loneliness gnawed at Drusilla's gut. That shit was the last thing she needed.

"The better to grope you with, my dear," the boy growled in

the girl's ear.

"Ugh!" Drusilla exploded, and she rushed to her locker.

Predictably, Michael was there waiting. Drusilla felt her breath catch in her lungs. He was dressed in the white shirt, leather jacket, and black pants combo. His square eyeglasses were low on his nose as if they were shades, as if he were some James Dean poster. A stinging went from her lungs to her eyes. Drusilla had worried about what this moment would be like, and now it was here. She found it worse than any horribleness her mind could come up with. She felt the wetness at the corners of her eyes. Drusilla blinked rapidly. Like she was going to cry in front of Michael Prince, as if.

"Hey," he said.

"Hey back," Drusilla replied after a deep sigh.

An uncomfortable silence fell around them like a dream. Drusilla breathed deeply to try and steady herself. Michael looked down and fiddled with his jacket zipper, awkwardly. It felt like a slow death, Drusilla thought as she watched him. Please say something, Michael, Drusilla begged him with her mind, but he didn't. Fine, Drusilla thought as she opened her mouth to speak.

"You look a little better today," Michael said, cutting Drusilla off before she could even.

"Um... thanks," Drusilla replied. "For once, your outfit doesn't suck."

Michael smirked at that. "How do you feel?"

"Uncomfortable," Drusilla replied, honestly.

"Sorry."

"You should be," Drusilla replied. "This bag is heavy."

"Oh!" Michael started. "Right, *shit*. Sorry."

Drusilla watched as he made quick work of opening her locker. He took her bag to hang it on the little, metal hook. Then, his eyes saw something. He stopped and scrunched his face on a sigh. Intrigued, Drusilla moved between Michael and the locker to see for herself. Michael slumped against the locker next to hers. Drusilla was surprised that Michael didn't try to stop her, or at the very least, try anything. It nearly hurt Drusilla's feelings. Then, Drusilla reminded herself that she was at school. She wasn't supposed to have feelings. She took a deep breath and reached for her books. A small brown box was resting on top of them.

"Oh-"

"Don't," Michael said making her stop. "I forgot all about that. Don't worry about it now."

"Damn it, Michael," Drusilla said. "What's in the box?"

"I saw them at the mall the other day. It made me think of you. It was before... it's probably going to piss you off."

"Before?" Drusilla asked, as if she didn't already know.

"Yeah." Michael was back to his zipper. He didn't seem to be in the mood to pretend.

Drusilla reached for the box. It felt leathery in her hands. A jewelry box. A little gold stamp on the oxblood box told her it came from Seven Sons jewelers. The expensive place in the mall where most people got their diamond engagement rings. The box opened with a little squeak. On a satiny little pillow sparkled two purple, glittery glass butterflies. It felt like a hand was squeezing Drusilla's chest. How many times had she admired these, but could never afford them? She looked up at Michael who was suddenly too close. His hand closed over hers, and the box snapped shut. He was very close. Drusilla forgot how to breathe.

"Michael..." She whispered.

"Is-"

He was cut off by the screeching overhead speaker. The voice was metallic and grating. Like nails on a chalkboard met a bunch of forks whirling in a blender, and then popped out a couple of screeching brats. To Drusilla's annoyance, Michael tried to cover her ears. How gallant, Drusilla thought, as she pushed his hands away to listen. The speakers switched off, and a brief moment of relief before...

"Attention all students," Principal Peep's voice echoed over the speakers, badly. Drusilla was sure her heart had sunk so low that it lived somewhere else entirely, like Spain maybe. "Please report to the auditorium. All students report to the auditorium, thank you."

Everyone pulled a U-turn. Drusilla felt as though the rest of her insides were being squished down with a potato masher. She looked around. Mary was nowhere in sight. Real panic gripped her by the soul. People were filing past. The red hooded girl and her big, bad boyfriend walked past, hand in hand. The girl gave Drusilla a very worried look. A look that Drusilla returned. Principal Peep's voice was over the intercom again. This couldn't be happening this soon.

“Hey, we should get going,” Michael said, as if all hell wasn't breaking loose.

“I can't,” Drusilla said, and she hated the panic in her voice. “I have to find Mary.”

Drusilla was off. She left Michael behind to struggle against the current of students. She felt the painfully comforting hand of Michael on her shoulder. Drusilla looked back. Michael's face was pleading. Drusilla didn't have time for this. She had to find Mary. Why couldn't he see that? Drusilla wrenched herself free from Michael and pushed harder against the tide.

“She'll be heading towards the auditorium.” Michael's hand was back on her shoulder.

“No, you don't understand, yet!” Drusilla's voice was breathless.

“Um... yet?”

“I have to find Mary *right now*!” Drusilla roared the last two words for emphasis.

“Okay, but it's smarter to head towards the auditorium instead of going against the crowds, I mean.” Michael's eyes seemed like two pools of very clear, cool water. Drusilla wanted very much to muddy them. “Just forget everything that's going on around you. Forget the panic. What makes sense?”

*

The auditorium was a dark, quiet place with fabric covered walls and velvet chairs. They made their way through. Michael attempted to hold her hand, but Drusilla was having none of it. She crossed her arms and turned away from him in a huff. Stress radiated off her. Well, we can't have that, Michael thought, as he tickled at the small of her back. Predictably, Drusilla swatted at him. Michael caught the attack and laced his fingers with hers. Drusilla fumed and yanked her hand free. She turned to glare at him, and Michael smirked at her teasingly. Drusilla blanched. Michael stopped. Backfire.

"I was trying to get you out of that dark cloud of yours."

"Not now," Drusilla grumbled. "Everyone can fucking see us."

"Ugh, you act like they pay your bills or something," Michael retorted.

Drusilla rolled her eyes and sat. They were in the very back row. Michael plopped down next to her. He scanned the auditorium. Most of the student body had found their seats and were waiting quietly. Some still milled about or were huddled in little groups. They seemed to be in worried conversation. Michael's eyes found Paul's little group. They were missing their leader. Damn, Michael thought. He was looking forward to giving him a good thrashing. Drusilla's fingers laced with his, and Michael was yanked back to the present. He smiled down at her and lifted an eyebrow.

"Shut up," Drusilla groaned, and then gave the room a once over. "I don't see Mary."

Michael looked, too. No Mary. "Give it a minute. She's probably still getting here."

"Or maybe a tree fell on her!" Her voice was a shrill whisper.

"That's not going to happen." Michael looked deep into Drusilla's frightened, violet eyes. Drusilla squirmed. "I promise."

"Hey!" someone barked.

Both Michael and Drusilla snapped to attention. Mary stood in the row in front of them with an ugly sneer on her face, George, on her heels. Drusilla's grip on Michael became deathly strong. Mary's eyes locked with his. He watched as Mary seethed for a moment, and then swallowed her rage. That's right, Michael thought at her. Pipe the fuck down. George looked from Michael to Mary, and his face fell a little.

"Well, this is cozy," Mary snarled, sarcastically.

Her eyes fell coldly on Drusilla for a brief moment, and then she was off. Stalking away. George shrugged at them, then followed, and so did Michael's eyes. He watched them go down towards the front of the auditorium. Despicable, Michael nearly said aloud, but he was smarter than that. Drusilla removed her hand from Michael's, and a very heavy sigh washed over her. Michael looked over to find Drusilla hanging her head. Michael snatched Drusilla's hand back and laced his fingers with hers. Drusilla gripped back.

"Well, there she is... not dead in the woods," Michael said as he swallowed the heat boiling up in him. "Not dead at all."

"Hooray," Drusilla said, flatly, to her feet. Then, in a whisper, "I just want this day to end."

"Students." Principal Peep's voice crackled over the electric screech of the microphone. "This morning is met with tragedy." Michael noticed a deathly hush creep around his classmates. "Early this morning, one of our own, Paul Hunt, was rushed to Elderberry Hospital." Michael felt the painful grip of Drusilla's hand on his. "I'm afraid he was crushed by a fallen tree in the woods. I must emphasize, yet again, that these woods are not safe and must not be entered. The trees are very old, and we have been informed that a recent infestation has made the trees more brittle and prone to collapse. Therefore, any students found in the woods at any time will face suspension for their own safety. As always, if you need to talk about this, or any other problem, my door is always open. Thank you."

"Way to go, Peep," Drusilla groaned to herself. "She might as well have dared the fools to go into the woods."

The student body sat in stunned silence. Michael felt heat boiling him to the bone. That stupid fuck got himself put in hospital. Michael inhaled sharply and deeply. How long would Paul be there? Three weeks, maybe? A month? How long would Michael have to wait before he could get his hands on him? Unbelievable, Michael seethed. He watched as the student body began to funnel out of the auditorium. What next? Michael wondered, darkly. Suddenly, Drusilla gripped Michael's arm, hard. He felt the pull and lick of whiplash as they were suddenly in the clearing of trees. Drusilla let him go. Michael fell to his knees as his head spun. The head rush grated against his already bad mood. Drusilla knelt down with him.

"What did I do to deserve that?" Michael demanded.

"You didn't have to put him in the hospital," Drusilla replied.

"What?" Michael picked himself up and dusted off his jeans. Drusilla's violet eyes were filled with suspicion. "I didn't get the chance."

"Bullshit, Prince." Drusilla sighed. "I remember what you said."

"Yeah, well," Michael began, "he beat the shit out of you. Did you think I was going to let him get away with that?"

"So, you try to kill him. That's your response?"

"No, Goddamn it!" Michael raged. "I never got the chance. He went and got hurt all by himself, like a big boy."

"So, you *were* going to kill him?"

"I wanted to, but I figured pounding his face in would have to do." Michael began to pace.

"You must really think I'm helpless." Drusilla's voice gurgled with disgust.

"No," Michael corrected. "I don't think that at all."

"Well good! Because I already beat the shit out of Paul. Did you really think I was going to take a beating from Paul Hunt?" Drusilla reached into her pocket and pulled out an orange pill bottle, and tossed it to him. "There."

"What is it?" Michael asked as he caught the pill bottle. He read the label. "What? You force fed him estrogen?"

"Michael," Drusilla groaned. "Open it."

Michael did as he was told. He squeezed the white plastic top and twisted. The rattle was not from pills. Inside were two blood-crusted teeth. Two back teeth. Drusilla moved closer to him. Michael's heart jumped as Drusilla's fingers closed over the hand holding the pill bottle. Their eyes locked. She was so badass, Michael thought, distractedly. Drusilla leaned in, and Michael mimicked the action not wanting to miss an opportunity. Her lips were an inch away.

"I take trophies," she whispered, before pulling away cruelly.

"Seriously?"

"Yep. Take that to your made up pit fighter club." And with that, Drusilla began fading.

"Oh, come on," Michael groaned. "You're making me walk back?"

"Yup!" Drusilla's voice echoed. She shimmered out of sight. Michael sighed and waited a moment before heading back to the school.

*

Drusilla moved through the halls. Art class was so far away. Frazzled by Michael, Drusilla had landed at the opposite side of the school. It was too early in the morning, and she was too tired to work anything magical so quickly. Dammit, Michael, she seethed. Then, hauled ass. The students did their best to avoid her. Which was convenient, but accusing glares greeted her at the beginning of every new hallway and lingered on her like a stain. Awesome, just what I need, Drusilla thought.

"Hey," George stepped in front of her. "Can we talk for a second?"

"What the hell are you doing?" Drusilla hissed.

"You need to get out of here."

"You need to not be seen talking to me." Drusilla scanned the hall.

"I mean it. People are talking. They think you went after Paul."

"Of course, they do." Drusilla sighed.

"Paul's pack is coming for you."

"Oh, goody," Drusilla said, flatly.

"You need to get out of here," George urged again.

"Fuck them. I'm not going anywhere."

"Damn it. Listen. Paul's not here to call them off."

"Like they scare me," Drusilla said with the roll of her eyes. "Besides, I have to take Mary home."

"How are you going to be able to take Mary home from the hospital?"

"What's this about a hospital?" Michael's voice asked.

"You have literally the worst timing," Drusilla said, spinning to face him.

"No, really, what's going on?" Michael demanded.

"Nothing-" Drusilla began, but...

"Hey, freak!" screeched Pan's voice.

Drusilla, Michael, and George looked over to see them. All five of Paul's group stood tensed for the fight. Faster than anyone could react, Michael walked over to the gaggle of boys. All five of their smug faces turned to shock as Michael's fist collided with Pan's face. Then, Pan's face collided with the dirty, tiled floor. Drusilla's insides locked up. She watched Paul's shocked gang for movement. Pan was getting to his feet. Michael circled to Pan's side.

"Grow up, Pan." Michael added a swift kick to his ribs. Pan rolled onto his back. Then, Michael began swinging at the rest as Paul's pack descended on him.

"Damn it." Drusilla sighed. "Get out of here, George."

Then, Drusilla jumped in. They were a tangle of fists and kicking for a long while. Drusilla's body screamed as already bruised flesh was freshly thumped. An arm attempted to wrap around her neck, but Drusilla threw her elbow backwards. It collided hard with flesh and bone, and the arm retracted. He wailed, and Drusilla jumped on another. Wrapping her legs around his middle, Drusilla dug her nails deep into the boy's face.

As they fell to the ground, she looked up to see another one of Paul's goons vomit violently at a gut punch, courtesy of Michael. Awesome, Drusilla thought as she rolled. Now, the fight would be a slippery one. The fist caught Drusilla square in the face. Then, a fresh kick to her mid-section. Drusilla crumpled. She curled into a ball. They were kicking her, mercilessly. Drusilla counted three different kickers. The sound of Michael scuffling with the others wafted past. Drusilla guessed he was fending off the other two. Then, a cracking sound as someone hit the wall. Drusilla wasn't sure who lost, but she didn't have time to find out. The next kick came for her head, but Drusilla was ready. She snapped her head up and caught the kicker by the ankle. She bit down hard. The bloodcurdling scream was very rewarding.

"Ah, the freak's biting me!" Peter Piper panicked.

Drusilla bit down harder with each kick that came her way and began yanking her head back and forth like she was rabid. A coppery taste filled her mouth. Hands yanked at her, but she wasn't letting go. She just kicked out wildly and sank her teeth in deeper, even when one of them grabbed her by the hair and began punching her in the side of the head. The person got off two punches before he was pulled away. The squeals Michael got out of the guy were gratifying. She kicked out again. Flailing her feet at the others who were trying to rescue their friend. Her captured prey was crying by now. It was clear he no longer wanted in this fight. He would be lucky if he got out with his foot, Drusilla thought. She clamped down on her new trophy with her hands for extra support and dug her nails in.

"Get the fuck away from her!" Michael roared.

The rest of them scattered. The one Drusilla had in her jaws was trying his best to crawl away, but Drusilla only yanked Peter back. Michael knelt down beside her and laid his cool, gentle hands on her face. It was clear what he was doing, and Drusilla would have none of it. She looked at him wild-eyed, bit down. Her prey's wails reminded Drusilla of something from the National Geographic. She liked it.

"It's okay. They're gone now," Michael soothed.

"Get that thing the fuck off me, man!" Peter half pleaded, half demanded.

"Shut the fuck up!" Michael gave the guy a hard punch to the thigh.

"Ah! What the fuck!" Peter cried. Drusilla began to chew.

"It's over, Drusilla. You can let go now." Michael gingerly tried to disconnect Drusilla from him. "It's okay."

*

Drusilla growled like an animal in response. Michael wasn't sure how to go about this. Blood pooled by Drusilla's face, and he wasn't sure how much of it was hers or Peter Piper's. Drusilla's body was mangled and bruised. George ran over to them, faster than light. He knelt down with them. Michael saw the worry in his large eyes, but he also saw how he did nothing during the fight. Michael tried again to detach Drusilla from Peter, but the boy screamed as she sank down deeper. Her eyes dared Michael to try to pull her free. She had lost it. Michael remembered what that felt like.

"We have to get her out of here," George panicked.

"I know..." Michael began.

"No, now! Someone's coming."

At that Drusilla unlatched and spat out a gelatinous red mass. "Why didn't you leave like I told you to, George?"

Peter Piper half scrambled, half limped away. Michael couldn't help wonder how much trouble Drusilla was going to get into for this. The police would probably have to get involved, but that wasn't something he could help right now. Michael scooped Drusilla up in his arms, and she immediately began to struggle. Michael held her tighter. He could see the pain in her face. She was really messed up. Then, Michael looked over to George.

"Can you make sure Mary gets home okay?" Michael asked George.

"Put me down!" Drusilla roared over them. Then, she twisted and yelped.

"Yeah," George replied, and he faded away.

Shit, George had power, too? Michael didn't have time to dwell on his shortcomings. Drusilla was thrashing again. In an attempt to not drop her, Michael clamped down on her, and Drusilla yelped. A pang of guilt went through Michael, but he shoved it somewhere for the moment. He needed to get Drusilla to the hospital. Drusilla flailed despite the pain, and despite Michael's increasingly tighter hold on her.

"I mean it -"

"Can you not right now?" Michael demanded as he headed for the nearest exit. "You're only damaging yourself more."

Drusilla wriggled and whimpered in response. Michael held her close and moved. Once he pushed a side door open with his foot, he walked past the track and field towards the student parking lot. Drusilla flailed and cursed the whole way. Michael felt like animal control trying to carry an irate cat out of a tree or something. His shiny shark of a car was in sight. Thank god, Michael thought. This walk was starting to take forever. Suddenly, a brutal head-butt caught Michael off guard. His ear rang. Not unexpectedly, Drusilla began repeating the process over and over.

"Ah, quit it!"

"I'm not going to the hospital!" Drusilla said as she flailed and wriggled to prove her point.

Michael was half tempted to drop her on the hard parking lot. His muscles ached with each new thrashing from Drusilla. Not to mention the bruises and scrapes he earned in the fight. That wall didn't feel very good when he was thrown into it. Michael gritted his teeth and marched to the car. Letting her legs drop, Michael opened the passenger door with his newly free hand and promptly dumped Drusilla in the seat. Fire ripped across his back as he bent down to get eye level with her.

"Do *not* make me chase after you." Drusilla just glared at him in response. Good enough, Michael thought.

Then, Michael made his way to the trunk and popped it open with the press of a button. He pulled out a half-used bottle of hydrogen peroxide. Then, he moved back to Drusilla, who was brooding in the seat. She glared at him some more. Michael sighed and struggled to one knee. He was pretty sure he pulled his back out. Michael twisted the cap off and put it to her busted lips.

"Swish and spit," he commanded. She did, and Michael was half ready to get a face full of it, but Drusilla spit on the ground. "You're going to be out of makeup by the end of the week, at this rate."

She looked up at him, miserably. Her purple eyes locked with his, and suddenly, this was worth it again. Michael helped get her legs in the car. Drusilla scoffed at this and did her best to yank them away. Then, with a grunt, she pulled the door shut before Michael could. With a sigh, Michael made his way to the driver's side. He discovered that he had a small limp. Oh good, Michael thought in annoyance. He plopped into his seat and winced at the reverberating pain that shot up his back. Then, he shut the door, and the silence was smothering. Michael started the car.

"Michael, I can't afford a trip to the hospital." Drusilla's voice shook. Her face was rigidly locked in front of her.

"I'll handle it," Michael said as they drove.

"Why?" she demanded.

"Just let me!" Michael stopped. He took a deep breath. He hadn't meant to yell. "I'm sorry. You don't have to worry about it."

*

Drusilla sat staring at the cream-colored walls in the cramped hospital room. The paper dress crinkled as she hugged her body painfully. She listened to the two arguing outside of her closed door. Drusilla could kick herself for not taking a Spanish class. The only word she recognized was cinco. Drusilla rubbed her legs together slightly. She needed to shave them. How long before her body wouldn't hurt enough to stop her. Curse you, Paul, and your damned accident. Though deep down, nothing felt like an accident.

The door opened, cutting Drusilla off from her thoughts. The woman was a head shorter than Michael, and her flawless skin was a shade darker than his, but her curly hair and plump mouth were just like Michael's. Her white lab coat had a shiny badge with the name Dr. Rita Prince laminated on it. Oh fuck, Drusilla thought, but said nothing. Michael's mother slipped a clipboard into its plastic compartment on the back of the door. Then, she moved like water over to Drusilla. The annoyance was plain on Dr. Prince's face. Gently, she tilted Drusilla's face up to meet hers, and with her cool hands pressed lightly on Drusilla's bruised face.

"Well, you have two black eyes, but your nose is intact," Dr. Rita Prince said as she moved down to the collarbone. Her jaw tightened in the same way Michael's did when he was annoyed. "Do you want to tell me what happened to you?"

"I got in a fight. It's not uncommon for me."

"Oh, so you call three broken ribs a typical Monday?"

"Fuck!" Drusilla sighed. "I can't afford any of this."

"Don't worry about that."

Drusilla looked up. “I don't have health insurance. I'm going to be in so much debt, I won't even be able to get a student loan for college. I'll have to go to that new community college, oh my gods! I'm never getting out of this town.”

“You need to relax,” instructed Dr. Prince in a cold voice. She put a hand on Drusilla's shoulder, and all of a sudden, Drusilla felt wonderful. A little dizzy, but wonderful. Of course, Michael’s mother was a witch. Drusilla could have kicked herself.

“Whoa... what spell was that?” Drusilla asked, lazily. She was beginning to see spots.

“Sit still. I need to set your ribs.” Dr. Prince placed her hand over Drusilla's middle. Drusilla felt the magic mingle with her own and felt bones sink back into place. “I can only do so much. The worse the injury, the harder it is to knit back together. You’re still going to have to take it easy for a few days. It'll still hurt,” Dr. Prince said as she moved to Drusilla's face. “But nothing will be broken, only bruised.”

“Why are you helping me?” Drusilla asked. The spots were becoming brighter now.

“It's my job,” Rita Prince said, bitterly.

The lights became a blinding brightness as Drusilla's head rushed. It was becoming harder to stay alert. The brightness was all there was, after a while. Its searing light penetrated everything. Drusilla screamed as the sweet blackness overtook her, and the waking mind give way to the slumber. It was blissful there in the dark. Nothing hurt.

*

Sunlight sliced through the blinds leaving the dust to sparkle in between. Michael watched the sleeping patient's chest rise and fall. He had been in better hospital rooms in his life. Then again, Michael reflected, he had been in worse ones, too. Michael stood and stretched, painfully. Then, he walked over to the door and closed it. This deserved some privacy, Michael thought. He walked back over to the bed and looked down. So peaceful.

“Wake up!” Michael snapped, with a resounding slap to Paul

Hunt's face.

Paul woke with a startle. Michael clamped his large hand on Paul's mouth, hard. Paul's eyes widened and scanned the room, frantically. His arm reaching for the panic button, but somehow it was out of reach. How could that have happened, Michael mused. He didn't much like how distracted Paul had become. He wanted Paul's full attention. Michael put his knee up, and then leaned it into Paul's injured midsection. Paul's screams died in Michael's hand.

"Don't *ignore* me, Paul." Michael felt himself creeping closer to the edge. Paul's eyes snapped back to Michael. "You and your shitty little friends, don't go near her again. You see her coming down the hall, you walk the other way. She doesn't even know you're there. Nod if you understand." Nothing happened. Michael leaned in harder. "That wasn't a suggestion."

Paul nodded, and Michael hopped off of him. He reached into his pocket and pulled out the remote panic button, and slowly, deliberately laid it on the table. Paul watched, wide-eyed. Fear dripped from him in buckets, and Michael ate every bit of it up. It would have been better if Paul cried, Michael thought. He also thought about trying to make him cry, but that felt like overkill somehow. Instead, he enjoyed Paul's misery.

"Don't make me have to come back for you." Michael let that thought linger in Paul's big, dumb brain for the moment. Then, he was gone, out the door like nothing ever happened.

*

Michael pulled the door open for Drusilla. She rolled her eyes at that and slumped in. He walked in front the car, and Drusilla's large eyes followed him from beyond the windshield. Michael got in the driver's seat and turned to Drusilla, who was regarding him. Something warm and fuzzy spread through Michael's battered body. Her dark lips twisted into a half smile. Things seemed to be improving.

"Well, your mom is hot," Drusilla said.

Michael's insides curdled. "Boner killer."

Drusilla huffed at that. “I was trying to... fuck it, I don't know what I was trying to do.”

“So, you want to bang my mom, now?” Michael teased as he drove. “Is that what's happening?”

“That's not what I meant. I-”

“Then, you want me to bang my mom?” Michael cut Drusilla a sly look. “I can't wait to tell her that.”

“Ugh, that's not... no, I don't... dammit... you creeper.”

“Hm... Good. I'm not sure how I would handle my own mother being competition.”

“I hate you.” Drusilla lapsed into thought. “It's cool your mom's a witch, though.”

“Yeah,” Michael said. “Too bad she is *pissed.*”

“Yeah. I could tell,” Drusilla replied. “But a lot of things make sense now. Like, why my magic didn't freak you out. Though, I kind of wish I would have known that going in.”

“Why? So you could've used some other way to push me away?”

Drusilla was silent for a long while. Michael had nowhere to be, so he just let her struggle with whatever. Drusilla's hands clasped in her lap, and she sighed deeply before looking at him. It was not a glare. No. She studied him. Michael was sure of it. He watched her watching him and waited for an answer. He knew what the answer was, but he wanted to hear it from her.

“What do you want me say, Michael?” Drusilla asked in a small voice.

“It's okay,” Michael said, dropping it. “I'm glad you aren't badly hurt.”

Drusilla seemed to crumple a little. “Yeah. You, too.”

“Well, be still my heart.”

“*Shut up,*” she groaned. “You mother isn't the only one that's pissed. What were you thinking, jumping into a fight like that?

“They wanted to hurt you.”

“Yeah, and because you decided it was punching time, I did get hurt.”

“You didn't have to jump in, too.” Michael bit back his harsh tone... barely. “You could have just sat back and watched.”

“No. I really couldn't.”

Michael pondered that. The sun was beginning to dip down. Nearly six o'clock. Shit, there went the day. “Well, at least the day's over. What a fucked day, too.” Drusilla didn't speak. “I wish...” but he couldn't. “Are you hungry?”

“I just want this to stop.”

The cracking of her voice felt like shards of glass in Michael’s chest. He looked over. Tears mingled with black makeup and ran down her face. Michael held out a hand for her to take, but she didn't. Instead, she cried into her hands like a child. Tiny, angry sobs and sharp gasps escaped her. Michael drove on. The school was up ahead, and Michael pulled into the parking lot next to her van. He killed the engine, but Drusilla kept crying. Michael put an arm around her shoulder. He was crumbling at the sight of her. Drusilla sobbed for a long while. Michael was failing to comfort her. He knew it, but he still tried. When Drusilla was all cried out, she looked around.

“What are we doing here?” she croaked.

“I didn't want your van to get towed, but I don't think you should be alone right now.”

“Ugh, you’re so sweet,” Drusilla groaned.

“So, I'm sweet. That's not my defining quality.” Michael's smile deepened as Drusilla glared at him.

“True.” Drusilla sniffed. “You also an ass hat.”

“True, but I'm not an ankle biter.”

Drusilla rolled her eyes. Michael was hoping for more of a giggle. He should have known better. Then, she just looked at him for a long while, and Michael looked back. The setting sun made her violet eyes glow lavender, like she was some predator in the dark. Her bruises looked almost like primal camouflage. He wanted to take her away from all this bullshit. Then again, he always seemed to want to do that. Maybe he *was* a creeper.

“It's because you like to be the hero,” Drusilla said, as if reading Michael's mind.

“What?” Michael's heart skipped. Could she read minds?

“That's why you’re interested in me. Isn't it?” Drusilla asked.

"I don't know why I like you, Drusilla. I just do."

"It isn't my sparkling personality?" Drusilla giggled at that.

"Haven't we had this conversation before?" Michael asked in an attempt to get her to stop downing herself.

"Probably. I don't remember. It's been a long week."

"Shit. It's only been a week?" Michael asked.

"Yup," Drusilla said, darkly. "Well, and some change."

"Well. I still like you," Michael said. "I'm not going to stop."

"I never said you had to stop," replied Drusilla.

Chapter 7

Drusilla and Mary rumbled along. It had been several days since Drusilla's trip to the hospital, and she was just glad it was Friday. Mary slipped into the front seat sporting a pink miniskirt and denim vest. Her belly button peeked out from underneath a rhinestone-crusted crop top. She popped her seat belt on and put her bare feet up on the dash.

"You need new clothes," Drusilla grumbled.

"It's supposed to be this short," Mary answered.

"Oh," Drusilla mused. "Well, do you want new clothes?"

"Always," said Mary.

"Fine, pull some cash out of my backpack. We can hit the mall after school."

"No," Mary protested, "you have to stay in after school and rest."

"Mary-"

"You promised, Dru," Mary spat. "You promised me, and you promised Michael. You haven't taken it easy one day since Monday. Do you want me to tell-?"

Drusilla slammed on the brakes and immediately regretted it. Her face scrunched together as she clutched at sharp pains in her gut. "I'm fine, Mary, okay? I just haven't had time."

"Make time!"

*

Michael waited by Drusilla's locker. He looked at the twisted thing and smiled. This shitty locker is the best wingman ever, Michael thought, as he saw Drusilla's brooding form come clomping towards him. Michael was pretty sure he could see heat lines radiating off of her as she pushed through the crowd. Another bad morning, Michael thought. Being injured really brought out Drusilla's surly side. She stopped in front of Michael, and her nostrils flared as she gave a sharp sigh. Her dark mouth was a tight line. Michael pushed open Drusilla's locker with a squeak.

"Thank you. Now, go away," Drusilla said as she deposited her stuff and slammed the locker shut.

"Anything you want to tell me?"

"Mary already chewed me out this morning. I don't need a lecture from you, too."

Disappointment radiated Michael as he sighed. "Why can't you just stay put and relax for a couple of days?"

"Just stop it, Michael," Drusilla groaned.

"Is it because Paul's back?" Michael asked. "Because-"

"No!" Drusilla screeched.

"Then what is it?"

"I have school, homework, actual work, my fucking dad, and all the other things I need to do at home. Not to mention mailing out essays for college and application forms. Michael, what time do you think I have to just lay around?"

"I'm only asking for a couple of days. Take a break from all of that and get better."

"Michael-" The bell rang. "Awesome. Now we're late."

Michael opened his mouth to speak, but Drusilla had already faded out of sight. So unfair, Michael thought, as he dashed off to class. He ran all the way to homeroom just in time for it to end. Damn, now he would have detention. Well, at least they'd *give* him detention. Like hell he was actually going. Michael spun on his heel and almost bumped into Drusilla. She grabbed his wrist, and Michael felt the tugging and warp-like rushing of a tunnel. Then, in an instant, he was seated in is class. He caught Drusilla's faint silhouette at the door as she shimmered away.

*

Mary pounded through the halls as if she were on a runway. Strategically flipping her hair and looking over her shoulder when needed. I am everything, she told herself. Her heels click-clacked loudly on the enamel floor, commanding attention. All the appropriate heads turned. Yes, Mary thought to herself, feeling powerful. I am fierce, she told herself. Paul Hunt made his way past Mary, and she flipped her hair. Paul's head turned. Mary locked eyes with him, and she was ripping him to shreds with her gaze. Her face cracked into a sinister smile. Then the moment was over. Satisfied, Mary turned the corner to begin a new hallway.

All badass curdled in her. Michael Prince. Next to Drusilla. Walking with her. Talking to her in public. Mary felt a hollow burning sensation burrow through her. Tears burned behind her eyes. No, Mary thought. She pulled her shoulders back and strutted her way down the hallway, like hot knives weren't driving themselves in and out of her with every step. *Boom boom boom* clicked Mary's heels. Finally, she was at the end of the hall. Almost over, she told herself. She flipped her long hair at the end of the hall. There were no survivors.

*

Mary slammed Tank's side door shut with a heave. Drusilla felt it like a stress-inducing jolt through her gut. Well dammit, she thought. This is the last thing I need. Mary rustled around in the back with all the ferocity of a wild animal. Drusilla started up Tank and rumbled out before anything unfortunate could happen. Mary slumped into the front seat and buckled up. Drusilla's heart pounded against her Adam's apple. The silence ticked on uncomfortably. What to do?

“I saw Paul today,” Mary said evenly, but her eyes were unmistakably filled with a fiery viciousness.

“Yeah, who knew he would be out of the hospital and back in school so soon?”

“I think it's bullshit,” Mary said. “Fucker should have died.”

"Yeah. The tree should have killed him."

"Hmm," Mary mused. "Maybe poison then. Something sweet and would take a long time to kill a man of his size."

"What?" Drusilla asked. "Mary, what are you talking about?"

"I'm just saying," Mary replied.

"What happened?" A new fear clung to Drusilla's bones like a fungus. "Did Paul do something?"

"You know what he did," Mary spat.

"So what do you want to do? It's Friday night," Drusilla asked in a desperate attempt to change the subject.

"Oh no, Bitch," Mary said with some relish.

"Mary. Don't worry about it, okay? I got beat up, it happens."

"You really must think I'm fucking stupid," Mary fumed. "You think I don't know what he did to you."

"Mary, everyone knows what he did to me."

"Oh? Everyone knows how he used to crawl into your bedroom at night? Does everyone know what he did to you then?"

"Mary you don't know what you're talking about. Okay?"

"I so know. Thin walls, bitch. Our shitty, little, lopsided house has thin walls. We might as well be living in a cardboard box," Mary sneered.

Drusilla opened her mouth and closed it again. The sinking hollowness spread. Drusilla blinked away the tears and did her best not to swerve the van. Mary turned to biting her nails angrily. Drusilla half watched as Mary ripped her long, beautiful nails down to the nub. Guilt gnawed at Drusilla's gut. Mary heard. Of course, she did. Drusilla wanted to beat her head against the steering wheel, but she was driving. Mary would rip those fingernails 'til they bled. Drusilla pulled into the shopping center and parked in front of her work.

"I'll be right back," Drusilla said before Mary started. "Want anything while I'm in there?"

"Nope," Mary said.

Drusilla hopped out with a little too much energy and winced. Then, she slammed the door shut and walked into the cafe. Mrs. Gooseberry leaned seductively against the counter with one elbow. Her beautiful pear-shaped body was draped in deep maroon. Her pose and face fell at the sight of Drusilla. Drusilla walked right over to the bar and rested her head on the cool metal counter. Mrs. Gooseberry's soothing hand rubbed her back.

"Baby, what happened?" Mrs. Gooseberry asked in a soft voice.

"I messed up," Drusilla took a deep breath, "after trying so hard."

"Baby, talk to me. What happened?" Mrs. Gooseberry tilted Drusilla's face up. "Tell me."

"I have to go." Drusilla popped up from the counter and turned to go.

"Drusilla Bonnet." Mrs. Gooseberry's voice rippled through, and she stopped. "Come back here and talk to me."

It was the mom voice. Dammit. She turned. "Fine."

*

Mary sat in Tank, watching Drusilla and Mrs. Gooseberry talking. Ugh, how long was this going to take. As she thought it, Drusilla stood and hugged Mrs. Gooseberry. Mary rolled her eyes at the gurgling, empty feeling in her gut and went to her phone. She scrolled with her thumb and sighed. No refuge for her there. The driver's side door opened, and Drusilla hopped in with a wince. Mary stowed away her phone and buckled up.

"Alright. Let's get you some dinner and then, home."

"And where are you going?" Mary asked

"I'm going to find a place to relax for the rest of the day."

*

George drove his beat-up green car down the road. Michael Prince was in the passenger seat. He leaned against his arm and looked off into the distance. What the fuck, George thought. He just wanted one normal game of basketball. Why couldn't Michael just be normal? George knew that dreamy look. It would only be a matter of time before he started asking about Drusilla Bonnet, and damn it, they had a deal.

"What's up with the trees around here?" Michael asked.

"Um... what do you mean?" At least this was new, George thought.

"They collapse a lot around here," Michael mused. "A lot of accidents involving teenagers. Isn't that weirdly specific?"

"Not really," George replied, feeling glad it wasn't a Drusilla thing. "The trees are old, and they have a beetle infestation, or something. The woods aren't safe because the trees keep dying and falling, but the city won't chop 'em down because the land is protected. They're some kind of rare species of oak, or something. No one goes in there except idiots who wanna show how tough they are, and a tree falls on them. That typically winds up being a teenager. We lose two or three a school year. Kind of sad how stupid people are, really."

"Really," Michael agreed, but he didn't sound satisfied. "Still, what if the trees had a little push?"

"Like from gnomes?" George teased.

Michael didn't continue the topic, and George was grateful for it. Maybe they would have a fun afternoon playing basketball. They pulled over to the park and saw Drusilla's van at once. Yeah okay, George thought darkly. He pulled up behind the van and looked over to Michael. He was pinching the bridge of his nose, and his jaw was clenched. This was going to go well. Michael threw the door open and hopped out. I should just drive away right now, George thought. Just turn the car back on and pull away. Instead, he watched Michael march over to Drusilla. She sneered up at him from the swing.

"Do I ever feel like I'm only the sidekick in this bullshit?" George asked himself. "Why yes, yes I do."

George unbuckled and got out of his car. Michael and Drusilla were screaming at each other at six paces. This was stupid. George moved to his trunk, pulled out his basketball, and began shooting hoops by himself. He made a three-pointer during a rather impressive screech from Drusilla. That's right, cheer for me, George thought, as he scooped the ball up again in a dribble. He shot again and missed.

"What are you even?" Michael yelled.

"I know," George answered under his breath. "That throw was way off."

"Oh, and you're so reasonable, aren't you?" Drusilla screamed.

"Thanks. I try. I really, *really* try," George replied as he tossed the ball again.

"I just want you to get better," Michael roared.

George's ball bounced back at him from the backboard. "You and me both."

"You know what, fuck you!"

"Well, fuck you back!" Michael's hoarse voice followed.

"Yeah, fuck this," George said as he grabbed his ball and headed back to his car.

*

Mary sat in the mall food court, nursing her lonely milkshake. She watched the pale whipped cream swirl with the artificial pink shake. Then, she took a pull of the shake from her straw. She looked up just in time to catch George taking a grease-stained paper bag from the burger place. She watched him turn to look over the food court for a spot and freeze like a cat in headlights upon seeing her. His struggle was painfully real. Mary sat, enjoying the effect she had on him. At least someone still gets it, she thought, as she waited to see if he was brave enough to approach. He waited a second longer than Mary would have liked and strolled over. You're a real man after all, she thought.

"Hey," Mary said in greeting.

"Hi, Mary," he answered.

"No Michael today?" Mary probed.

"Nah."

"You're hiding from them, too?"

"I just need a *break*, you know?"

"Yep, I do indeed," Mary said as she patted the empty part of the booth next to her. "Wanna hide out together?"

*

"I don't need this from you," Drusilla sighed.

"I just want you to get better," Michael said.

Drusilla and Michael were sitting on the swings now. They were screamed out. Drusilla wasn't sure when she had sat down on the swing, but she hoped it was after Michael did. Michael's crystalline eyes looked tired. She was wearing him down. Good, Drusilla wasn't sure how long she could hold up this momentum.

"I am doing the best I can, Michael."

"I just want you to take care of yourself-"

"Damn it, Michael. I don't need you to parent me. I already have two very stressful... you know what, never mind. Just stop." Drusilla's fire died, pitifully.

"You don't like daddy play. Got it. Sorry," Michael replied.

Drusilla smirked despite herself. "Well, now..."

"I was trying to lighten the mood," Michael groaned.

Drusilla felt it bubbling up again. Those pesky feelings. The need ate at her. Fighting this was becoming positively painful. She took a deep breath and tried to let it out in one long rush. No dice. Michael was looking at her. He was always looking at her. Enough was enough. This would end in tears, and Drusilla wasn't going to go through that again if she could help it.

"Why couldn't you have just fucked Mary like everyone else?" Drusilla sighed heavily. That hurt to say out loud, but it was better than what would happen if this shit continued.

"Man... no mood lightening. Got it," Michael sighed. "Fine, okay. First off, because yuck. Second thing. She's like sixteen going on nine. Could you imagine what that would be like to deal with on a daily basis? Well, never mind. You know exactly what that's like. And then, there's you."

"What about me?" Drusilla almost snarled.

"You're a badass. I almost ran you over in that parking lot, and I thought you were going to rip my guts out through my mouth, or something. You take trophies after fights. Nothing fazes you. You're like this awesome warrior woman. Do you have any idea how attractive that kind of badass is in a woman?" Michael finished.

"So, the only reason you like me is because I'm a huge bitch?"

"Yeah, at first," Michael held his hands out and let them drop, "but I enjoyed the glimpses you gave me of the real you. You're interesting and beautiful-"

"I am not beautiful. You take that shit back."

"I'm not going to pretend you're something you're not. You'll just have to get used to it."

She couldn't breathe. Drusilla stood and made her way to Tank. A cold shock ran down her throat and mingled with her innards. She could feel Michael on her heels, but she was almost to the van. Her fingers fumbled with her jingling keys. Michael's hand gripped her elbow. Drusilla could have yanked her arm free easily, but she didn't. Instead, Drusilla turned to face him. Michael's puppy-dog face was cramp inducing.

"You don't have to go. I'll go," Michael said, and he looked around. "Hey, where did George go?"

"George?" Drusilla stopped, and a sinking feeling hit her in the stomach. "Ugh, now I have to give you a ride. Unbelievable." Michael was staring at her. Drusilla groaned. "Well, get in."

*

"All he wants to talk about is Drusilla this, Drusilla that. I just want to grab him and say 'Dude, I don't care'. Even if I did, he wouldn't listen," George sighed.

"At least you can talk about it. I'm tired of the bubble of silence. I can't say what I really want because of all the bullshit she has to deal with. It fucking sucks." Mary tipped her empty cup over and watched the sticky thing roll.

"Yeah, but she has been through a lot."

"See?! That right there. Right *fucking* there! You got to share your feelings, and I didn't say a thing, but I open my mouth and wham! Judgment." Mary picked up her plastic paper cup and tried to scrape the sticky sweetness with her dirty straw.

"I was just saying."

"Yeah, everyone is just saying. Drusilla, the martyr. Do you know how hard it is to live up to Little Miss Victim? I'm not even on his radar."

George felt a stab in his gut. "Yeah. I know how that feels."

"But, you see me." Mary suddenly brightened.

"Yeah." George suddenly felt like a fly in a spider's web.

"At least something still makes sense." Mary's voice took on a husky quality.

George's heart felt like it was imploding. He would never make Mary's radar. Not a chance in hell. She inched closer to him, and George could feel her steamrolling over him. She was using him just like the others, and he would be discarded, too. He was just like the others. She put a tiny hand on his thigh, and it began moving upward. George felt each inch as if Mary were burrowing her hand into his chest. She leaned in unbearably close, and George felt less than worthless.

"Your eyes are very brown," Mary said. Her hot breath was sweet as it hit him in the face.

George took her hand by the wrist and gently removed it from his crotch. He stood up, feeling filthy. Mary looked so lost. Her green eyes watered, and her little mouth was in a perfect *oh* of shock. George felt as brittle as Mary looked. He escaped. One crushing step at a time, he walked away from her and made his way to his car.

*

Drusilla pulled up to the little, blue house. It looked similar to hers, except Michael's house didn't lean, and Drusilla's house was a faded shade of mustard. Michael actually only lived a street or so down from her. Michael's shiny toy car was parked neatly along the curb. Everything looked idyllic, and Drusilla hated herself for liking it. It all left her shaken slightly. Michael's fingers locked with hers and brought Drusilla crashing back to reality.

"Are you okay?" he asked.

"I'm fine." She wrenched her hand from his.

"Okay," Michael said, and he got out of the car. "Thank you."

"What?" Drusilla spluttered.

"For the ride." Then, Michael smiled.

"Oh." Drusilla looked at him awkwardly.

"Well, see you at school," Michael said, and with that, he closed the passenger side door.

*

For Michael, the next few weeks were nothing short of a dumpster fire. George had cut Michael off completely. He wouldn't answer Michael's calls or texts. George would turn the other way when he saw Michael coming down the hall. The cold war between them was sudden and unexplained. It would be easier if Michael knew why his friend hated him so much, but no. Instead, Michael was left to stew in his own ignorance.

Drusilla was occupied with Mary, who seemed to have become an even bigger monster than ever. Her outfits became increasingly revealing. Her heels became higher. Her makeup, more intense. The look in her eyes was hungry and cruel. Mary had abandoned her gaggle of friends to the winds. She was now a lone predator, and everyone knew it. Only Drusilla was safe. Everyone else was meat. That was probably Michael's fault, too. The ugly glare that Mary would shoot him every time he saw her was unmistakable. Nothing compared to Drusilla's ability, but with time, Mary would be just as hard.

Michael passed Paul Hunt, of all people, in the hallway. How does it feel to be just like him, Michael thought to himself, as he sneered at Paul's smug face. Paul's brainless goons circled him and laughed like hyenas as Paul followed Michael with his eyes. Bring it, you fuckup, Michael thought at him. His muscles itched for the chance to pound Paul. Michael longed for the feeling of his fist going through Paul's skull. Killing Paul suddenly felt a little too natural. Michael broke eye contact with the brute. Michael wouldn't be denied the one pleasure that was left to him.

He hooked a left and made his way to Drusilla's locker. He saw her walking towards him in a black poncho and her square sunglasses. Her stubby hair pulled back into two prickly pigtails behind her ears. Michael didn't bother to put on any bravado. There was no point to it. Drusilla's dark mouth had turned sorrowful and stayed that way. She stopped beside him, and a tiny shiver rippled through her. Michael reached out to take Drusilla's hand, but she retreated beneath her poncho.

A sudden, but steady, click-clopping sound made Drusilla jump. Michael looked past her to see Mary stalking through the hall in her sexy predator walk. She was dressed in the shortest, most frayed and faded pair of denim shorts Michael had ever seen. Her breasts nearly exploded from the tank top. She flipped her long hair as she passed them, and her green eyes did their best to burn holes into Michael's skull. Michael watched with a hollow pit in his stomach. Mary grabbed a guy by the front of his shirt and slammed him up against a locker with a loud crash. Before the guy knew what was going on, she was on him - jamming her mouth on his and grinding against him with unrestrained fire.

"She's doing this to punish me," Drusilla croaked. "She doesn't even talk to me anymore. She won't listen to me. I can't even remember the last time I saw her eat. She's just crashing and burning to spite me. I can't stop her."

Michael tried to pull her in, but Drusilla only turned into her beat up locker and laid her head against it. Michael rubbed her back and listened to Drusilla's heavy breathing. She was wrong. This wasn't her fault. This was his. Michael knew it. A moment later Drusilla pulled herself together and wiped her eyes underneath the sunglasses. Without words, Michael opened her locker, and Drusilla deposited her things and her black poncho. Then, she looked at him through her dark glasses. Her hand found its way into his.

"Thank you," she said.

"Don't worry," Michael said. "I'm right here."

Drusilla tilted her head at that remark. Her eyebrows furrowed, and Michael knew he had said the wrong thing again. Then, with a start, she pulled her hand free of his and dispersed into shadows. It was as if she was letting him know that he may always be here, but she wouldn't. Michael sighed and made his way to homeroom, where he was sure he'd see Mary leaving a dripping trail on her way to her desk next to his. He walked down the hall miserably and saw George at the end of it. Awesome, he thought darkly. George's eyes glared right past Michael, and Michael followed his gaze to Mary's display. How much more pain would the people he cared about go through because of him? Michael had to ask that over and over again.

"Damn it!" George said through gritted teeth.

The bitterness in his voice took Michael aback. "You ok-"

"Who was talking to you?" George growled before he turned and stalked off.

It was the first time George said anything to him in a long time. Michael felt like he was shot. The bell rang, and Michael stayed long enough to watch Mary dismount before heading to homeroom. He didn't hurry. What was the point? They kept giving him detentions, and he just kept not showing up. After that, they'd give him in-school suspensions, and he'd just go to class. Nobody stopped him. He found his way to his seat just in time to see Mary runway her way in and slide into her seat. Michael thought about saying something to Mary, but thought better of it. He would only make matters worse.

*

After school, Drusilla searched the halls. Where was she? Mary was nowhere to be found. After combing through the building, Drusilla ran out to the parking lot. There, she saw Mary leaning against Pan's green, little, zippy car. Pan's swagger was unmistakably dangerous. Oh no, you don't, Drusilla's thoughts snarled. She marched right over there. Blood thumped in her veins like drums on fire. She reached them. Pan's hand was an inch from Mary's thigh.

"Mary!" Drusilla barked. Mary and Pan both jumped. Then, Mary turned her hate-filled eyes on Drusilla. Drusilla had no time for guilt or misery. Pan's face turned smug, and Drusilla felt as though she could breathe fire.

"Mary, you're not going with him."

"I can do whatever the fuck I want, bitch!" Mary sassed.

"Yeah," Pan added, "you aren't the boss of her. Piss off, Freak."

"Mary-"

"You heard the man. Piss off." Mary's voice was like venom.

"Okay then," Drusilla said.

In one fluid maneuver, Drusilla shoved Mary into Pan's zippy car with one hand and snatched Pan's arm with the other. She gave his arm a little twist. Mary jumped up, but Drusilla was ready for her. She nudged Mary back with her boot. Mary bumped into Pan's car again, tripping over her long, spiky heels. Mary fell. She tried to stand, but Drusilla put a booted foot on Mary's middle and held her down.

"Hey-" Pan began.

"Pan, go home and jerk off with your uninjured arm," Drusilla said as she twisted his right arm until she heard a pop.

Then, she lifted the foot that held Mary at bay and smoothly kicked Pan in the side of the face. Drusilla scooped Mary up and slung her over the shoulder. Mary thrashed and flailed, but Drusilla's grip was iron. She carried the feral Mary to the van, slid the side door open with her free hand, and dumped Mary into the bowels of Tank. Then, slammed the door shut.

*

Drusilla had to kick the front door open to get in. Mary's thrashing wouldn't stop. They could hear their father bellowing, but neither girl cared. Drusilla struggled to get Mary in the house. Glittery nails dug into Drusilla's flesh. Drusilla cursed, struggled into the drab living room. Their father yelled from the kitchen area, but Drusilla couldn't understand him over the racket Mary made. She brought Mary to the bathroom, and getting her in there was even harder. Mary kicked out hard, and her foot put a hole in the wall.

"Damn it, Mary!" Drusilla bellowed. "I'm trying to help you."

"Get off, bitch!" Mary roared and yanked Drusilla by the hair.

Drusilla huffed and let Mary drop to the linoleum floor with a thud. Mary struggled to get up, but her too tight clothes and heels betrayed her. She thudded hard on her butt. Drusilla crouched down by her wild sister. A feral look glinted in Mary's green eyes. Drusilla sighed and sat cross-legged on the floor, blocking Mary's exit. Mary swiped at Drusilla, and Drusilla easily gripped the arm. Mary struck out with her free hand. Drusilla batted Mary's hand away, and Mary screeched in frustration. As expected, their father rushed in.

"What are you doing?" he demanded.

"Mary had a bad day at school today," Drusilla answered, calmly. "I've got this under control. You can leave now."

"Don't you talk to me like that!" he exploded.

"Get the fuck out, Daddy!" Mary roared.

Their father's shocked expression mirrored Drusilla's. He slowly backed away. Awesome, Drusilla thought, darkly. She turned back to Mary's sorrowful face. All wild fury had gone from her eyes, leaving a cold hollowness in them. For a while, Drusilla and Mary watched each other. Where to begin, Drusilla wondered. Then, Mary moved. She crossed her arms slowly and looked away. She was locking up. Wonderful, Drusilla's inner monologue moaned.

"Don't talk to him like that," Drusilla said. "It's not his fault."

"Are you kidding me?" Mary growled. "He treats you like shit, and you're defending him?"

"No, I'm protecting you."

"From what?" Mary demanded. "From him?"

"Yes," Drusilla said, flatly. "He can turn on you in an instant, Mary. Remember when I was the favorite? Now, look at us."

Mary didn't say anything. She just sat there with her arms crossed and her face turned away. Drusilla could see the wheels in Mary's head turning. A darkness came over her like a shroud. Drusilla was losing her Mary, and she knew it. She could see the path ahead of Mary. It was a dangerous path. A downward spiral that only promised pain. This had to stop.

"Mary-"

"What?" It exploded from Mary's mouth suddenly.

"Okay. I get you're mad," Drusilla took a deep breath, "but you can't do this to yourself." Mary closed her eyes against the words. "You don't want to turn into me, Mary. My life sucks."

"You have Michael," Mary whispered.

"No, Honey-"

"Bullshit!" Mary screeched, her face snapping in Drusilla's direction like a whip. "You have him wrapped around your little fucking finger, like some... like some... I don't know what, but like that!"

"Michael doesn't love me-"

"Then why isn't he all over me?"

"Because. I'm nothing more to him than some conquest. Michael wants what Michael can't have. The second he has me, he'll be gone. Moved on to the next like... like that."

"Then why not go for it? Get it over with."

"Because I'm better than that, Mary," Drusilla answered truthfully. "And you're better than this."

"This feels like bullshit," Mary said. "Remember the mud? You said you thought he loved you. You can't lie in the mud. Which means you're lying now."

"It's the only thing that makes sense," Drusilla sighed. "He may very well think he loves me, but it wouldn't last. It's not real."

"He fucking loves you! He fucking loves you, and you're hiding under some bullshit lie. Who the fuck loves me?"

"I love you."

"That's not enough," Mary said.

It was like a slap in the face. Drusilla felt her heart crumple. "Well, turning into me isn't going to fix anything. It just gets you more alone."

"Well, what's the fucking point? I can't be you. I can't be..." Mary stopped and shut her eyes on a sigh.

Drusilla wanted to bash her head against the toilet. "This isn't about Michael at all, is it, Mary?"

"Fuck off," Mary snapped.

"This isn't going to make Mom want to come home."

"This isn't about Mom," Mary grumbled. "Don't be stupid."

“Mary-”

“Fucking leave it alone!” Mary roared. “Who the fuck asked you to begin with?” Mary threw out her arms, and a gust of power pushed Drusilla back. She slid into the hallway. Mary stood smoothly, but Drusilla could see the tremble in her eyes. “I’m going out now. If I were you, I’d let me.”

*

It had been a full three weeks since Mary Bonnet's locker performance, and George was still pissed. How stupid he had been. He saw Mary for who she really was now. A bratty tyrant who chewed men up and spat them out. She'd never love him. She didn't love anyone. I might as well have been jerking off to the thought of Stalin with tits for fuck's sake, George thought, as he punched a wall.

“Having a bad day?” Michael said.

“Shouldn't you be up Drusilla's ass somewhere?” George retorted.

He watched as Michael shrugged and walked on. George did the same. He made his way past the same faceless people and the same stupid lockers. He passed Paul's gang. Paul stood in the middle and was talking nonsense as his friends laughed around him. Must be nice being that stupid and getting rewarded for it.

“Yo, George!” Paul called after him. George sighed and turned. “I'm throwing a party on Friday. You should come?”

Fuck it, George thought. “Sure.”

“Awesome,” said Paul. “Bring a costume. It’s a Halloween party.”

Considering Friday is Halloween, you dumbass. “I’ll do that”

“Cool.”

“Yeah.” George turned and made his way to class before Paul could open his mouth again. On the way, he passed Shelly Lots. She held her tapestry in her hands and an intense blush on her face. There was a dream-like quality about her heavy lidded eyes. They fell on him.

“Hello, George,” she said in greeting.

"Hey, Shelly," George replied. "Having a good day?"

"I'm off to see Principal Peep," Shelly informed him. "I need to ask her advice."

"Well, have a good day," George said, and he grabbed his personal power. Then, he slipped through the halls before anyone else could pester him.

*

Drusilla sat in Study Hall. Something wasn't right. She tried to open her sketchbook, but she quickly closed it. What was that sinking feeling? Drusilla looked around. Students filed in. She was in her seat. She saw Michael stroll in, so everything was normal there. Michael took his normal seat next to her. What was wrong? Drusilla looked around. Hmm. Michael's fingertips brushed the flesh of her arm. Drusilla shivered and looked at him.

"Thinking about me?" Michael teased.

"No," Drusilla said. She felt her cheeks burn, and Michael's smile burned hotter. "Doesn't something feel off?"

"Off?" Michael asked.

"Yeah. Something's not right."

Michael looked around the room. "Well, that weaver chick isn't here today. What's her name?"

"Shelly." Drusilla's eyes cut straight to the empty seat where Shelly from art class normally sat with her tapestry. "But she was in art this morning."

"Maybe she got sick," Michael offered.

Drusilla's gut called bullshit. "I don't know."

"Do we even know her?" Michael asked.

"She's in my art class," Drusilla replied.

"Hmm..." Michael mused. "Want to check it out?"

"What?"

"Once the bell rings, we can duck out a side door, and you can bring us back without anyone knowing."

"Where, the woods?" Drusilla laughed. Then she saw Michael's face. "No, I'm not going back in there."

"Something doesn't feel right in those woods, does it? Deep

in your gut, something feels wrong. Like maybe, something bad could happen," Michael said.

Drusilla's insides felt like her stomach acid was boiling its way through her. "Yeah, but like you said... she probably just went home."

"I'm going to check it out," Michael said as the bell rang. He got up and stowed his books in his bag. He leaned down to Drusilla's ear. "Feel free to tag along... that is, unless you're too scared."

*

A few moments later, Michael entered the woods with Drusilla in tow. Michael had to fight to keep the smile off his face. He listened to Drusilla's feet crunching in the October leaves. Halloween was right around the corner. Michael couldn't help imagining spending it with her. Something caught Michael's eye, and he stopped. Drusilla bumped into his back.

"Ah!" Drusilla squeaked. "What are you doing?"

"Look." Michael pointed at the area of fallen trees.

"This is the spot from last time," Drusilla said for him.

Then, Drusilla stopped. She was looking past him. Michael opened his mouth to ask, but Drusilla walked past him and stooped down. She stood and turned to show Michael what she found. A wet and muddy tapestry. Michael swallowed hard. Something was wrong. He could feel it now. Something terrible happened to that poor girl. Drusilla tilted her head and stooped again.

"It's a compact," she said as she showed him the blue plastic thing. Then, she opened it. "The mirror cracked."

"Well, what does that mean?" Michael asked.

Drusilla shrugged. "No idea, but she was here." Then, Drusilla turned her head around to look. "Maybe she's still..."

A dark, shadowy lump moved behind a tree. "Did you see that?"

"Yes, Michael. I saw the incredibly creepy, shadowy figure," Drusilla said with forced neutrality. "Why do you think I stopped talking?”

“Okay, that's enough,” Michael said. His skin was crawling. “We need to leave.”

He moved to Drusilla, and she grabbed him by the wrists. Michael felt the familiar wobble and tug. They were gone in a rush, and as fast as her power came, it spat them out. Michael looked around. The air was thick with chlorine. They were in the gym's poolroom. Drusilla threw Michael's hands down and turned to head for the door. Michael followed after her.

“I'm sorry.”

“For what?” Drusilla asked.

“I don't know. People have a way of just dropping dead at this school.” Michael replied.

“They go into the woods. The trees are weak and old.” Drusilla shrugged, though Michael could feel the undercurrent of worry in her words. “It's natural selection. If something happened, they'll find a body. They always do.”

“What if she needs help?” Michael asked, but he knew her answer before she voiced it.

“I don't think she needs help anymore.” Drusilla took a deep breath. “Can we please change the subject?”

“Yeah,” Michael agreed. “So, what are you doing for Halloween?”

“Probably horror movies.” Drusilla shrugged.

“Really?”

“Yeah. Mary and I...” Drusilla stopped herself. “Well... anyway. Why do you ask?”

“No reason. It just seems so pedestrian for you. I kind of imagined you going all out.”

“Oh...” Drusilla said. Then, she looked at the ground. “We should get to class.”

*

Mary sat in the passenger seat of Tank. Drusilla buckled up and waited for Mary's latest attack. Mary picked her nails and did her best not to bite them. Drusilla swallowed how much those nails cost to maintain. Instead, she watched Mary fidget. Mary's eyes flicked in Drusilla's direction for a brief moment, then she went back to her nails. Drusilla sighed and drove off.

"So, you missed it today," Mary said flatly. "Everyone got called into the auditorium today."

Shelly. "Who?" Drusilla demanded.

"Nobody. The school had some cops come to remind us that the woods are off limits, and that anyone caught in them will be punished." Mary grumbled. "So pretty much, they aren't telling us who, but someone must have."

"Shit," Drusilla sighed.

"Yeah. It's getting bad this year. There probably won't be any of us left by the end."

"Maybe we should just run away," Drusilla said.

"What?"

"I'm not kidding. Maybe we should leave. I'll get a new job, and you can finish school somewhere else."

"I don't think that's going to work out the way you want it to," Mary said.

"Yeah. Probably not." Drusilla's mind flew right to Michael.

Chapter 8

Halloween, Michael sat on his floor mattress. He had done nothing to improve the state of his room. In an attempt to stave off boredom, Michael pulled out his phone. Maybe browsing the web would help. The Internet was shit in this town, but some nights it pulled through. Michael watched a few Let's Plays, and was easily bored. He contemplated porn, but there were only so many times a man could beat off a night. What a bullshit Halloween, Michael thought. And with that, he threw his phone.

Michael pulled himself up and made his way into the kitchen. His mother was at work, and his father had long gone to bed. Michael popped open the fridge and surveyed its contents with despair. Closing the refrigerator, Michael moved back to his phone. Porn and chafed dick it is, he thought grumpily. Michael picked his buzzing phone up. George. About time, Michael thought as he swiped and put the phone against his ear.

"Hey. It's been a while," Michael said.

"Yeah." George's voice was fighting over the sound of chaos and shitty music. Then, sudden quiet. "I had to go outside. Listen, I need your help."

Michael's heart sank. For a moment he thought he was getting his friend back. "Sure. What do you need?"

*

Michael pulled up to the house. It was a nice house. Paul's parents must have made good money. Michael parked and got out. The music boomed through the walls of the home. Michael could see shadows in house. It was a pretty good party. Shame he wasn't dressed up. Michael made his way into the house. Monsters in costume mingled in Paul's house. Now, where was she? Michael thought. He spotted George doing his best to contain her. She was a hot mess. Mary Bonnet bent over – her long blond curls falling like a waterfall – and vomited spectacularly all over the hardwood floors. Hurl splattered at her feet, and George tried with all his might to keep her from slumping down into it. God dammit, Michael thought, as he made his way over to them.

"We need to get her outside," Michael yelled over the music.

"What does it look like I'm trying to do?" George yelled back.

Together, they pulled Mary's dead weight from the bumping house. George had her by the shoulders, and Michael lifted her up by the knees. Drusilla was going to have a stroke when she saw this. Michael wasn't looking forward to that. Mary sagged and turned her head. More vomit, all down one side of her hair. All over George's arm. He gagged, and Michael caught his eye. Don't you dare, Michael said with his eyes. They put her down in the grass. Mary got on all fours and vomited even more.

"Fuck, how much is in her?" George asked.

"How much did she drink?" Michael fired back.

"I don't know. I didn't bring her here. I just found her like this."

Michael could feel Mary's vomit splatter against the legs of his pants. He looked down at Mary. She burped and slumped over. Half in the chunky puddle, she cried like a baby. Michael and George dragged her out of her own bile and turned her on her side. Mary cried and hiccupped. Michael had never seen anyone so wrecked. He caught George's worried eyes, and he knew they were thinking the same thoughts.

"Mary, how much did you drink?" Michael asked.

Mary just cried.

"Maybe she took something, or someone might have slipped something in her drink?" George offered.

"Someone better not have." The thought burned in Michael. "We have to get hold of Drusilla. She's probably freaking out."

Mary was buzzing. She giggled and almost rolled back into her own vomit, but George stopped her. He reached into her pocket and pulled out her phone in its pink, glittery phone case. He handed it to Michael. Michael looked at the picture of a long haired Drusilla squished against a younger Mary. They looked so happy. Michael swiped with his thumb and put the phone up to his ear.

"Mary Marie Bonnet!" Drusilla roared.

Michael pulled the phone away from his ear. And now I'm deaf, he thought as his ear rang. "No, not Mary."

"Who the fuck-" Drusilla began.

"It's me."

"Me who?" Drusilla demanded.

"Michael Prince," Michael said. "Where are you?"

*

"Fuck out the way! Damn trick-or-treaters!" Drusilla yanked her head back inside the vehicle. Her heart was breaking ribs as it pounded. She drove as fast as Tank would allow. Stupid, stupid, stupid, Drusilla thought, over and over again. Tank skidded as Drusilla yanked the steering wheel right, and she hit the gas. She zoomed down the neighborhood and saw Paul's house. Slamming the brakes was not the best idea. Tank skidded to a stop in front of Paul's loud house, and Drusilla heard something in the van make an unpleasant crack. Michael and George did their best to help Mary stand upright. Guilt threatened to throttle Drusilla. She opened the door and stepped out.

Mary pushed herself away from the guys and rushed towards Drusilla. She promptly tripped and crashed to the grass. Drusilla, George, and Michael rushed to her. Mary cried, and Drusilla pulled her up by the elbow. Drusilla looked Mary over for injury. There would be no saving her sexy shepherdess costume, but other than that, Mary seemed like she would be okay.

"I've been looking everywhere for you," Drusilla said calmly.

"I'm sorry," Mary sniveled.

"I know."

"Are you mad?" Mary asked.

"No, Sweetheart. I'm not mad." Drusilla could have killed Mary dead, but she put an arm around her sister.

"I don't feel so good," Mary squeaked.

"Wanna throw up on Paul's car?" Drusilla soothed. "Would that make you feel better?"

Mary, tearing up, shook her head. Drusilla looked up at Michael and shrugged. Then, she led Mary to the passenger side, buckled her in, and turned to the guys. She mouthed a thank you, and then made her way to the driver's side. Drusilla started the car and began to drive slowly back home. Mary curled up into a little ball and moaned to herself.

"So, are we done with this now?" Drusilla asked. "Can we put out-of-pocket Mary away for a little while? Maybe whip the bitch out around college?"

"Okay," Mary croaked.

"How much did you drink?" Drusilla asked. "Did you take anything?"

"No, I didn't take anything," Mary answered. "I just drank some shots. Maybe a little beer."

"Okay. What was in the shots?"

"One had whiskey, then I did some vodka Jello shots, and a few tequilas," answered Mary.

"Well, buckle up. You're going to be sick all night."

"Ugh... I think I left my knife at the party," Mary groaned.

"Knife? Mary, why do you have a knife?" Drusilla demanded.

"It's okay, I found it." Mary hiccupped as she pulled out a medium sized kitchen knife.

Drusilla slammed on the brakes. Tank screeched to a stop, and there was another distinct cracking sound, but Drusilla didn't care. She unbuckled her seat belt and turned to Mary. She reached to snatch the knife, but Mary flailed her knife arm wildly. Drusilla flinched away from the blade. The knife clanked against the hard metal of Tank, and Mary dropped the knife with a little shriek. It plummeted dangerously close to Mary. Drusilla's heart might as well have been tap dancing.

"Are you fucking insane?" Drusilla roared. "You could have really hurt yourself! What made you think that was a good idea?"

"I'm going to throw up again," Mary groaned.

"I don't care! Where did you get the knife, Mary?" Drusilla slammed her foot on the gas.

Mary clamped her hand over her mouth in response.

"Do not yak in this van, Mary," Drusilla said sharply. "Swallow it."

They pulled up to the house. Darkness. Their father wasn't home. Drusilla helped Mary out of Tank and held Mary's crunchy hair back for her while she threw up water. Then, Drusilla half carried her sister into the house. She took Mary to the toilet and plopped her down by it. Drusilla lifted the lid, and made her way into the kitchen to grab some water bottles and a heavy pot. A note on the fridge told Drusilla that her father was out of town on business for the weekend. Awesome, Drusilla thought as she rolled her eyes and pulled out her phone. She dialed his work cell and listened to the ring tone. Please go to voicemail, Drusilla thought. Please go to voicemail.

"This is Barnabas Bonnet of Bonnet Cars and more," his cheerful voice answered.

Drusilla froze. It had been forever since she heard her father's civil voice. She wasn't sure how to react. Fuck my life, she thought.

"Hello?" her father asked. A woman giggled in the background. He didn't even sound irritated.

"Um... Dad." Drusilla began and braced herself.

"What do you want?" His voice dropped into its familiar tone of disgust.

"I had to pick Mary up from a Halloween party. She's throwing up. I'm just letting you know since you're out." Drusilla wanted to shrivel up and die.

"Oh... was she drinking?" he asked.

"No," Drusilla lied flatly. Why did she even bother? "I think she's just sick."

"She probably just had a little too much candy," he replied. "You know she has a sweet tooth."

"Yeah, probably." Fucking moron, Drusilla thought. "Well... I need to go check on her."

Her father hung up without another word. Drusilla wiped her eyes and went back to help Mary wash the puke off. The costume was trash. She helped Mary into an oversized shirt. After that, she took Mary to her room and gave her the large pot. Drusilla arranged Mary on her side with the bottles of water. She looked down at Mary. More tears came, and again, Drusilla wiped them away before they could fall. Quietly, she got up to leave the room.

"I was there to kill him," Mary croaked. "Paul. That's why I went. Because of what he did to you."

Drusilla swallowed hard. "Is that why you got super fucking drunk?"

Mary nodded. "I was going to seduce him. Get him alone..."

"I never asked you to do that, Mary."

"Yeah," Mary said, and she closed her eyes.

Drusilla left the room and shut the door behind her. She scrubbed out the tub and showered. After that, she made her way to her room. Then, dressed in an oversized band shirt - Bitch Fury - and her favorite purple and black striped underwear. She fondled the little lacy bow for a moment and sank into bed. It was time for a death-like sleep.

"Happy fucking Halloween to me," Drusilla said as she watched the clock tick off the last few moments of October.

Her phone buzzed on the side table. What now? Drusilla pulled her phone up to glare at it. She looked at the alien number and frowned. If I'm lucky, it's a crazy person come to finish me off, she thought, then answered in case it really was. She leaned back in her bed and braced herself for whatever fresh hell was about to be thrown at her.

"What?" Drusilla demanded, with as much growl as possible.

"Trick or treat," said a familiar voice.

"Oh good. It is a crazy person," Drusilla sighed. "The door's unlocked. I prefer to be murdered with a cleaver. Butcher knives are super overdone, and none of that phone cord strangling nonsense. I want people to see what my insides look like."

"Ha!" Michael barked with amusement. "Sorry to disappoint, but I'm about to fall over dead, I'm so tired.

"Well, don't let me stop you," Drusilla sassed. "Michael, how did you get my number?"

"From your sister's phone," Michael answered.

"Oh... of course you did." Drusilla sighed.

"Is she okay?"

"Yeah, she's finding out the hard way what happens when you mix every alcohol in sight, but she'll be okay." Drusilla curled up in her blankets. They were soft and they snuggled her back. She closed her eyes and began to relax. As far as the end of this miserable day could have gone? Talking to Michael wasn't so terrible. At least on the phone, anyway.

"How are you holding up?"

Fairies fluttered in her stomach. "I'm tired."

"Me, too," Michael said before Drusilla could ask.

"Well," Drusilla took a deep breath. "I'm glad you're home safe."

"Well... I mean, about that..." Michael said, and then paused just long enough to cause worry. "Promise you won't be mad?"

"No!" Drusilla sat up in a panic. Please no. Please no. Her eyes caught the silver gleam of Michael's car outside her window, Michael leaning against it. "No! Damn it, Michael. Why?"

He started to walk towards her window. "I wanted to make sure you got home okay."

"So, you followed me?" Drusilla raged.

"Yeah. I did that," Michael whispered.

He reached the window. Drusilla's heart jumped to her throat and fell. She dropped the phone and slid open her window. The mesh screen was all that stood between them. Michael's eyes were pleading. Drusilla felt a sudden urge to pluck them out. Michael's phone arm dropped to his side. Everything seemed to be spinning. What to do? What to say? Drusilla didn't know. How to make this not so... Fuck!

"It's been a shit night," Drusilla sighed.

"I know," Michael replied.

"I don't know if I can do this right now," Drusilla breathed.

"Do what?" Michael's voice was soothing. Drusilla hated how much it soothed her.

"This... complicated thing we..." Drusilla had to growl to try and cover up the way her voice cracked. It didn't work. She knew it didn't.

"Okay," Michael soothed. "So, let's skip it. Tonight, let's pretend we have it all figured out."

"I don't think it works that way, Michael."

"I don't think you want to be alone tonight," Michael countered. "Unless... Do you want to be alone?"

Drusilla shut her eyes on a shudder. "Michael, why?"

"Me neither," Michael confessed. "Maybe tonight... we could give in a little? Nothing would happen that you aren't comfortable with."

"So, you just want to cuddle?" Drusilla sassed

"I'd like that," Michael replied.

"Michael." The fairies in her stomach began to nibble. She looked into his exhausted face, and she wanted to. Drusilla hated how much she wanted to. This would bite her in ass. She just knew it. This is what came from wanting... like with... Drusilla swallowed that thought down. "If I say yes, we're going right to bed. No kissing, no talking, and no sex. Agreed? Oh, and this doesn't mean we're dating."

"Whatever you need," Michael replied. "Meet you at the front door?"

"I don't know..." Drusilla huffed. "Maybe? I want..." Damn it. "Fine, but this means nothing."

"As you wish," Michael replied, and Drusilla could tell by his smile he didn't believe her either.

Drusilla hopped off her bed. She moved through the dark house to the front door and popped her head outside. No Michael. Well, that was odd, Drusilla thought as she stepped onto her warped front porch. Michael slid out from the bushes and pulled her into him. Un - fucking - fair, Drusilla thought as his arms surrounded her. It shouldn't have felt that good. She buried her face in the hardness of Michael's chest. He held her so close, it hurt. Drusilla never felt so comforted and so terrified. His scent was clean and musky. Drusilla half worried how she smelled.

"Don't be scared," Michael whispered.

Drusilla thought about lying. Telling Michael she wasn't afraid, but she knew he wouldn't let her get away with it. So, she hid her face for as long as possible and enjoyed his strong arms around her. Milking it for all it was worth. Her heart thudded harder than ever, and Michael's hands left trails of fire in their wake. They lowered to the small of her back, and Drusilla burned. She took a deep breath and was overpowered by his closeness. This was too much. Michael tilted her head up to face him. His big eyes where like pools of water. They rippled when he smiled.

"Ready for bed?" Michael asked.

Drusilla nodded. Then, pulled away from him only to lock her fingers around his. Michael drew her hand up and kissed the back of it. Drusilla was a puddle of stinging nerve endings. She wanted to pull her hand away, but instead, she pulled him inside. Michael closed the door behind them. Through the dark, she led him to her bedroom door and stopped him there. Freeing her hand, Drusilla pressed a finger over his lips. They were soft. Like rose petals. They would be, Drusilla thought. She moved to Mary's door and cracked it open. Then, popped her head in. Mary was still on her side. She looked up at Drusilla.

"It's alright. I'm just checking on you," Drusilla whispered.

"Who's here?" Mary breathed.

Drusilla didn't want to answer.

"Oh, I see." Mary's voice betrayed her tears. "I'll try not to be an asshole in the morning."

"I love you, Mary," Drusilla said. "You know that, don't you?"

Mary nodded and rolled over. With a heavy sigh, Drusilla shut the door. She turned and made her way back to the obedient Michael. When she opened her door, Michael's hand wound around hers again. Light flooded the hall for a moment, and she pulled him in. She felt, more than heard, Michael shut the door behind them, and they were in her room together. What had she done? Her hands shook, and the bed was unmade. She should have thought more about this.

Drusilla quickly straightened the covers. Her fingers fidgeted. Turning to smile apologetically at him, Drusilla nearly swallowed her tongue. Michael's eyes flicked up in a flash. The hungry expression on his face was replaced with forced neutrality. Their eyes met, and Drusilla knew he had been staring at her butt. She tried to give Michael her best glower, but what came out was a grimace.

"If it'll make you feel any better," Michael said, "I can make us even."

"What? Are you going to moon me now?" Drusilla said, automatically.

"Do you like butts?" Michael chuckled.

"I haven't given it much thought." Drusilla bit back her frown.

Michael lifted a bushy brow at that and took his shirt off. Oh, what the fuck? Drusilla thought, as heat consumed her. She felt the hardness of his body, but now faced with it.... Drusilla didn't know how to react. Michael's baggy clothes hid most of the uncompromising muscle beneath. He was broad shouldered and beautifully sculpted. Scars ripped along Michael's hairy torso and arms. They were deep and gnarled. Drusilla read the pain in each of them. It caused more heat in her than she was comfortable with. She traced the scars with her eyes. A particularly nasty one ripped through his left shoulder and snaked midway down his chest. She found herself liking that one the most. Michael slipped off his jeans. More muscles, more hair, and more scarring. Drusilla would have swooned if she weren't so terrified.

"So, you like what you see," Michael said as he casually flexed in his boxers. Drusilla quivered so much that she failed to roll her eyes. Michael moved towards her. Drusilla's shiver graduated to a full-blown quake. She was sure Michael would be able to feel the floor vibrating. Michael reached for her. His fingertips brushed against her cheek, and Drusilla flinched. Michael's face faltered. "You don't have to be scared of me."

"I know," Drusilla said to her feet.

She was rooted to the carpet as Michael slipped his arms around her chubby middle. Then, her knees betrayed her to gravity. Drusilla buckled. Michael caught her with a chuckle. He held her up with ease while she regained the ability to stand. Drusilla's mind whirled. Michael was bigger and stronger. Stronger than she could have ever imagined. Like a fucking animal. Michael smiled down at her. Drusilla did her best to enjoy the mingling of terror and excitement in her. Mostly, it made her feel queasy.

"Should we get you under the covers?" Michael asked.

Slowly, Drusilla nodded. Michael's smile was a hungry one. He pulled the blankets back and gestured for her to hop in. Drusilla took the way out and got into her bed. Michael fell in after her, and he pulled the covers up around them. Drusilla curled up into a little ball of defeat. Michael was around her again. His knees came up to nestle behind hers, and his arms caged her middle. Drusilla was trapped in human contact, and her unwillingness to be parted from it. At least she put up a good fight. For whatever that was worth. The light blared in the room. Every detail of this train wreck was on display. Michael kissed her shoulder.

"You're trembling," Michael whispered.

"I know that." Drusilla was too tired to snap at Michael, but she tried her hardest.

His hands found the gap between shirt and panty, and tickled slightly. The pleasure jabbed through her gut and mingled with the terror. It sent lightning up her spine. Tears welling up in Drusilla eyes, and no amount of swallowing them back would save her. How stupid was she? They would crash and burn like they were the Hindenburg. How much baggage would she have after this one? Drusilla bit back tears for as long as she could, but she also needed to breathe. Breathing won out, and a quiet sob escaped her. Embarrassment and fear wracked her bones. Michael pulled her closer. He pressed his lips to the edge of her ear. Drusilla let her tears spill onto the pillow in silence.

*

Drusilla was crying. She was doing her very best to hold it in, but Drusilla wasn't fooling anybody. She curled up against Michael and took very controlled breaths into her pillow. Michael tightened his hold on her. He wanted her to feel safe. So much had happened to her. In that moment, at least, he could help her feel safe. Then, the floodgates broke and sobs rushed out. For a long while they lay together. Drusilla emptied herself, and Michael got to be there while she did.

"Drusilla." The need in Michael's voice reverberated through the room. He stopped and took a deep breath. This needed to be about her. "Do you want me to get you some water, or maybe a snack?"

"Why are you here?" she said, resolutely at the wall.

Michael rubbed along her upper arm. "Because I-"

"Don't!" Drusilla snapped. "You don't mean it."

"I was going to say because I want to be here, but okay?" Michael replied as gently as he could. "But since we're talking about it, I would mean it."

Drusilla's body relaxed on a very heavy sigh, but she looked like her insides had just been pulverized. "Damn it, Michael-"

"I mean it," Michael said again.

Drusilla freed herself from Michael and clung to the edge of the bed like an angry cat. Michael watched as she twisted away. The hem of her shirt lifted an inch or two more, and Michael spotted a purple splotch on Drusilla's skin. His heart sank. Who hurt her this time? How many asses would he have to kick to keep this from happening again? A surly, frustrated energy clogged his lungs.

"Is that a bruise?" Michael asked, gently.

"I have a bruise?" Drusilla swapped fear for confusion. "Where?"

"On your back," Michael said. "You have a big purple bruise. I just saw it."

"No...? Oh, wait," Drusilla said. "Do you mean my tattoo?"

"You have a tattoo of a bruise on your back?"

"Yes, Michael." Drusilla rolled her eyes. "I scraped up all my tips for months to get a tattoo of a bruise on my back. Like I don't get them for free all the time."

Michael's stomach dropped to the rim of his asshole. "Um..."

"That was supposed to be sarcasm," Drusilla said awkwardly. "Wanna see it?"

"Yes, of course... I mean." Michael's face felt very hot. "Sure."

Drusilla twisted and lifted the back of her shirt. Massive purple butterfly wings burst from her shoulder blades. They stretched down Drusilla's rib cage. The tattoo was expertly done. Each detail painfully needled in. The blood rushed from Michael's head, and he wrapped Drusilla up in his arms.

"It's only a tattoo," Drusilla whispered.

"I prefer tattoos to bruises," Michael muttered.

"Me, too," Drusilla sighed.

"I'll make sure no one ever hurts you again," Michael promised.

"Michael, I don't need..." Drusilla began. "You don't..."

"I know you don't need a hero, but could I be yours, anyway?" Michael asked.

Drusilla gave him a worried look and laid back down. She curled up into her protective shell. Michael snuggled against her again and hoped he added an extra layer of armor. His fingers rested on the tender gap of skin. The feel of her body against his was incredible. She was his, and Michael knew it. The light glared around them, but Michael was unwilling to get up. Drusilla reached over him, and with a wave of her hand, they were plunged into darkness.

"Is there anything you can't do?" Michael asked, and the second it came out of his mouth, he knew it sounded cheesy.

"Plenty, actually. Most of the magic I've learned is spells of convenience. Blinking, switching lights on and off, and stuff like that. I'm still learning," Drusilla said drowsily.

"That's more than I can do," Michael mused.

"You have your own magic." Drusilla sounded half asleep. "You just have... to find it..."

Michael nuzzled her closer, and Drusilla relaxed a little. Michael smiled to himself as he planted a kiss on her burning cheek. He couldn't see, but knew the little blush fairy bloomed there. Drusilla's back pressed against Michael's chest and stayed there. All his now, Michael thought. Maybe in the morning, they'd go out for pancakes, or something. Michael fantasized about it for a little. Drusilla snuggled deeper into him, and soon, little snores escaped Drusilla. Michael settled in and closed his eyes.

Chapter 9

The cold, gray light greeted Michael's eyes. He lay on his back. Drusilla's frame curled up against him. Her hand rested against his chest. Her fingertips mingled in his hairy chest. Michael looked down at her. A sweet smile played on her face. Instinctively, Michael held her closer, as if she would be taken away. Instead, she inhaled deeply, and smiled wider. Heat bloomed in Michael's lungs. Smile for me like that all the time, baby. He didn't dare speak it. They laid like that for a long while. Michael's eyes took in the room. A Bitch Fury poster hung on the far wall. It was a good enough band. If you were into angry, shrieking women. Luckily Michael was, but what he kept falling back to was the purple string of butterflies. Maybe it was the glitter, and the way it sparkled all the colors of the rainbow when his eyes unfocused.

Michael rested his free hand above his head, and his knuckles brushed against the spines of books. He looked down at Drusilla sleeping and pulled one at random. The book was heavy. More like a binder. The cover was plastic, faded, and yellowing. Crude tulips in a stenciled basket defaced the cover. Michael ran his thumb along the plastic pages. A photo album. He cracked it open and began flipping through baby photos, birthdays, and trips to the zoo. Somewhere in the middle, he stopped.

The photo of a dark haired child in hunter green. Drusilla was maybe six or seven, and a blond baby Mary was sitting in the dirt. It looked like they were making mud pies. A young woman bent over them. Her long, dark hair pulled back in a ponytail. She tilted her face up to smile for the camera. The sunlight hit her in the face and illuminated her unsmiling purple eyes. There was a coolness there that the smile didn't melt. Drusilla's mother. An Ice Queen, Michael thought. Emotion pulled Michael down and attempted to drown him.

Michael shut the book and carefully slid it back into place. He turned back to Drusilla. Purple orbs lifted to look at him. Feeling caught, Michael smiled down at her. Drusilla smiled back. Her eyes were warmed by the action. Drusilla held him tighter, and relief ran through Michael. Drusilla crawled up to be face to face with him. Michael's hand slid down, and he cupped her bottom without thinking. Drusilla snuggled him fiercely.

"You're still here," she said, sleepily.

"Where else would I be?"

"Um... I don't know." All sleepiness drained out of her in a rush. She lifted herself up to look at him. "Your bed?"

"Nonsense," Michael replied. He hooked an arm around her as she fell back into snuggling against him. "I'm here."

"Okay." She moved her hand up to Michael's shoulder and ran her fingers along the jagged scar. "So, what happened here?"

"Change of subject? Smooth," Michael mused. "Broken bottle."

"How?" She looked up at him skeptically.

"Sometimes people threw things in the pit. My opponent picked up a bottle. I was beating his ass, and he had a lot of money riding on the fight. He used it. It didn't help him much."

"What?" Drusilla pushed herself up and looked at him for a long while. "But that pit fighting stuff was bullshit. You were just making yourself sound big, or whatever."

"I don't need to sound big." Michael reached out an invitation for her to lie back down. "That's how I could afford that spiffy car, and my college fund, and... and I told you all this."

"Michael, what did your mother think?"

"Why do you think we left Michigan?" Michael countered.

He watched as Drusilla pulled her knees under her chin. His

inviting arm ignored. Worry plagued her face. He could almost see Drusilla calculating each scar on his body. Each second glance brought more and more discomfort. Like she was figuring out some complex equation. Michael vaguely wondered what the total would be. At least she cared. He had been with women who found them sexy, but never really bothered to think anything else. Like they were tattoos, or something. He had also been with women who took one look at his body and ran screaming. Michael sat up and put his arm around her. She looked up at him with misted eyes.

"So, you fought in some filthy pit. Where people would throw beer bottles and stuff at you?"

"And won a *lot* of money doing it," Michael said cheerfully.

If Michael had to put a word to the look Drusilla threw him, it would be incredulous... maybe irritated. Though her eyes didn't narrow. Teeth raked against Drusilla's bottom lip. Michael ran his fingers along Drusilla's hand. Absentmindedly, she grabbed it and laced her fingers with his. Little pink butterfly patches burst across her cheeks like a spell. It sent a pang of need through Michael. He scooted closer, and Drusilla lounged against him. His arms wound around her, and there was a novelty to the opposite of her pushing him away. This was how things were meant to be, Michael thought.

"Well, I guess we both have scars," Drusilla sighed.

"Mine are only skin-deep."

"Fine," Drusilla said, flatly. "Rub it in."

"I'll rub something," Michael teased, then stopped. "If I kissed you right now, will it freak you out?"

"Don't kiss me if you don't mean it," Drusilla's whispered.

"I mean it." Drusilla began to shrink away, but Michael held her firm. "Drusilla..."

He gave her a moment to stew, and then went in. She gasped, but Michael was quick to stop her mouth. Their lips grappled, and soon their tongues and teeth joined the battle. Drusilla clung to him for dear life. Nails dug into Michael's back, but the pain only made it more exciting. The skin on Drusilla's thighs prickled Michael's hands, but he moved to softer pastures.

His hands slipped beneath the shirt, and before long, he was lifting it up over Drusilla's head. Michael cupped the small breasts in his hands. His thumbs brushed over her pink, little nipples, and Drusilla gasped against his mouth. Her thick thighs wrapped around him, and they were breathing the same breath. Michael watched Drusilla's eyes dilate, and then more kissing.

"Okay," Michael said. He pulled away and began to untangle himself from her crushing thighs. Drusilla's hurt face made him lunge in for another quick kiss. Then, Michael reached over the edge of the bed for his pants. Sadness radiated off Drusilla in waves. He pulled his wallet out and snagged a condom. Then, returned to her with the square of cellophane. She pounced at him, mouth first. As if he would leave her, Michael thought. He slipped her panties down. Drusilla began to lock up under Michael's hand. He shrugged out of his boxers and slipped into the condom.

"Don't be scared," Michael soothed. He rubbed her in ways he had only imagined and never really thought he'd get to in real life. He wasn't wasting any time.

Drusilla clung to him with all her might. She was crushing. Michael only kissed her harder and longer. After a while, she went limp in his arms. He pulled back to see the dazed look in her eyes. Michael guided her knees up to rest by his sides, and Drusilla was kissing him again. Her mouth furiously attacking his with all she had. Michael felt nails rake painfully down his back. He eased into her, and she moaned uncomfortably. All wildness left her, and Michael pulled back. Drusilla looked up at him and panted. Had he hurt her? Then, her strong hands came up to cradle his head and pull his face down on hers by the ears.

*

Mary rolled out of bed. Her brain was head-butting the inside of her skull. Staggering to her feet, Mary pulled on some shorts, opened her door, and stumbled into the hall. Vomit nested in her throat like a lump of clay. This was happening. Get to the bathroom, bitch. The wall was awesome for leaning on as Mary's stiff legs took her to the bathroom, little by little. The toilet was Mary's best friend. It gratefully took her hurl and flushed it away. Mary rinsed her mouth out at the sink and made her way back into the hall. She cracked Drusilla's door open a peep in without knocking. Whatever was going on, she wanted to catch off guard.

Drusilla and Michael were sleeping, so that did happen. It still hit her like a sucker punch to the smut pocket. Drusilla's eyes opened, spotted Mary, and fell. Sadness radiated off of Drusilla like heat. Sorry, Mary mouthed. Go back to sleep. Then, she shut the door and tried not to realize that Drusilla didn't seem to be wearing a shirt. Defeat washed over Mary, and she made her way to the kitchen. Mary did her best to get over it. She knew she never stood a chance, but it still sucked. Mary picked up the house phone, punched in her father's cell, and waited for the ringtone.

"What do you want, Freak?" her father's words cut.

Motherfucker, I will break you! "Hi, Daddy."

"Oh hey, Princess." His voice adopted its normal happy tones, but it was too late. His words were like imitation butter. "How are you feeling?"

Like you even care. "I'm feeling a little better."

"That's good, Princess." His voice was cloyingly sweet. Too bad Mary hated sweet.

"Yeah, so, when are you coming back?" Mary thought she'd scream if he called her princess one more time.

"Not until Monday, Princess."

"Oh, okay." Fuck you, you piece of shit.

"There's pizza money in the bread box. It should last you till I get back."

"Okay, Daddy." No, don't bother asking me what happened. That would be too real. "I was just checking on you."

"Thank you, Princess." He paused. Mary could hear a woman murmuring something in the background. It sent a shiver up Mary's spine, oddly. "Listen, Princess. I have to go, okay?"

"Sure." Whatever. Mary was done anyway.

"Okay, Bye bye." Click.

Mary looked at the phone. Bye bye? Was she nine? She didn't

bag three guys a week to be seen that way. Had he always treated her like this? Of course he has. Mary was treated one way, and Drusilla another. She used to think that their father hated Drusilla and loved Mary. Now, she could see the truth. There was a default dealing with Drusilla and default dealing with Mary. Mary was pretty sure that their father didn't even remember their names. These are my children, Freak and Princess. Fine then, you fucking robot. Have it your way. She could assign a label to him just as easily. He can be ATM, or maybe Cash Monster. Mary popped open the breadbox and pulled two twenties out. Yup, Cash Monster.

*

Drusilla slipped into the hall. Mary looked at the receiver end of the phone in disgust. Then, she slammed the phone down into its cradle. Awesome, Drusilla thought. Mary reached for something in the breadbox, then Mary moved into the kitchen. She opened the fridge. Her eyes moved from left to right, over and over, as if she were reading a book. Then, she groaned and slammed it shut. Mary turned and froze.

"Hey," Drusilla said in greeting. She hated the meekness in her voice, but there it was.

"How long have you been standing there?" Mary sounded frightened.

"Not long."

"Oh," Mary sighed. "Where's your new boy toy?"

"That's not funny, Mary," Drusilla groaned

"Oh, come on, Drusilla," Mary replied. "It's a little funny."

"Fine," Drusilla admitted. "But it isn't nice."

"Look," Mary sighed. "I'm doing the best I can with this."

"Mary, I-"

A knock at the door cut her off. What now, Drusilla and Mary thought. Drusilla moved to the door and looked through the peephole. It was Ronda. Red hood over her lank, brown hair. What the hell? Drusilla looked back at Mary, then nodded her head toward the hall, silently telling Mary to go back to her room. Drusilla waited until Mary had complied, and then opened the door.

"Hi, Drusilla," said Ronda. Her voice was raspy.

"Hi, Ronda," Drusilla answered, slowly.

"It's been a while," Ronda said to her feet. "The house looks... well."

"What do you want, Ronda?" Drusilla said as gently as she could muster.

"Shelly Lots is dead." Ronda's deadpan voice shook a little.

"Dammit!" Drusilla's insides burrowed deep down and hid in their own little oubliette. Drusilla so didn't want to be right about that. Something solid was suddenly against her back. Strong arms curled around her, and Drusilla burned.

"Holy shit," Michael's low voice thundered above Drusilla's ear. "How?"

"How do you think?" Ronda threw her hands up. "God! You people are so wrapped up in your own little story that you're missing what's going on here... Why'd I even bother?"

Drusilla looked past Ronda to her boyfriend in a tiny, beat up red car. Too much, she thought. The words attempted to murmur their way out of her mouth, but Drusilla swallowed hard. She would be constructive. "Why would Shelly ever want to mess around in the woods?"

"I don't know, but I can see the writing on the wall. Wolfgang and I are out of here. I just thought I'd give you a heads up since everyone always blames you."

"Thank you," Michael said.

"Yeah." Then, Ronda stood there awkwardly for a long moment. "Well, good luck with everything, or whatever." She walked back towards the car and stopped halfway before she turned. "You guys should leave, too. Before it gets you... Don't die, okay?"

They watched her turn and walk to the car. Ronda hopped in, and the red car pulled away. Michael pushed the door closed, and Drusilla watched the scene be shut away. Something ripped its way through Drusilla's chest. It exploded, and Drusilla kicked the door wildly. Michael's hold on her tightened, but Drusilla sank to the dirty floor.

"Fuck!" she roared. Her voice shattered into a billion pieces.

"Breathe," Michael soothed. He crouched down with her.

"I fucking told you something bad happened to her." Drusilla's voice felt fragmented. Shards of it plunged into her lunges. "I knew it!"

"I know, Baby," Michael soothed.

"Who died?" came a small voice.

Drusilla gulped down her rage and her tears before turning to look at Mary. She looked so fragile. Drusilla could have kicked herself. "Shelly Lots."

"Oh." Mary's voice was hollow. Tears slid down her rosy, little cheeks. "She was nice."

"Are you okay?" both Drusilla and Michael asked.

"Yeah." Mary shrugged as if she was fooling anyone. "It happens. We go to the woods and don't come out. Then, the adults tell us not to, but we do, and don't come out."

Drusilla wiped her face and pushed herself up. "Yeah, but it's still awful."

"Yeah," Mary said. "I'm going to take a bath. Do any of you need to pee or... or take dumps? Drusilla? Butt sex always makes me want to shit."

Drusilla winced and shook her head. Mary shrugged. Drusilla watched her broken little sister go. It was a whole new kind of hell to play in. Drusilla turned and fell face first into Michael. Their arms wound around each other, and Drusilla felt Michael's lips press against her scalp. They stayed like that for a moment longer than Drusilla would have liked, but she didn't move until Michael let her go.

"Are you hungry?" Drusilla asked.

"Yeah, I could eat," Michael replied, "or we could go back to bed."

"Fine, you win," Drusilla said after a full thirty seconds.

"How are we going to spend the weekend?" Michael mused, suggestively.

*

Michael waited by Drusilla's locker. He didn't have to wait long. Spotting her in a plain, black dress with black and white stockings and fishnet sleeves, he waved. Drusilla lifted a paper cup in response. She passed it to him and took a shaky sip from her own. Michael lifted the tiny opening of the plastic lid to his nostrils and inhaled. Green tea. Drusilla stared at her feet. Michael reached for her, but when he touched her, she flinched and looked up at him with haunted eyes. Michael leaned in for a quick kiss. Drusilla pulled away.

"Not here," she whispered. The little pink butterfly patches appeared on her face.

"Why not?" Michael asked.

"You know why," Drusilla replied.

"Paul will never hurt you again," Michael promised.

"It's not just him," Drusilla said. "You know that."

Just then, Paul and his goons walked past. They looked at the pair. Michael watched Drusilla's stillness. Her purple orbs followed the pack until they turned the corner. Michael wanted to grab her dramatically and tell her everything was going to be alright. He knew that would have gone over like a lead balloon, so he didn't. Drusilla huffed and hugged herself.

"Nobody's going to do shit," Michael assured her. "And if they try, I'll break them in fucking half."

Drusilla rolled her eyes at that. "Michael..."

"You think I won't?" Michael asked as he put his hands around her hips.

"Yeah," Drusilla sighed, sarcastically. "Totally what I think."

"That's what I love about you. Your unwavering faith in me." Michael leaned in.

Drusilla pulled away slightly. "What did I just say?"

"I know. I'm sorry," Michael said. "But after school, you're mine."

He watched with gratification at the look on Drusilla's face. He spun the combo to her locker and opened it for her. Drusilla pulled the books out and deposited her things. Then, she closed the locker and turned to him. She opened her mouth to say something, but Michael slipped his hand in hers, and she froze. Drusilla took a deep, shuttering breath. Michael enjoyed that she began to pant.

"We might as well be screwing on the desks," Drusilla breathed.

"Nah," Michael replied. "You're too classy for that."

"Ha ha," Drusilla groaned back, pulling her hand away. "Bring puns to the table."

"Oh shit," Michael laughed. "It's pun versus pun, now."

"What?" Drusilla demanded. "Where was my pun?"

"Bringing *puns* to the *table,*" Michael spelled out for her. "Like buns to the table."

Drusilla paused for a long moment. Then, "*Oh*! That wasn't intentional."

Michael shook his head and then grinned at her. The bell rang, and Drusilla threw her hands up in acute exasperation. She looked at Michael as if this were his fault. Then, she grabbed him. Michael was hurled through those familiar between places as Drusilla blinked with him. She turned to him and pressed her lips aggressively against his. Michael curled around her, and he deepened the kiss. They hurtled through the magic, locked together for what felt like forever, but before he knew it, Michael was in his desk in homeroom. He watched her outline shimmer away, her words still lingering in his ears.

"To tide us over."

Michael's mouth stretched into a stupid smile. He looked over to Mary, who was dressed in sneakers, jeans, and a fitted top? That wasn't normal. Her hair was in a lazy braid down her back. Okay. Maybe she got whatever she needed out of her system? Maybe this would be easier than he originally thought. She looked at him with a glimmer of contempt in her green eyes. Maybe not.

"You have," Mary stated flatly, "black lipstick absolutely *all* over your face."

"You're not dressed up today," Michael responded as he wiped his face with his hand. The black smear on his hand confirmed that he had only spread it around his face more.

"There's no point anymore," Mary said. "No one left to impress."

"There's still George," Michael offered.

"Ha!" Mary barked, bitterly. "He rejected me. Not that it matters anymore, anyway. I'm fasting till college."

Mary turned her attention to the clock, and it was as if Michael weren't even there. Well, okay then, Michael thought as he began to daydream about Drusilla's mouth. His face leaned against his propped-up hand. The way she- the bell cut through his daydream and happy mood. Mary swept up her books and left homeroom. The faceless occupants of the room did as well. Michael stood, grabbed his things, and left homeroom. The halls were crowded and stupid.

*

George slipped through the halls and spotted Drusilla. They made eye contact for a few seconds, and then she slipped into the art room. George weaved through the crowds, carried to the right place and the right time by the magic. He wasn't sure why or how, but he didn't question his gifts too much. Not even when the magic bumped him right into Mary. She turned to glower, but when she realized who she was glowering at, Mary's face fell. They stood awkwardly as the crowds bustled past. Mary began to twirl her rope of golden hair around her fingers, but seemed to remember something and stopped.

"Sorry," George said

"For what?" Mary said, flatly.

"Bumping into you."

"Oh," Mary sounded hollow. "It's whatever."

George watched her go. He had his own hollowness to deal with. He would have to be more careful next time. George made his way to class, though class proved to be less important. Michael sat some seats away from him. He openly stared out the window. George doodled in the margins of his history book and did his best not to think about Mary. An impossible task, indeed.

*

By lunchtime, George was just feeling bitter. He slipped through the lunch line and got his serving of daily slop. The lunchroom was its normal, awful, crowded mess. He looked at the table he normally sat at and cringed at the people sitting there. Then, his eyes fell on the only other open table. Drusilla and Michael ate their lunches out of brown paper bags. Michael's arm inched around Drusilla's shoulder. She scowled at him, and he removed it. George looked away, his eyes locking with Mary's. She did not look away. How long had she been staring at him?

George took his plastic tray over to Michael and Drusilla's table. They both looked up in surprise as he stood there. George noticed Michael's hand tighten around Drusilla's for a moment, and Drusilla's eyebrows met in the middle for a brief moment. An awkward moment passed. Then, George put his tray on the table. Then, he took a seat. Drusilla's worried face scanned the table behind George. He really wished she wouldn't. In fact, George wasn't sure this had to be such a big thing.

"Um... what are you doing?" Drusilla hissed.

"Making a choice," George answered.

"Do you know how much trouble you're putting yourself in right now?" Drusilla asked.

"You don't have to, man," Michael added.

George looked up to find Paul Hunt's narrowing eyes. "I'm not afraid of them."

"Cool," Drusilla said, not sounding like she thought it was cool at all.

*

Mary sat in the passenger seat of Tank and looked away as Drusilla and Michael sucked face just outside of the driver's side window. This is all bullshit, Mary thought as Drusilla slipped into the driver's seat. Drusilla cranked the van to life, and they were off. Mary wanted nothing more than to be in her dark room with her plants, but Drusilla turned the wrong way out of the parking lot. What now? Mary was sure she couldn't handle any more today.

"We haven't had an Us Day in a while," Drusilla said.

"No, we have not," Mary agreed. She was not thrilled by the idea of having one now. "Where are we going?"

"I have no idea," Drusilla replied.

"Yippee," Mary groaned, and then pulled out her phone. She began to look up gardening tips.

"Fine," Drusilla sighed, and drove.

*

The van pulled to a stop, and Drusilla hopped out. Mary looked around. It was night. They had pulled into a gas station. Drusilla was feeding money into the pump. This bitch is going to go all night, Mary thought. Then, her mind drifted to her undone homework. Tomorrow was just going to be a *treat*! Mary snagged Drusilla's phone and began to snoop. Drusilla's phone had three messages. Ten guesses from who, Mary thought as she swiped the screen with her thumb. The phone buzzed. Incoming call. A lovely picture of Michael picking his nose greeted Mary's eyes. He clearly was not aware of the photo then, or now. Good for you, Bitch, Mary thought at Drusilla. Good for you. She slid her thumb to ignore.

Drusilla hopped back into the driver's side and cranked Tank to life. They drove and drove. How *long* was this going to take? Drusilla's phone wasn't *that* interesting. Mary began snooping through Drusilla's email only to find junk mail. Why not put this in your spam, Mary thought as she did just that. She looked up again, and they were driving through the woods. The clock read midnight. Ugh.

"Are we running away, or something?" Mary spat.

"Where do you want to go?" Drusilla asked.

"Philadelphia," Mary replied, without hesitation.

"Why there?"

"Because everyone runs away to New York."

"We don't have the gas to get there," Drusilla confessed.

"Adventure tease."

Drusilla chuckled at that. It was nice. Drusilla was getting to her. Damn it! Mary decided to look out the window, but Drusilla's reflection was smeared all over the thing. The dark world around them made the window even more reflective. Mary was trapped, and they both knew it. What bullshit, Mary thought.

"So," Drusilla began, and Mary felt danger, "I hear there was a George incident."

"No shit," Mary grumbled. "He sits with you now. I'm sure he told you all about it."

"Actually, no," Drusilla interjected. "Michael told me."

"Fucking loud mouth."

"Yes," Drusilla agreed. "Maybe not his best quality."

"He's also needy," Mary said, holding up Drusilla's phone. "He texted you a bunch of times."

"Mary, get off my phone." Drusilla snatched the thing away.

"Fine," Mary snapped. Drusilla said nothing. She just drove. Mary went back to staring out of the window. The trees whizzed past. "I didn't hear anything... about Shelly."

"That's because no one's talking about Shelly," Drusilla replied.

"Bummer."

"Yeah, want to get pizza?" Drusilla asked.

"We always get pizza," Mary replied.

"I know," Drusilla agreed. "Burger?"

"You're going to eat a burger?" Mary called bullshit.

"I'm sure they have a veggie burger somewhere that doesn't taste like plant asses."

"Wanna bet, Bitch?"

*

George dropped his things off at his locker and picked up the books he would need for the morning. He shut the locker door with a clang. Mary was there. She leaned against the locker next to him in jeans and a snug pink top. A pale, tie-dye like smear stretched across her ribs. It was like a bully scene from a bad 80's teen movie. Mary's face was placid, though her eyes smoldered. A part of George still wanted her, but the rest of him just wanted her to go away.

"Boo," she said softly.

"What do you want, Mary?"

"Just saying hi," Mary sighed.

"Why?"

"No reason." Then, she walked off.

Unfair, George thought. He had been trying so hard to get Mary to notice him, and now that he didn't want her, he couldn't be rid of her. He shook the Mary incident off and began the trek to class. Fucking Mary Bonnet, he thought. He kicked and accidentally struck a student in the back of the leg. He went to call out an apology to the poor girl, but she kept going as if nothing had happened. George was confused, but went on with his day.

*

After a passionless art class, stupid math test, and completely drab science lab, Drusilla made her way down a little used hall. One of the lights was broken. It flickered, and no one had ever gotten around to fixing it. Nor did they get around to replacing the other lights that didn't work at all. Drusilla paused at a glass covered bulletin board. Old newspaper clippings and photos lay behind it like some sort of morose shadow box. Her eyes locked on her own face, and Drusilla nearly gagged. She wore the airhead grin of ignorance. Paul's meaty arm wound around her shoulders. Pulling her too close. It was practically a headlock. Her hair nearly reached the hips of Drusilla's old, lanky boy body. Yuck.

"I miss it, too," Paul's voice echoed through the hall. Drusilla had a hard time trying to figure out if it was real or imaginary. She chanced a glance. Paul stood there, almost too close.

"Why, Paul." Whatever, let's rabbit hole this, Drusilla thought. "You miss having a free hump toy. Willing or unwilling."

"Come on. It wasn't like that," Paul said. "We looked happy."

"I look like a prey animal," Drusilla replied. "Speaking of which, no fist to the face? What gives there?"

"You will never forgive me, will you?" Paul said. "No matter how many times you kick my ass."

"I fucking loved you." Drusilla's words left a bitter aftertaste in her mouth, but it was no lie.

"I knew that," Paul said as the bell rang.

"And you still did those things me." Drusilla's bitter voice turned icy.

"Nothing happened that you didn't ask for," Paul retorted.

"You fucked me, and you never gave me a choice. You grabbed a hold of me, and it was go time." Drusilla growled. "You told me you loved me one night, and the next day you practically curb stomped me. What part of that was I asking for, you piece of shit?"

"Yeah, well, I handled things badly. It was confusing."

"I was wearing the dress you bought me." Drusilla's laugh was frozen. "You're right. I would have been confused, too."

"I didn't think you'd wear it here." Paul's face turned red. "When you told me you wanted it I thought..."

"What? We'd play dress up?" Drusilla's hands balled into fists. "Have a fucking tea party, Paul?"

Paul didn't reply.

"You're pathetic," Drusilla said, and then she looked at the shadow box. Its contents burst into purple fire for a brief moment, and then all were ashes.

"Those old pictures of us where the only thing that made me happy," Paul said, more to himself than to Drusilla.

"Sucks, doesn't it?" Drusilla killed any emotion in her voice.

"Yes, it does." Paul's eyes closed on a sigh, and they didn't open for a while. "Do you think this could make us even?"

"Even, Paul?" Drusilla said his name the way she used to. Before everything went to shit. He opened his wet eyes to look at her. Then, she went in for the kill. "Nothing will ever make us even."

Drusilla enjoyed the way grief consumed Paul. She just stood there and watched Paul implode. He locked eyes with her until he could no longer take it, and then Paul left. Drusilla stood alone in the abandoned hallway. She looked at the blackened glass. This had been a good day after all. Then, Drusilla realized she was late for lunch. Michael would probably be having a cow about now. Drusilla rolled her eyes and made her way to the lunchroom. She so wasn't in the mood for any kind of tantrum he would pull.

Chapter 10

Michael drummed his fingers against the imitation wood table. The lunchroom raged around him. Where was she? George was gone, too. Something in Michael's gut felt very wrong. He was just about to get up and start looking for them when the doors pushed open. Drusilla made her way over to the table and slid in next to him. Their hips touched. Michael opened his mouth to speak, but Drusilla cut him off with a kiss. Her fingers locked into his hair. Michael felt eyes burning on them. How hard would this make things for her? Screw it. He grabbed her. Pulled her against him hard and rode her mouth with his till the end.

"I'm sorry," Drusilla said.

"It's okay," Michael said with a smile.

Drusilla's lovely eyes searched him. "Don't do that."

"What?"

"Pretend everything's fine because you don't want to rock the boat."

"I..." Michael stopped. Drusilla's purple eyes narrowed dangerously. "Look, I was worried, but you're fine."

"I didn't mean to worry you," Drusilla said, and then she pulled out her brown paper bag.

Michael watched her for a moment. Then, he dug into his turkey and cheese. They ate in silence. Michael wanted to say something, but Drusilla was militantly focused on the green tortilla wrapped whatever. Probably sprouts or... Eyes. They burrowed into Michael. His head snapped up to face the watcher. Paul Hunt. Who the fuck else? Paul gave a tiny nod. Michael felt his jaw tighten. Drusilla's chilly fingertips pressed against his cheek. She turned his face to meet her worried eyes. She leaned in for another kiss. Her mouth tasted like spinach and avocado. When the kiss broke, Drusilla's forehead rested against his.

"What did he do?"

"Nothing," Drusilla replied. "This time at least. He just wanted to talk."

"He tried to talk to you?" Michael face contorted with rage. He turned cold eyes on Paul

"Yeah." Drusilla wound her arms around him, comfortingly. "I need you to not go crazy right now, okay."

Michael took a few steadying breaths. "Is that all he tried to do?"

"Thankfully," Drusilla sighed. Then cheerfully, she said, "I did make him cry."

"Maybe Paul needs to be hit with another tree."

*

George put away his books. It was the end of the day. About time, he thought. A tug at his elbow. George slammed his locker closed and turned to face Mary. Keep cool, George told himself. Mary's eyes lingered uncomfortably. He just wanted to go home, but no. Selfish Mary Bonnet needed the floor, apparently. George crossed his arms and leaned against the lockers. Let's get this over with. Mary pursed her lips. Oh god, George thought. Maybe she just wanted him to look at her. How long was this going to go on?

"I'm sorry," Mary said, and she walked away.

*

Mary sat in the passenger seat. Drusilla kept her kissy face appointment with Michael mercifully brief. Drusilla hopped in, and they were gone. Mary scrolled through her phone. She was comparing prices on winter flowers. Her phone buzzed. A text message from an unknown number. Mary slid her thumb down. A long, greasy smudge added to the other oily smears. She really needed to clean out her phone. That distracted her for a few minutes before she could get to the message. All old numbers had to go. Then, she wiped the screen shiny with her sleeve.

"Hey, Mary," the text said.

"Who the fuck is this?" Mary typed back.

"George."

Okay? "What do you want, George?"

"I accept your apology."

"How did you get my number?" Mary typed, and waited. No response. The message was marked as seen. Awesome.

"Did you give George my number?" Mary asked her sister.

"No," Drusilla replied. "Although, he did go through your phone to get my number on Halloween, so..."

"Sneaky fucker," Mary groaned. She hopped back on her phone to type. "I'm not going to bang you, if that's what you're after."

"That's not what I'm after," George typed back.

"I don't get guys anymore," Mary announced. "I'm cutting off all my hair and becoming a lesbian."

"Don't cut your hair," Drusilla said.

"Fine," Mary sighed. "I'm keeping my hair and becoming a *lesbian*!"

"Yeah, Mary. That would last," Drusilla replied.

"Sass!" Mary declared, throwing her hands up in mock outrage.

"Yes, Mary," Drusilla replied. "All of the sass."

*

Drusilla filled the espresso maker. The beans clanged as they filled the hopper. The cafe was empty. Blissfully so, Drusilla thought. The door opened, and the bell rang. Just kidding, Drusilla told herself. She plastered a working smile on her face and prepared to greet the customer. Principal Peep walked in. Drusilla dropped the act and gave her a tiny wave. Peep giggled to herself and walked over to the counter.

"Drusilla, it's been ages since you've paid me a visit," Peep said as if Drusilla were in her office and not the other way around. "Everything going okay?"

"Yeah, for now," Drusilla said with a shrug.

"Good," Peep said with a grin. "Is my big sister here?"

"I'm here," Mrs. Gooseberry said with a cheery smile. Drusilla rushed to pull three paper cups, but Mrs. Gooseberry put a chubby hand on her arm. Drusilla stopped. Mrs. Gooseberry pulled out an envelope of cash and handed it over. "Thank you for coming in today, Drusilla. Take the rest of the night off."

"Oh?" Drusilla questioned, but she took the envelope.

"Atta girl," Mrs. Gooseberry said with a wink.

Drusilla looked to Peep. Her smile widened. Suddenly, Drusilla felt her guts drop out. Peep tilted her head questioningly. Drusilla pulled herself together and smiled back. Drusilla turned to Mrs. Gooseberry. Mrs. Gooseberry pulled her into a fierce hug. Drusilla's heart leaped, and then plummeted. It made her nauseous all of a sudden. She didn't want to let go, but Mrs. Gooseberry released her. Drusilla bit back a sudden wave of tears. Damn hormones making her feel all crazy, she thought darkly.

"I'll see you tomorrow." Drusilla smiled as hard as she could.

"Yeah, baby." Mrs. Gooseberry smiled back.

Drusilla and Peep nodded to each other, and Drusilla got out as fast as she could. It wouldn't do to have a fit of hormones right there between the two adults who actually got her. Like she needed that shit. The crisp air hit her in the face, and Drusilla was grateful. She took a deep breath and tried to get a hold of herself. She took the orange plastic bottle out of her bag and glared angrily at the little blue pills. Something small and dark fluttered onto her shoulder. Drusilla plucked it off with her pointer finger and thumb. It was a little, black feather that swayed in the wind. How odd.

*

Mary sat in a hard plastic chair in the mall food court. George approached with a tray of burgers and soda cups. Mary's insides felt like they were going to fly out of her mouth and strangle them both. She tapped her foot rapidly and watched George divide the burgers and fries. Mary already regretted this. To stop her mouth, she unwrapped her burger and bit into the huge thing like she owned it. She should have asked him to get her two. This was stressing her out. George munched on some fries. Spit it out, Mary thought at George.

"About that thing that happened between us," George started.

"I'm not sleeping with you," Mary said.

"I'm not asking you to," George replied. "I thought we went over this?"

"Then, what did you want from me?" Mary asked. "You seemed to like me well enough, but you weirded out on me."

"That's because I don't want to be one of your fuck boys, Mary."

"Well then, what do you want, George?"

George took a bite. Mary was about ready to leave. "I wanted more than that."

"Ugh, why?" This was making her want to explode.

"Because I like you," George replied.

"Like *genuinely*?" Mary asked. "Like, be my girlfriend type stuff?"

"Yeah." George's voice took on an awkward quality.

"I'm sorry. I think I'm having a stroke or something. What?"

"That makes two of us."

Mary ate furiously. This was too much. How the fuck was she supposed to deal with this? George watched her and smiled. After Mary inhaled her burger, she began cramming fries down her gullet as fast as she could. Next, Mary sucked down her large soda as if George would yank it away. Soon she was sucking the dregs of watered-down root beer. George was almost laughing at her. Mary wanted to punch him in throat.

"If you hurl, I won't clean it up."

"Oh, fuck you," Mary spat.

“Do you kiss your mother with that mouth?” George laughed.

Mary blanched at the comment. “No... no I don't.”

“Oh.” George swallowed hard. “I shouldn't of...”

“It's fine.” Mary made a decision. “I guess now we're even.”

“It's not about even,” George said.

Mary sat back, and looked at him. “So, what now?”

“Do you like cheesecake?” George asked.

“Oh my god, yes!”

*

The day was a bitter one. Michael walked Drusilla to her locker and opened it for her. Two dead students in one night. Unheard off, Drusilla had said. Another assembly. Principal Peep urged them to be cautious. In one ear and out the other. Drusilla squeezed his hand, and Michael squeezed back. Michael had liked Ronda and her boyfriend. They never messed with Drusilla, and that was likable. They were found in the wreckage of that zippy, red car they drove off in. The huge tree had fallen on them as they were cutting through the woods. In the end, not so much of a short cut and more a crush.

Mary sat next to George at lunch. They seemed to have worked something out. Their hands were somberly linked beneath the table. Drusilla leaned her head against Michael’s shoulder and wouldn't touch her spinach salad. By the time the bell rang, she just wrapped it up and placed the salad back in her brown paper bag. They spent study hall playing a quiet chess game, and Drusilla was losing. Really, she wasn't trying.

The next day there was another morning assembly. More students were killed. The three pigskin brothers were looking for cheap carving wood, and *crunch*. The police were going around from classroom to classroom, informing the student of the dangers of the weak trees and placing a ban on anyone entering the woods. Drusilla stopped talking. She hid behind her large sunglasses and did her best to wipe the tears away when no one was looking. Only Michael noticed.

*

A few more weeks went by, and everything seemed to slip into an easy rhythm. It was nice. Easy to be in. Michael kissed Drusilla goodbye for the day. She and Mary drove off to do what they normally did, and Michael hopped in his own car to go do what he did. That day, he was going to the park to shoot hoops with George for a little and dodge calls from his mother. His parents were fighting worse than ever, and Michael just wanted it all to go away. As if he summoned his mother, Michael's phone buzzed. Nope. Not today. Hoops with George and a quiet bid for information.

George kicked his ass. They played for hours. Michael goading him into rematch after rematch, but George was on fire in a way Michael had never seen before. He could guess where it came from, though. After being all played out, they hit the mall for burgers. They ate bacon double cheeseburgers and fried cheese sticks. Secretly, Michael hoped that the Bonnet sisters would be there, but no luck. George seemed in a cheery mood. Michael wanted to wait for George to bring up the topic, but he wasn't getting to it fast enough.

"So, how are things going with Mary?" Best to start off easy.

"Okay," George said, but he couldn't hide a wide grin.

"That's good," Michael said. Then paused. How to word this? Fuck it. "So, what's really going on with the trees around here?"

George froze for a second. Discomfort ripped through his easy happiness. "What do you mean?"

"I mean, I don't think it's beetles, or whatever they are saying."

"Yeah. I know," George sighed. "It is pretty weird."

"And there have been a lot of deaths this year," Michael added.

"Yeah." George was silent for a moment. His brows crunched together in the middle. "Can we talk about something else? I'm not feeling the most comfortable with where this is going to lead right now."

"Sure." Michael was just about to give up when it hit him. "Do you still have that yearbook?"

*

After hanging out with George, Michael could think of nothing to distract him from going home. George was unwilling to part with the yearbook, much to Michael's annoyance. His phone buzzed again, and again, he ignored it. He was on his way home anyway. If she nagged him about it, he could lie and tell his mother that he left the phone at school. He leaned against the side of his car, pulled up Drusilla's face, and started typing with his thumbs.

"What are you up to?"

Silence. Then, three little dots shuffled. It was annoying.

"Where are you?" Drusilla typed back.

"On the way home," Michael typed. He counted to three before he sent it to at least feel suave.

"Okay," she replied, almost at once.

"I could take you to dinner instead," Michael typed.

He waited, and waited. Drusilla didn't respond. The tease, Michael thought as he got into his car. He started it when his phone buzzed once. A message. About time. He pulled the phone out and unlocked it with a swipe.

"Come home for dinner." His mother's message burned against Michael like a brand.

"Never mind. My mom is nagging me about getting home. Another time?" Michael typed.

"Okay," was her reply.

"Well, if you didn't want to go out, all you had to do was say so," Michael said out loud. Then, he pocketed his phone and started the car.

In the privacy of his own car, Michael allowed himself to sulk. He would have to suck it up when he got home. At least until he got to his room. The drive was unfortunately short, and Michael sat in his car in front of the tiny, blue house. He felt trapped, and he hated it. He sat there, waited and watched, until he could crush his bitter feelings down. Until he could keep a neutral expression. When he did, he pulled himself out of the car and walked to the front door. He took a deep breath and hoped things would be quiet tonight. He opened the door.

"Well, it's about time," Michael's mother said in crisp English.

Michael didn't answer. He just walked in, and stopped. Drusilla sat – cheeks ablaze with fairy blushes – on his couch. Next to his mother. She looked shyly up at him, and he couldn't even enjoy it. Because she was in his house. On his couch, *next to his mother*! Michael's mind raced. How did he deserve this? How? What did he do that landed him in this? He quietly shut the door behind himself and entered the room. His mother looked smug. How nice for her.

"Hi," Drusilla said, meekly.

"Hey, babe," Michael sighed. He hung his coat up. If he knew walking into the woods would guarantee he'd be crushed by a falling tree, he would walk right out that door, but Drusilla's little butterfly blush patches were on full display. That was reason enough to live, but now his mother was about to ruin it all. Like always.

"I stopped for coffee this evening-" Michael's mother began to say.

"I can see that." Michael fought to keep his tone even.

Just then, his father walked in, and Michael wanted to die all over again. His father was holding two mugs of something hot in his paint-stained hands. He wore his working clothes, which were splattered sweat pants and a ripped, paint-smeared shirt. Would it have killed him to put on a clean shirt when Drusilla came over? Michael noticed his mother eyeing the ragged thing, and he knew that she was thinking along the same lines. Awesome, Michael fumed. Why couldn't his parents be dead? But he instantly regretted that.

"Hey, Michael," his dad said. "Want some tea?"

"Hey, Dad," Michael replied. "No, I'm okay. Thanks."

"Honey, we have company over," Michael's mother started with that tight, yet civil tone. "Why not change-"

"So, you want me to change?" Michael's father started, less civil.

"Your shirt, dear," Michael's mother's replied. "I would like it if you changed your shirt."

She was calling him dear. This would fall apart quickly. Michael rubbed his face with his hand, and sighed. His eyes met Drusilla's, and she was looking at him with concern. She looked like she wanted to go over to him, but her butt was glued to the old couch. His mother had a way with people. Michael thought back to every girl he ever brought home to meet his mother. First voluntarily, then less so, over the years. Classic her, Michael thought. Dinner with the parents was usually the beginning of the end for Michael and his girlfriends. He looked at Drusilla fondly, as if she were already gone.

*

To say that Drusilla instantly regretted getting roped into dinner at Michael's was an understatement. It was a long, *long* night of quickly killed bickering and words unspoken between Michael's parents. None of them kind words. Michael looked as if every moment was slowly, painfully killing him. His tired eyes lingered over Drusilla, apologetically. She wanted to grab his hand under the table, but they were seated painfully, just out of reach.

Drusilla ate her tasteless, half cold dinner and spoke when she was spoken to. Mostly, all she had to do was feign compliments on the food and dodge simple questions. Towards the end of the dinner, Drusilla got the feeling that Michael's mother wasn't satisfied. Rita should have known better, Drusilla thought. This was only uncomfortable. She should come have a dinner at Drusilla's house where people throw plates, and Mary threw like a pitcher. She'd have a blast, then. Maybe some wicked scars, too. Come on lady, don't waste my time.

"So, Drusilla," Michael's mother started. "I understand your mother is Aneira White?"

Michael froze. His mouth became a very thin line of disapproval. He narrowed his eyes at his mother. Rita Prince did not miss that. Drusilla's mouth spread into an easy smile. So suddenly, it was go time? Oh goody. She cracked her knuckles under the table, and her eyes locked with Rita's. She must have sensed something because Rita lifted her eyebrows in a small surprise.

"Unfortunately," Drusilla said, pleasantly.

"Oh." True surprise escaped Rita. It danced on Drusilla's tongue as she tasted it. "We went to Elderberry with her."

"How unpleasant for you," Drusilla said in the best imitation of her mother she could whip out. "I'm sorry."

Rita froze. Suddenly, she was sucked right back to the bad old days. At least, Drusilla was assuming they were bad. Anything having to do with Aneira Bonnet was a bad scene. Rita looked haunted all of a sudden. Yeah, Drusilla thought. Bring that shit up again. I dare you. Out of the corner of her eye, Drusilla could see a vague shadow of Michael. He wasn't moving, but she couldn't see his face. She couldn't let herself want to look at him.

"Well, yes," said Rita. "I take it her departure hit you hard?"

A roaring silence buzzed in Drusilla's ears. She could feel hot anger reverberating from Michael. Don't hate me for this, Michael, she thought desperately at him. A slow, wide grin spread across Rita's face. Drusilla mirrored it, wickedly. Rita's smile faltered. "I was very happy to see her go."

"Oh?" Rita swallowed hard. "I take it you didn't approve of her parenting style?"

"I don't think much of mothers who let their personal problems bleed into their parenting style. It shows a degree of weakness." Drusilla let that sink in with a smile. She couldn't look at Michael. Her facade would crack if she knew his feelings. She took a bite of the cold corn. "Don't you agree?"

Rita smiled back, but didn't ask Drusilla any more questions. Was that really it? Drusilla wondered. Rita was giving up already? She was lucky Drusilla wasn't her mother. If she was, she'd have that woman slitting her own wrists and painting bloody poetry on the walls. Still, Drusilla was painfully aware of how much like her mother she was. Damn it. Drusilla had to get out of this without any more ugliness. She was sure Michael wouldn't talk to her anymore. She could cry about it later. Right now, she had to find a way out. Dinner was almost over. Rita went off to whip up some awful dessert involving chemically loaded whipped topping. She just had to keep from looking at Michael, and-

“Could you pass the salt, Drusilla?” Michael said, evenly.

And *damnit*! Drusilla did her best to breathe deep without anyone noticing. Then, she grabbed the salt and held it out for Michael to take. Her eyes locked with his. She couldn't help it. She could never help it. Double dammit! Michael looked insistently at her. Damnit! Damn it damn it damn it, and now her mask was breaking. Triple damn it and a half, she thought.

*

Drusilla's van was still at her job. Michael and Drusilla left the house and walked over to Michael's car in silence. Drusilla's unreadable face made Michael's insides squirm. He had hoped for something when she had passed him the salt. Some kind of reassurance that they were okay. He had tried to let her know, but he was greeted with a stone wall. Michael unlocked the car and opened the passenger door for her. Drusilla got in, buckled up, and looked straight ahead. Like Michael wasn't even there. He shut the door and bit back tears before hopping in the driver’s side. She was looking out of the passenger window now. Why did this always turn into his fault? Like, every fucking time! Michael started the car and they drove.

“I'm super sorry,” Michael said. Not that it mattered anymore because fuck him, right?

Drusilla's hand came up and pulled Michael's away from the wheel to lock fingers with him. He glanced sideways, but Drusilla was still looking out the window. They drove almost aimlessly. They passed the parking lot a few times, but that was because the town was so small. Drusilla didn't mention it. She just squeezed his hand, as if checking to make sure it was still there.

When, finally, Michael could not think of a way to take, and they had been driving around for what was probably hours, they pulled in next to Drusilla's van. It was a big, terrible monster that was going to take her away. Michael would never see her again. Drusilla looked up at her van. She didn't move to get out, and neither did Michael. They just sat there, hands locked together, in misery.

"Please talk to me," Michael pleaded once he could no longer take the heavy silence. He was looking at the back of her head. Another brick wall, but finally, she turned. Her eyes, red raw like hamburger, making stained tears, still falling to her cheeks.

"I'm sorry," Drusilla whispered.

Michael was out of his seat belt and had her in his arms before the cry could escape her dark lips. She broke down. Drusilla cried the same way she kissed, like it was a battle. Michael held her close until she was quiet, and they were rocking back and forth together. He was never letting her go. They were going to spend the rest of their lives in this parking lot, huddled together in his car.

"I shouldn't have gone there," Drusilla said once she was all cried out.

"You never have to again," Michael said. "I'm sorry my mother forced you to come over in the first place."

"It was just so tempting," Drusilla sighed. "She went for what she thought would hurt me the most, and I ripped her for it. I'm not even sure I could help myself."

"I thought you were brilliant," Michael murmured. "You would have seen that if you had looked at me."

"That's your mother, Michael," Drusilla sighed. "I just threw down with your mother. I didn't care what it cost me. I didn't care that I could have lost you."

"Is that why you wouldn't look at me?" Michael whispered. "You thought I would hate you because you weren't taking my mom's crap? I thought you were mad at me."

"I'm sorry," Drusilla breathed. "I just couldn't stand it if you hated me."

It was the closest she ever got to saying I love you. "Yeah. I know how that feels."

Drusilla lifted her head to kiss Michael. It was a sweet and tender thing. Another first, but Michael didn't dwell on it. He slipped his arm around the small of her back and pulled her in to deepen the kiss. Her tongue darted between his lips, and their head movements fell into a rhythm that was hypnotic. Drusilla's hands moved up Michael's arms to rest on his neck, and Michael was grateful. Then, she yanked his head back by the hair in a surprise attack that caused him to gasp more out of surprise than pain. Her mouth jammed hard against his, and it lit a fire in him. He kissed her hard until the fire was slaked, and Drusilla was curling up against him. A happy, feral thing. His feral thing, like he had fed a raccoon too many times. Michael hummed contentedly. He liked the thought.

"Michael?" Drusilla asked in the dark.

"Yes, my love," Michael said, trying out the new term of endearment and finding it lacking.

"Let's never be like them," Drusilla breathed.

"I don't want that either," Michael agreed. "We'll be better than them. Just promise me you'll tell me if you have a problem and not lord it over me."

"I promise, if you promise you won't ever ignore that there is a problem."

"My dad doesn't do that," Michael replied.

"Mine does," Drusilla sighed

"Okay," Michael agreed. "I promise."

Drusilla curled up against him, and her phone vibrated between them. She growled softly and pulled it out. Light blinded Michael for a moment. Drusilla swiped the phone with her thumb and read the message. Then, she swore, and the sinking feeling crept into his gut the way it always did when they had to part. Drusilla lifted her head, and they kissed for a long while. Michael wasn't ready to let her go. He was never ready, though. He knew that. She pulled away suddenly, and a growl ripped from his mouth that he didn't mean to utter aloud. Drusilla looked at him, a shocked expression on her face.

"What was that about?" she asked.

"Drusilla, I..." but Michael didn't really know. "I'm sorry."

Drusilla lifted her eyebrows at him. "Look, my dad actually

noticed that I wasn't home. Which means, I have to go yell him under a table for the better part of the night."

Michael felt worse. "I'm sorry."

"I'm going to be super bitchy tomorrow," Drusilla added. "So, save the sorry for something more than this. Because I'm pretty sure you're going to hate me in the morning."

Drusilla opened the door with a smile and went to leave. Michael watched her go, and then he had an idea. "Hey, Drusilla?"

"Michael, I have to *go*," she said as she stuck her head back in the car.

"I know, but real quick," Michael said, "winter break is coming up.

"I know that."

"Do you wanna do something?" She tilted her head at him. "We could go... somewhere... like..."

"I'll think about it." Drusilla smiled. "Good night, Michael."

"Good night," Michael said back, but Drusilla had already shut the door on his words.

He watched her hop into the van and crank it to life. The headlights came on, and Drusilla drove off. Michael's phone buzzed. He looked at it as if he didn't already know. He looked at his mother's happy smile. He was so pissed at her. He just watched the phone ring and ring. Then, her face faded. Michael sighed, feeling a little guilty, but then the phone came to life on a buzz. His mother's smiling face, taunting him. Michael pocketed the phone and drove.

*

"Your son isn't answering his phone," said Rita Prince as she walked into the kitchen.

"Quit calling him that. Like you want nothing to do with him. We made him, Rita, and we decided to keep him. Pushing him away isn't going to change that," Charles Prince said. He was elbow deep in the dirty dishes.

"What is that supposed to mean?" Rita snapped.

"Come on, Rita. We both know what I mean." Charles rinsed

and repeated. "You can't keep this up and expect Michael to put up with it?"

"Is that what you do?" Rita spat. "Put up with me?"

"You know I do, Rita," Charles answered. "You pushed me away a long time ago. What do you think Michael's going to do if you keep pushing him away?"

It was like a slap in the face. "I didn't push you away. You scuttled away because you can't handle an ounce of responsibility around here."

"That's bullshit, Rita!" Charles spat. "I haven't done my share? Who worked two jobs and sold paintings to put you through medical school?"

"Yes, and you haven't worked a day since. I-"

"I haven't worked?" Charles spun to face her. "I didn't stay with the baby while you went climbing hospital ladders? My paintings didn't keep food on the table during the lean times? Who took care of Michael when he got sick? Who suffered through every single tantrum? I did. I made sure he was fed. I made sure his homework was done, and done right."

"Yeah, well, you missed it when he was out being a criminal."

"Oh, please. Like you noticed," Charles spat back. "Like you *ever* notice anything!"

Chapter 11

"I can't wait!" Mary cheered in a singsong voice. "This is going to be so awesome! I'm going swimming!"

This was getting on Drusilla's nerves. She floored it over a bump in the road and they bounced up. Drusilla felt her butt cheeks lift a full inch from the seat. The safety belt threw her back down. Mary whooped and giggled. Mary reached for the radio, and some shitty pop song blared through the grainy speakers. Are we there yet? Drusilla silently whined. Another bump. This one Drusilla had not meant to hit, and another squeal of delight from Mary.

"Mary," Drusilla groaned. She leaned over to shut off the radio. "It's December."

"We're going to the lake!" Mary cheered in response. "We're going swimming!"

"Mary, it's freezing out. You can't go *in* the lake." Drusilla was already wishing this trip was over.

"With our boyfriends!" Mary said, as if Drusilla wasn't trying to talk to her.

"Yes, we both have boyfriends. Said boyfriends are taking us to a cabin by a lake for winter break. Ugh, that rhymed. Anyway, we're going to have a wonderful time. Now *please* shut *up!*" Drusilla moaned.

"Why aren't you excited about this?" Mary asked.

"Something's finally going right for us. That, like, never happens."

"I know." Drusilla's stomach dropped. She turned down their street. "Do we have everything?"

"You act like we didn't just buy everything," Mary snarled.

"Sass, Mary," Drusilla shot back.

"You bet your bunghole," Mary just about roared. "And I'm going to keep sassing you until you cheer the fuck up!"

"Fair enough," Drusilla sighed. "You win this one."

"Huzzah!" Mary cheered. "Eat it, ya-"

They pulled up in front of the house. Drusilla and Mary caught sight of the car. It was shiny and navy blue. Not a car either of them recognized. Drusilla's stomach clenched. They sat in the car for a long while and watched. The car was parked in the driveway. Okay, Drusilla thought. Their father's beat up car was next to it. So he was home and he had a friend over? Did he even have friends? Something didn't feel right. She looked over to Mary who was doing something on her phone.

"The car's a rental," Mary said as she looked up. "I did a search on the plates."

"Okay," Drusilla replied. "Do you have everything packed?"

"In my room, but-"

"Awesome." Drusilla took a deep calming breath. She could fade into Mary's room, grab her shit, and fade back. Then Michael could drive the whole way, but then Drusilla would never know who was there. Decisions, decisions... "Wait for the boys. I'm going in."

Drusilla hopped out of Tank and made her way to the crooked, little house. She took out her keys and fitted the right one to the door. The lock turned, and Drusilla waited a beat. Just get the crap and get out, Drusilla repeated twice before she turned the doorknob and pushed the warped door open, with some difficulty. She walked into the living room. Her father wasn't in his normal lazy chair. A woman's back was to Drusilla. A waterfall of inky hair fell to her waist. Drusilla heard her father say something from the kitchen, and the woman's laugh was like an early frost. Drusilla was frozen to the spot. Oh no! The woman turned, and Drusilla's own purple eyes stared back at her.

"Andrew." Her voice was glacial. "You're home."

"Who?" Drusilla answered, without missing a beat. She had to fight hard to keep her voice twice as frosty.

"You look..." Her eyes traveled over Drusilla. "Well, at least you cut that hair."

"It reminded me of someone..." Drusilla paused to run her own eyes through her mother's long locks. "Weak."

"I was visiting with your father." Her voice was honey with a hint of poison. Drusilla knew that tone all too well.

"How awkward for you," Drusilla said, adopting the same tone, only with twice the venom. "Well, don't let me stop you."

"Oh? Too busy to spend time with your own mother."

Drusilla leveled dead eyes in her mother's face. "Look into my eyes, old woman. Do you really think-"

"What the fuck is taking..." Mary's voice died with a little gurgle.

"Mary-" their mother began.

"The fuck is this bitch doing here?" Mary roared, and Drusilla felt power in that roar.

"Honey-" Their mother pushed past Drusilla, like an afterthought.

"Who the fuck was talking to you?" Mary demanded. An inferno swirled in Mary's throat.

Drusilla watched as their mother's face blanched. Their father crept into the living room, but said nothing. Coward, Drusilla accused with her eyes. This bullshit was on his head, and they all knew it. How bad was this going to get? Drusilla's eyes snapped back to their mother. Her lovely face was becoming blotchy. If she flipped, what were Drusilla's chances of getting Mary out? Drusilla's mind was spinning. She looked at Mary. She was pulling her golden earrings out and pocketing them. Oh damn.

"Mary, go back out to the car, please," Drusilla commanded evenly.

"Princess-" their father began, but Drusilla cut him off with a killing look.

"It's okay. Mary, go back to the car and wait for the guys." Drusilla searched the fire in Mary's eyes for any sign of intelligence. She was tomato red, her fists were balled up, and you could feel a crackle in the air. "We're almost out of here."

"Good," Mary said, more to her mother than to Drusilla. "I don't want to be here. Not with a punk bitch that dips out on her own family and doesn't have the stomach to stay gone!"

Drusilla sighed and looked at her mother. Her icy purple eyes narrowed at Drusilla, and Drusilla scoffed. "Oh, what did you expect? A welcome back party?"

The hand flew across Drusilla's face. Mary screamed in bloody outrage and charged. Drusilla got between them to shield Mary. It was too fast for Drusilla to react. Her mother pushed, and Drusilla fell sideways. She attempted to twist away, but Drusilla came crashing into the entertainment center. Glass shattered and wood splintered beneath Drusilla's right side. Raised voices exploded into a cacophony of confusion. She had to get to Mary. Drusilla struggled to get to her feet, but pain shot up her back like a bolt. She couldn't get up. She didn't dare open her eyes.

"Mary, get out!" Drusilla roared blindly.

Someone yelled, but the words were drowned out by Mary's unintelligible screaming. Now Mary was probably being beat. Then, the sounds of a struggle. Drusilla tried again to move. Pain ripped through her back again. Her body flailed. Everyone was yelling and banging around. She had to get to Mary. She had to keep Mary safe. The sound of more things breaking, and someone crashed into the wall next Drusilla. She could hear the plaster buckle and cave. The sound of a body slapping against the floor and a decidedly feminine cry. Mary! Drusilla struggled to get free. Hands were on her. Powerful arms pulled her up to her feet. Drusilla struggled her hardest.

"Baby, don't open your eyes," Michael said in her ear. His fingertips brushed glass out of her face. "Don't try to stand. I'm lifting you up. Okay, easy."

"I have to get to Mary!" Drusilla struggled against him harder.

"She's outside," Michael said as he lifted her off her feet. "She's okay. Try to relax."

The sound of a fight still raged behind them. Drusilla curled up into a ball and did her best to shut everything out. Michael was moving, and the awful sounds gave way to fresh air. Drusilla could hear Mary whimpering, but the sounds of George soothing her were there, too. That made Drusilla relax, finally. Michael sat her down on the hood of his car and asked George for a water bottle. He tilted her head up. Drusilla's neck screamed, and a whimper escaped her tightly pursed lips.

"I'm going to rinse the glass off of your face," he explained, and then proceeded to dump freezing cold water over her face. Most of the water went up her nose. Michael's fingers brushed her eyes. "Okay I'm going to bend you over. Try to blink a bunch, okay?"

Drusilla managed it without getting glass in her eyes. She looked up at him. Michael's face was a worrying mix of anger and sadness. She looked over at Mary through the windshield, sitting in the backseat of Michael's car. George cradled her in his arms. George's eyes locked with hers, and Drusilla looked away. She looked up at Michael again. He opened his mouth to say something, but a muffled thrashing sound cut him off. What a dumpster fire this all is. Drusilla fought back tears. As if it was a battle she could ever win.

"I need to get Mary out of here." Drusilla hated the desperation in her voice, but there it was.

"I need to get *you* out of here," Michael countered, or agreed. Drusilla didn't know which.

"Same," Drusilla agreed, and she allowed Michael to help her into the passenger seat. He buckled Drusilla in. Then, he booked it to the driver's side.

"Holy shit," George said. "Look at your arm."

Mary exploded into a fresh wave of wailing. Drusilla was going to kill George. Kill him dead. Michael buckled himself in and looked back at Mary. Then, his eyes turned to George before he started the car and drove away. Drusilla hugged her arms around herself in an attempt to not get blood on Michael's car upholstery. Mary cried for what felt like forever. Drusilla looked over at Michael. The muscles in his jaw rippled as he tensed them. Turning back to look at Mary meant risking blood and pain, so Drusilla settled for watching Mary from the side mirror. Mary didn't look hurt, but most of her was wrapped up in George. After a long while on the road, Michael pulled into a convenience store. The building looked like a white painted barn.

“Hey, Mary?” Michael asked. Drusilla watched Mary's head perk up in the mirror. Michael handed back a wad of bills. “Can you get a first aid kit? Spend the rest on whatever you want.”

“I'll go with you.” George punctuated his words with a kiss to the side of Mary's forehead.

A sense of dread flooded Drusilla's lungs as she watched them go. Drusilla watched the trees outside her window. They swayed dangerously. The last thing she wanted was to look Michael in the eyes, but his reflection was watching her in the glass. A hand came up to pull her arm free, and Michael's fingers locked with hers. Drusilla had to swallow back tears or be consumed. The comforting squeeze came, and Drusilla knew there was no avoiding this. Resigned to her fate, she turned to face Michael's hard eyes only they weren't hard. Sadness dripped from them. It was almost worse.

“So, that's your mother,” Michael said. His wet eyes blinked. Drusilla knew what he was trying to do, but he did it a little too late. Two fat tears slid down his cheeks.

“I'm sorry.”

“For what?” Michael cradled her stinging face in his hand. “Drusilla, Baby... you never have to go back there.”

“I can't talk about this right now.” Drusilla leaned her forehead against his. It helped to quiet her thumping cranium. She was running out of room for swallowed tears, so she let them fall freely for a moment.

“Okay,” Michael soothed.

The back door opened, and Mary tossed a plastic bag in before scooting in herself. George followed with a white metallic box. Michael backed out to get gas. He looked at his phone. Then, they were off again.

A half hour later, they reached the cabin by Elderberry lake. George's family owned it. It was huge. More of a log mansion. A wide wraparound porch looked like it went right around to the water. Mary seemed to forget all about the day's events as George led her to the doorstep. He pulled a key out and let them in. Lights illuminated the windows. Michael helped Drusilla out of the car. She looked back at the seat. Blood was soaked into the seat on Drusilla's left side.

"I'm sorry," Drusilla breathed.

"It'll wash out," Michael said as he put an arm around her. "It's not a big deal."

"I'll clean it."

"Let's get you cleaned up," Michael countered. "Don't worry about the seat."

"But the car-"

"Is meaningless compared to you. Fuck the car." Michael began to sound frustrated. He stopped and took a deep breath. "Drusilla, you're my girlfriend. Can I take care of you, please?"

Drusilla didn't say anything. Instead, she looked at him. Michael scooped her up again and carried her into the cabin like they were newlyweds. It was a pretty big cabin. An antler chandelier hung from the ceiling, and the stair's banisters were polished logs. George and Mary were nowhere in sight. Michael found the nearest room with a bathroom, and put Drusilla down on the edge of the Victorian style tub. She allowed him to remove her top and let him turn her away to look at her wounds.

"Shit," Michael swore. "She got you pretty good."

"How bad?"

"We should have taken you to the hospital," Michael replied. Drusilla looked back at his determined face. Michael sighed. "Fine, but this is going to hurt."

"It already hurts," Drusilla growled.

She braced herself as Michael dug into her arm with tweezers. She grunted against the pain as Michael pulled something out. The sound of glass hitting ceramic met Drusilla's ears. Michael splashed something that burned over her cuts, and Drusilla had to clamp her mouth shut to not cry out. A warm hand rubbed her back, and Michael made soothing sounds as the pain passed. Then, he went back to it. What felt like forever actually only took about five minutes.

Drusilla lay in Michael's arms. Cleaned and wrapped up with gauze. They were in the big bed. It was soft and smelled heavily of fabric softener. Drusilla had a hard time keeping her eyes open.

“I really hope we didn't pick George's parents’ room,” Michael said. “That would be weird.”

“Yeah,” Drusilla mused. “Though, I think it might be a guest room or something. It's on the first floor.”

“Maybe his mom's a screamer, and they didn't want to wake the kids.”

“Yuck,” Drusilla laughed.

Michael snuggled up closer. “Should we test it out?”

“I could just text Mary and have her ask.”

“No, let them rest.”

“Right, *'rest'*.” Drusilla said adding air quotes with her fingers.

Michael's soft chuckle brought a smile to Drusilla's lips. She leaned over and kissed him. It was a brief and lazy thing. Michael pulled her in and gave her a real kiss. A spasm ripped down Drusilla's back, and she yelped. Michael pulled back immediately. Worried eyes searched her face. Drusilla leaned in and pressed her lips against his. Michael responded a little easier. Drusilla's hand slipped under his shirt. It was stupid how easy this was.

*

Michael slipped out of bed. It was the middle of the night. Drusilla rolled over and curled up into the fetal position in her sleep. That always saddened Michael. He made his way to the bathroom to take a leak. While doing so, he looked over into the sink. The shards of glass and splintered wood still lay there. Drusilla's blood mingled in the mess. He should have taken her to the hospital. The cuts were deep, and the bits were embedded in them pretty hard. Drusilla was going to have scars. Michael grabbed some toilet paper and cleared out the sink. No use having Drusilla see it. He needed to get Drusilla out of that house somehow. Michael made a mental note to check his finances and flushed. When he got back into the bed, Drusilla propped herself up.

"Hey," she moaned, sleepily. "Where did you go?"

"To the bathroom," Michael whispered. "I didn't mean to wake you."

"It's okay," Drusilla said as she snuggled up in his arms.

Michael planted a kiss against her scalp.

"That was nice." Drusilla's eyes were barely open.

"You're nice," Michael shot back.

"I love you." She sounded half asleep, but she looked at him. "I mean it, Michael."

"I know, Baby," Michael replied. His heart leapt out of his chest and started mosh-pitting.

He held her close as she drifted off. Michael pulled the blankets up to cover her better, and Drusilla nuzzled him in her sleep like a kitten. Hers, he was hers. Finally. Michael closed his eyes and imagined taking Drusilla far away. Where she wouldn't have to deal with anything remotely resembling the day's bullshit again. He reached for his phone and slid his thumb across the screen. Drusilla flinched against the light, but she didn't wake. Michael checked his accounts, and frowned. He wasn't comfortable with the amount of "start over" money he had. Michael calculated how much he would need for winter break and popped the rest into savings. Then, he made his way to Craigslist.

*

Mary pulled George's shirt over her head. It fell to her knees. She looked down at his naked, sleeping form. George may have been rail thin, but the man was tall. She pulled on her underwear and kissed her boyfriend's cheek. George smiled in his sleep and rolled over. He snuggled a pillow fiercely. Mary slipped out of the room and went downstairs. She didn't think much of the wilderness decor, but the cabin was huge. The kitchen was empty and might have been the size of her whole house. Her eyes caught the back of Drusilla through the sliding glass door. Mary slid the door open, stepping out to a massive porch and the cold. She made her way to her sister and plopped into the wood chair next to Drusilla's spacious bench.

"Hey," Drusilla said as she hugged a quilt tighter around her. She looked sad.

"Did you get fucked last night?" Mary asked in an attempt to lighten the mood.

"Mary." Drusilla turned annoyed eyes to look at Mary. "Come on."

"Me, too. Really took me to pound town," Mary said with a wink. Drusilla sighed heavily in response. Okay, no laugh. Mary swapped topics. "Where is your boy toy?"

"Sleeping."

"Mine, too."

"Well, that's something," Drusilla replied.

They sat for a long while and looked at the water. It was very still. Mary wasn't sure she liked that. She wished she had a stone or something to throw at it. See if it was real. Touching had a way of destroying illusion. Their mother had thought them that. Mary's chest lurched at the memory. She looked over at Drusilla's down turned mouth and brooding eyes. Then, her purple eyes slid in Mary's direction, and Mary watched as Drusilla's mask came up. Mary's heart sank.

"What she did wasn't okay," Mary said.

A tiny tear slid down Drusilla's face. She rubbed it away hurriedly, as if Mary wouldn't see. "Yep."

"We should kill her," Mary sighed. "We probably have enough power between us to get away with it."

"We aren't killers, Mary."

"Everyone's a killer given the right circumstances," Mary pointed out. "She can't get away with what she did, Drusilla."

"Just let it go. We're on winter break. I'll handle it later. Don't worry."

"This is bullshit!" Mary exploded. "She-"

The sliding glass door slid open with a rasping sound. They both looked back to see Michael and George, both shirtless and bleary eyed. George shivered and made his way over to Mary. His cold fingertips were comforting as he bent down. It was a short peck of a kiss, but it was nice all the same. Michael slid in with

Drusilla. It looked like they barely fit on the large wooden bench. Michael held her close, as if one of them would try to pull Drusilla away. The only thing missing was a territorial growl, Mary thought.

"What's up?" George asked.

"We're plotting to kill our mother," Mary answered.

"Mary," Drusilla groaned.

"Fine," Mary snapped in disgust. "I was planning. Happy?"

Michael's eyes locked with Mary's for a moment, and the silent approval Mary glimpsed there unnerved her. All that fur and scar tissue. What kind of animal was Drusilla screwing? Mary didn't have an answer. Drusilla seemed happy enough, so... Mary dropped it. She looked up at George. His plump lips stretched into a smile. This was good. George was the real prince here, Mary told herself. Then, she stretched up for another kiss.

"Do you want to go on a food run with me?" George asked. "There's no food in the house."

"Fuck yes, I do!" Mary cheered. "I am, like, starving!"

"Okay then, let's get dressed," George replied.

"Why?" Mary giggled.

*

Drusilla watched Mary as she stood and took George's hand. They were off. Back through the sliding glass door with a grating sound. Michael slipped his arm behind Drusilla to gently squeeze the pudge at her hip. Drusilla yelped and winced as pain rang through her in a sharp throb. Michael sat up and steadied her with his other hand. Drusilla took a deep breath and blinked back tears.

"I'm sorry," Michael soothed. "I forgot you were hurt."

"I'm always fucking hurt." Drusilla was tempted to push him away, but she didn't. Instead, she lounged into him. "I'm so tired of always getting hurt."

"I don't like it either, Drusilla." Michael's hot breath hit the back of her ear. "We should probably clean those cuts again."

"Damn it," Drusilla sighed.

"If they get infected, it'll hurt worse."

"I know that," Drusilla growled. "Fuck! Why does my mother have to mess everything up?"

"I'm sorry I wasn't there to stop her," Michael breathed in her ear. "I'll be damn sure to be there the next time she's there to do something."

Michael stood. Drusilla had to cling to him as he took back inside. He carried her back through the house, working doors and light switches with some quick maneuvering. Drusilla buried her face in his neck. She was resigned to the destination, but was enjoying the ride. They slipped through the bedroom and into the bathroom. Drusilla looked away as he put her on the toilet. She did her best not to wince as Michael unraveled her bandages. Life was dramatic enough as it was. No yelps of pain. Instead, Drusilla clenched her jaw. Michael splashed hydrogen peroxide over the cuts. Pain ripped through Drusilla's arm in a wash of fizz.

"I know," Michael said, as if she had cried out. "Almost done."

"It doesn't hurt that bad," Drusilla lied.

"Well, you'll probably get your revenge soon enough," Michael said in a teasing voice.

"What do you mean by that?"

"Nothing," Michael said and kissed her fresh bandaged arm. "All done."

"What are you up to, Michael?"

"Drusilla, honey, don't worry about it."

"No, tell me."

He kissed her hair and lifted her off the toilet instead. Drusilla bit into his shoulder angrily. Michael winced, but didn't drop her on the way to the bed. Drusilla wasn't appeased. Michael was up to something, and she would figure it out. Michael placed her on the bed and slid in with her. Drusilla was prepared to let Michael know that she could walk just fine, but his mouth crashed against hers. For a long while she let herself be distracted.

*

George drove down the dirt road his family drove down

every summer on the way to the little local market. Mary sat in the passenger's seat of Michael's car. Nervously, she smoothed out her little green dress. It was a summer item, but paired with cream leggings and a thick sweater, Mary insisted she was warm enough. She seemed lost in thought, George noted. Probably thinking about her mom. It was a rough situation. Everyone remembered when Aneira Bonnet left her family. Everyone was talking about it. The pride of the White family, abandoning her husband and children. All the adults were talking about it, at least, but from the looks of things, Mary's mother was better off gone. George pulled into the tiny parking lot and killed the motor.

"Oh!" Mary flinched out of her daydream. "I'm sorry. I was miles away. Did you just say something?"

"We're here," George said gently, and he was rewarded with one of Mary's warm smiles.

"Cool. Do we have a list?"

"No. Should we have one?" George asked.

"Fuck it," Mary said happily, then she got out of the car. "Lists are for Drusilla and bitches, anyway."

Mary shopped for food like she was shopping for clothes with her friends or something. Like it was an awesome time. Like the money would never run out. She danced around George, tossing anything and everything that caught her eye into the cart. George didn't mind. He liked watching her go. She ran to a shelf and had to hop a few times to get two kinds of sugar filled cereal. She tossed both in, and off she went again. Before George knew what had hit him, the cart was almost overflowing. He didn't know how to tell Mary they had too much food. They pulled into the checkout lane, and Mary helped George load the food onto the conveyor belt. By the time the checkout guy finished scanning, their bill was over two hundred dollars. Mary looked shocked and a little embarrassed.

"I only brought twenty dollars," Mary said, meekly. "Um... I guess let's go through everything, and decide what stays and what goes?"

"It's okay," George said as he pulled out his wallet. "I got the rest."

"But..." Mary's voice died in her throat as she watched George pull out his plastic credit card.

"Don't worry, Mary," George said with a smile. "Now we have food for the whole trip."

He could tell by the way she looked at him, that something was wrong. He slid his card. Then tried to help Mary pile all the bags back in the cart, but she insisted that she had it. They loaded up the car, and George opened the door for her. Mary slipped in and buckled herself in. George waited for her to give him another winning smile before he closed the door. They pulled out and began to head back. On the way, they stopped for gas and again, he paid with his card. Mary looked at the thing like it was a gun.

"I almost forgot your father is *the* successful toy maker," Mary said.

George didn't know what to say to that, so he shrugged. He didn't want to go into explanations of why he wore second hand clothes and drove his beat up, old car. He didn't want to find out if Mary would be like most other girls. He didn't want to see Mary look at him with dollar signs in her eyes. Now the moment was here, and her eyes were void of dollar signs. Instead, there was a fear there. Suddenly, George wished for dollar signs.

"I was always going to pay for the food," George said, finally. "It was cool you brought money."

"Oh," Mary said, and her cheeks flushed. "Well, yeah. I don't expect you to pay for me."

A heat filled George's lungs. Mary's fingers laced with his, and George drove off. The drive back was nice. A light snow broke through the clouds, and Mary gasped at the sight. It was really beautiful out. George found himself feeling glad that Mary had insisted on buying four different kinds of hot cocoa. He could see himself snuggling with Mary under the covers. A fire lit in the fireplace. This trip was going-

The tree came crashing down out of nowhere! George would have never noticed it if Mary hadn't screamed. He yanked the wheel left. The car turned too sharply. They skidded and slid sideways towards the falling log. George slammed the brakes and hoped for the best. The tree crashed into the street right next to the car on Mary's side. The trunk of the tree shattered into splinters on the street.

"Oh fuck, Oh fuck!" Mary panted.

"Are you okay?" George demanded.

"Oh fuck! Oh fuck!" Mary's voice was becoming shrill between sharp breaths.

"Honey," George brought her trembling eyes to face his steady ones. "You're okay. We're okay. Okay? It's okay. We're okay."

Mary hyperventilated. George looked past her at the crumbling wood. They could probably drive over that. The trees were probably ripped to hell. He turned his attention back to his frantic girlfriend. He kissed her, letting his relief flow through their lips to hopefully calm her. She clung to him like she was on the edge of a very high cliff side. George held her close until she calmed down enough to let go. Mary wiped the tears out of her eyes, and George drove gingerly over the crunched tree. It was dust by that point, but he had a feeling that Michael wouldn't be pleased with George bringing his car back with a flat. He hoped the tree didn't scratch up the paint.

*

"Whelp. I guess the car's name is Hel now," Michael sighed as he looked at the damage to the right side of his car. It was scratched beyond recognition.

"I'm sorry, Michael," George said again. "I'll pay for the body work."

"Dude. Don't even worry about it," Michael said with a shrug. "Nobody's hurt, and the car runs. That's the best we can ask for."

"Whoa," Mary said. "Why aren't you, like, totally killing us right now?"

"Because the tree could have," Drusilla said. Her arms hugging her oversized shirt clad body as if she could contain the worry.

"That," Michael sighed. "Let's get the food in and eat. We

can worry about the rest later."

Michael opened his trunk with a squeak. He pulled out most of the plastic bags and carried them in. Drusilla wasn't far behind him. Two bags dangled in her hand. Michael looked down at Drusilla's bags and scooped them up. Then, he headed for the kitchen to put the food away. There was so much of it. How would they eat it all before break was over? If the trees didn't kill them first. Michael huffed. The trees were wrong. He knew it from the beginning, and he shut it out of his mind. Michael felt it in his gut. So many students, dead. Too specific a target. What was the- a soothing hand at his back. He turned, and Drusilla fell into him. He bent down and kissed her. What if she was next?

"Just let me stay here for a good five minutes," she moaned, and buried her face in his chest.

"Stay as long as you like," Michael murmured.

"Ewah! Are you guys going to fuck in the kitchen?" Mary just about screamed.

Michael sighed heavily. "Yes, Mary. We're going to screw right here on the kitchen floor."

"Please don't!" George called teasingly from the hall.

"Sass!" Mary shrieked, as she pointed an accusatory finger in Michael's direction.

"Mary," Drusilla lifted her head to say. "Michael doesn't know about sass."

"Oh really?" Mary demanded excitedly. "Because from where I'm standing, he looks like a little sassafras!

Drusilla resumed the buried state of her head in Michael's chest. Her shoulders shook as muffled giggles escaped her. Michael shook his head at that whole thing. Mary stood there, hands on hips and glowered at Michael. What was he supposed to do with this? Give her a cookie or something? Experimentally, Michael reached into a grocery bag and pulled out one of the boxes of cookies. He broke the seal and reached in for one. Both females watched his hand as he pulled the cookie out and offered it to Mary, wordlessly.

"But what does it mean?" Mary groaned, and rolled her eyes. Then, she stormed out of the kitchen. "This is madness!"

“Um... I'm sorry?” Michael looked down at Drusilla. “What was I supposed to do?”

“Call her sass back,” Drusilla answered, as if it were the most obvious course of action to take.

“What is even with you people?” Michael couldn't even.

“It's a stupid game we play sometimes,” Drusilla answered.

“The sass is not stupid!” Mary's voice called from the hall.

“The sass is just sass!” Drusilla called back.

“Sass!” Mary exploded.

“The sassiest in the land!” Drusilla replied.

They waited for the reply, and waited, and waited, and - “You're a Sasquatch!

“Nope! That took longer than five seconds!” Drusilla called back.

“Fuck!”

*

Winter break went by too fast for Drusilla. And just as she was getting comfortable with the idea, they were packing to go. Their last night at the cabin, they stuffed themselves with the last of the food. More out of the need to be rid of the food than true celebration. Michael made love with her. They were doing a lot of that as of late. Each time became easier for her. Less to worry about and more to enjoy. She loved him. She had even said it out loud. She knew that wasn't a dream, but she was content to pretend it was.

The ride home felt unfairly short. Drusilla watched the familiar bland houses and streets of Elderberry flow by like poison. Drusilla wasn't ready. She was never going to be ready, she told herself, so there was no point in complaining. Besides, it wasn't like the trees were any less dangerous out in the woods. Drusilla looked back at Mary. She was somberly picking at her nails. Drusilla sighed, and Michael gripped her hand. Drusilla gripped back. The car turned, and they pulled into the shopping center. Michael parked right outside of the strip of shops. Reluctantly, she let Michael go.

She looked up at the shopping center. There was a supermarket, the sports store, the abandoned store that might have been a cafe once along time ago, and the old pharmacy. Confusion radiated through her brain. Why did I want to stop here, Drusilla thought.

“Do we need groceries or something?” Mary said as if reading Drusilla's thoughts.

“I don't remember why we stopped here,” Drusilla replied. She felt stupid.

“Yeah I don't remember either,” Said Michael.

“Weird,” Added George. “I know you said something about stopping here for... Nope, no idea.”

“Can't have been that important then,” Sighed Drusilla. Something nagged at her mind, but she couldn't figure out what.

Chapter 12

They sat in the car. All four of them looked up at the house with a knot in their stomachs. Mary leaned against George for all it was worth. She found herself needing his sturdiness suddenly. Time seemed to tick on, and the motor ran. Mary half worried about the amount of carbon emission from car idling. The other half just wanted to drive off and never look back. Only she wasn't driving. She didn't even have a learner's permit.

"You don't have to go back in that house," Michael said, cutting down the silence like the rain forest. "Neither of you have to go back there."

"Michael, please," Drusilla cried. "Not right now, okay?"

"I... we could get something to eat?" Mary offered.

"I just want a shower," Drusilla replied somberly.

Mary watched her get out, sling her bag over her shoulder, and walk towards the house. Mary stayed behind and clung to George. She wasn't as ready as Drusilla seemed to be. So, she sat and watched Drusilla walk halfway up the dead lawn. Michael Watched her. The closer Drusilla got to the door, the more panicked Mary felt. Drusilla stopped and looked back at them. Mary glared at her back defiantly, but she knew when she was beat.

“It'll be okay,” George said, finally. “Go be with your sister.”

“Yeah, George is right.” Michael's voice sounded very tired.

“Give us five minutes,” Mary said. “We'll be back out.”

“Mary-” George began, but...

“Give me five minutes.” Mary tried her best not to snap. “Please.”

Mary got out of the car before the guys could keep flapping their lips. She made her way up the yard towards Drusilla. Drusilla looked at Mary with a little sadness in her eyes. Mary pulled a yellow flip knife from her pocket. She palmed it and slid the blade open with her thumb. Just in case. Drusilla reached out for Mary, but Mary slapped the hand away with her free one. Drusilla sighed and walked toward the door. Mary was quick to keep in step with her. They stopped at the door and looked at it.

“I see you have your rape knife,” Drusilla remarked.

“Yeah,” Mary replied. “It feels appropriate.”

“I suppose it does,” Drusilla sighed, and she opened the door.

They entered the half mangled living room. The wrecked entertainment center was mostly swept away. Only fragments remained. A sheet had been stapled over the person-sized hole in the wall. Their father sat in his chair and pretended they didn't exist. A new one for Mary. She knew he did that to Drusilla when he didn't want to deal with her, but it had never happened to Mary before. Good thing Mary no longer gave a shit about him. Drusilla took Mary's hand. Mary gave it a little squeeze, and they made their way down the hall to put their stuff down.

“We should go out for dinner,” Mary said as they sat on Mary's bed. “The guys can take us.”

“We just spent two weeks with them,” Drusilla replied.

“And?”

“And maybe I just want to be alone right now, Mary.”

“Okay, fine. You and I could go to that vegan place you like to eat at.”

“You hate that place,” Drusilla said. “Are you really that afraid to be here?”

“Yes.” Mary looked Drusilla dead in the eyes and lied. “I'm

terrified."

"Okay," Drusilla said. "We should shower first."

Mary pulled out her phone and began to text.

*

Michael got the text and looked back at George. "We will be right out after a quick shower," Michael read out loud for George.

It didn't take very long. Drusilla got back into the seat and buckled herself in. Her eyes never left her feet. Michael looked at Mary from the rear-view mirror. She winked at him from George's snuggle. Michael drove off towards the only pizza place in Elderberry. Mary hopped out of the car as soon as it stopped, and George wasn't far behind her. Drusilla sat in the passenger seat with her hands in her lap, her eyes still on her feet.

"I'm sorry," Michael said. He gripped both her hands with his own large one. "I know you like being the strong one, but she's your mom."

"I don't even know how to handle this," Drusilla said to her feet.

"We'll figure it out together," Michael replied. His hand rested on her locked ones.

"I just want us to get out of this fucked town." Drusilla finally looked at him. "How are we supposed to do that with no money? I can't find a job. What are we going to do?"

"We'll think of something," Michael said, knowing all too well that he had it taken care of already.

It looked like Drusilla was going to say something, but a knock at Michael's window cut her off. Aggravated, Michael turned to see George's worried face. Michael rolled down the window. What now? George slipped his phone into his pocket, and he leaned down to look at them better. What? Michael wanted to shout, but he thought it instead.

"More students were killed over winter break," George said. "Apparently, Paul had a winter break rager in the woods."

"Wow. Did Paul...?" Drusilla asked.

"No," George replied.

"Well, no silver lining there," Drusilla said hollowly.

"We'll be in in a second," Michael said, a sick feeling sinking in his gut.

"Where's Mary?" Drusilla said. Her voice was dead in her throat.

"Inside. She's picking out a table," George answered.

Drusilla hopped out of the car and walked in. Michael watched through the pizza place's windows. She moved over to Mary and slid into her side of the booth. Mary fell into her arms and she was sobbing. Mary's friends. Michael felt it in his gut. The barely noteworthy mean girls that Mary was blowing off. They must have gone down. George confirmed it a moment later, and then he too went to Mary. Michael watched the three of them from his car. They were huddled together in grief. No trees for them, Michael thought darkly. They were his now. The trees couldn't have them. He got out of the car and went in to add something comforting to the mix.

*

"Hey, let's talk." Michael slipped an arm around Drusilla's back and pulled her into a lonely hallway. It had been a couple of weeks since Drusilla's mom, and a few days before the funerals of Mary's friends. Drusilla had spent nearly every morning in Principal Peep's office. Michael and Drusilla passed a burned out diorama, and the lights flickered. Michael wasn't sure if they were allowed there, but Drusilla snuggled close, and a dull stinging burned through him. Soon, the weeping would come, and it was painful to know that all Michael could do was watch.

"I'm fine," she said before Michael could ask, but her voice cracked.

"I don't believe you," Michael said. He hugged her against him despite his soreness. Drusilla's head leaned against his shoulder and her lips came up to press against his neck.

"I don't believe me either." She hugged him sharply, and Michael winced. Drusilla stopped. She pulled away from him and just looked at him as if she knew everything. "Who have you been fighting."

"Um..." Michael felt the wad of cash throbbing through his wallet. It wasn't enough, but it was something. "I-"

Footsteps. Brisk ones came from behind them. They turned to look. Michael *knew* they weren't supposed to be there. A student was also using the nearly abandoned hall. She was short with long, dirty blond hair and overalls. She got closer. The girl's faceless head nodded an automatic courtesy greeting, and then she moved on. As if she had somewhere to be. Michael froze. All worry of the not-yet-a-fight gone from him. It was like his brain was trying to unsee it, but couldn't.

"You saw that right?" Drusilla breathed.

"Yeah, I think-"

"She didn't have a face, right?" Drusilla stood strong, but her eyes quaked with terror.

"Right," Michael confirmed. "She had no face."

"Okay." Drusilla let out a deep breath. "I'm just making sure I wasn't losing it."

"Okay, let's never go down this creepy ass hallway again," Michael suggested.

"Agreed." Drusilla's voice quaked a little.

They turned on their heels and moved briskly into the crowds. Both Michael and Drusilla looked for faceless students that weren't there. Every face looked averagely bored. Misery abound, Michael thought, and he pulled Drusilla closer. Michael did his best not to wince. She held him just as hard. It was weird, Michael thought. To see her scared like this. He couldn't think of any time when Drusilla wasn't staunchly glaring shit in the face and threatening to wreck it. Ever since her shitty mother...

A tickle at the back of Michael's throat made him clear it, but it only intensified. In his arms, Drusilla was shivering. Her pudgy body quaked against him so hard that she started to make him shake in response. He looked down at her. She was looking at someone. Okay. Michael followed her gaze. Paul Hunt and his group, well, what was left of it. Only Paul had a face, his eyes locking with Michael's. Paul put his hands up. No trouble. Michael looked past him at Paul's dwindled gaggle. They had faces before. Michael remembered pounding them in with his fists. His throat burned. Pan and Peter Piper were gone now. What did the rest of his goons look like? Michael couldn't remember.

"What the fuck is happening?" Drusilla whimpered.

"Let's get out of here," Michael said, and without waiting for her to respond, Michael led her through a side door.

*

Drusilla was fighting tooth and nail to suck down her fear. She had seen a lot of weird shit in her life, but this was... How did she not see them before? Something in her back squirmed. She tried to flex it, but it only caused her back to spasm uncomfortably. Michael walked her to Tank, and Drusilla saw that Mary and George leaned against the large, black van. Both looked freaked out as hell. What monsters did they find?

"Well, they look shaken up," Michael echoed Drusilla's thoughts.

"Maybe they saw something, too," Drusilla said sarcastically.

Mary noticed them and ran over. She grabbed onto Drusilla and sobbed ridiculously into her. Drusilla looked over at George and wondered wildly if he was going to jump in this, too. Instead, he simply walked over to them and gently pulled Mary off. She crumpled into him instead. He looked at Drusilla with haunted eyes, as if he would never be okay again. Drusilla wouldn't blame him if he wasn't. Michael cleared his throat and everyone looked at him expectantly, but the only thing that came out of his mouth was a dry, hoarse coughing. Drusilla thumped him on the back, but Michael only coughed harder into his fist.

"You okay?" Drusilla and George asked, almost at the same time.

Michael sucked in a breath and nodded. "Yea. It's a throat tickle."

"But you saw them, too?" Mary asked.

"Yeah," Drusilla replied. "We saw them."

"They're not real," George began. Drusilla was ready to inform him that if they could all see them it would reason that they were in fact very real, but he cut her to the quick. "I mean, I don't think they're real people. Like a spell maybe, or some kind of..."

"Like a golem?" Mary offered.

"Or something," George replied.

"Well, why?" Drusilla asked next.

"To hide the deaths?" Michael guessed.

"What deaths?" Drusilla and Mary asked stupidly.

"All the ones that can be covered up. Like a lot of students were killed this year. Maybe those things are meant to camouflage it, or hide how many students went down, or..."

"From who?" Drusilla asked.

"School administrators, government school boards, companies who may have invested in the school," George ticked off with his fingers. "Anyone who would stand to lose money if the school had too many deaths on its hands or had to close."

"Yeah." That made a sort of sick sense to Drusilla. Even public schools were a business, weren't they? Drusilla made a mental note to look it up later.

"So, they aren't here to hurt us?" Mary's question was a whimper.

George shrugged. "I don't know, my love."

"*No*," Michael said. His voice stretched in thought. "I think that's what the trees are for."

"What do you mean?" Drusilla was almost accusing, but as soon as it came out of her mouth, she felt her stomach lurch in a sickening way. Like she realized somehow she always knew. She looked at Mary and saw it click for her, too. Then, George's eyes found hers, and she knew that he was trying to see if Drusilla felt it too.

"Yeah," Michael agreed. "I thought something was wrong when we were attacked in the woods."

"You were attacked in the woods and you didn't tell me?!" Mary roared at Drusilla.

"They were only trees," Drusilla shrugged, but if felt absurd. As if she had said 'they were only bullets'. "I'm sorry, Mary. I didn't figure it out."

"I bet that's part of the spell, too," George guessed. "Maybe it drugs us, or I don't know. I'm not the best with magic. Maybe we get preoccupied somehow."

"That's not hard," Drusilla and Mary said at once.

"So whoever is killing us is putting in fakes to pad the school and distracts everyone somehow, maybe? That way no one notices a difference while they work," Michael worked out. "Who do we think, and why?"

"Mrs. Gooseberry knew something," Drusilla said suddenly. Where was Mrs. Gooseberry? Drusilla didn't know. The last time she saw her- "I used to work at the cafe, Damnit!"

"*Okay?*," George clearly had no idea where that came from.

There was a long silence. Drusilla clung to Michael's hand, hard. He squeezed it back. Her other hand was taken up by Mary's tiny one, and she gave Drusilla's hand a sharp squeeze, too. Drusilla felt the fear in it, and she looked at George who was reaching for Mary's free hand. They stood there, hand in hand, like some bullshit production of the Wizard of Oz, but none of them cared how they looked. Fear rippled through them, and Drusilla was no longer sure how she was going to keep her little sister safe.

"We're leaving," Michael said suddenly. "We can pile into Drusilla's van and just never look back.

"The van isn't going to get us very far," Drusilla said. "My magic is barely holding the screws together as it is."

"Okay. Then everyone pile into Hel," Michael amended.

"What are we going to do about money?" George asked.

"I keep all my money in my backpack," Drusilla said. "I have about three, maybe four hundred dollars right now. I've been saving up my tips. You know from the cafe I used to work at!"

"Oh! I remember that now," Mary said. "Wait-"

"Can we focus?" George asked her. "Why do you always have all your money on you?"

"In case I ever needed to get Mary out of here."

"Aw, Dru," Mary cooed.

"That or bottom surgery," Drusilla added.

"Hey! I thought we were supposed to be focusing?" Michael growled. Then, when everyone stopped, "That will get us pretty far out of town, and I have some money saved up. What about you two?"

"I keep all my money in a bank like a normal person," George said. "I use my debit card."

"I think I have some change in my purse," Mary offered. She pulled it up to start going through it, but Drusilla shook her head at her. Mary dropped the bag.

"Okay, let's go," Michael said.

"What about our things?" Mary asked.

"What about them?" Michael asked.

"It's just stuff, Mary," Drusilla added. "Right now all that matters is that we get away. We can figure the rest out later."

*

They were on the road. Passing thousands upon thousands of dangerous looking trees. Michael didn't call his parents. He didn't want to have that fight right now. He just wanted to get the hell out of there. It would probably be easier to get them to leave, too, if he was already somewhere else and they had to come get him. So far no trees moved against them, but he kept a sharp eye on them as they whizzed past. The large green sign for the interstate came and went in a rush. Almost out, he thought. Drusilla's warm fingers clung around his free hand. They were almost free. Free from bullshit students, and difficult parents, and murdering magical trees.

The tree was as large as a semi-truck. It was crashed neatly across the only road out of town. Cop cars, and their police officers were out and investigating. One in an orange traffic vest turned her faceless head in their direction. Everyone in Michael's car froze. The faceless cop walked over to them with a friendly wave. Her dark skin stretched thin over her skull. Michael lowered his window. The cop bent down with a two-finger salute. Monster charades, Michael thought darkly. How kick ass?

"Hello, officer," he said with false cheer. The faceless cop gestured towards his car and towards the fallen log like some deranged mime. "Yeah, we were going to the next town over to visit my grandmother. I see a tree fell. I hope no one was hurt." The mime cop shrugged and spun her gloved finger. "Yeah, I better turn back. Guess I'll have to see her some other time." The mime cop waved with a few curls of her four fingers, and Michael had to suppress a shutter as he rolled up the window and made a U turn.

*

No one spoke on the drive back. George watched the trees go by. Whoever was doing this was powerful. He didn't voice his thought. He knew he didn't need to. Mary whimpered into his shoulder. George was afraid for her. He wished his father was rich enough to have a helicopter he could use to get them out or something. The nearest airport was the next town over, so that was out. The nearest body of water was the lake, and that was just a lake. Michael coughed and turned on the radio. Static. Weird. Michael coughed some more, and Drusilla rubbed his arm.

"Are you okay?" she asked softly.

"I need to pull over," Michael said as he spun the wheel to park on the shoulder. "I'm sorry, everyone."

"Let's go to the park," George said, with a sudden idea.

"What?" Drusilla asked.

"We can regroup there. No one ever goes there, it's mostly a field. No trees."

*

Drusilla had to drive for Michael. His car was surprisingly hard to drive after driving her large, rickety van for so long. Michael sat in the passenger seat and nearly hacked up his lungs. What was going on with him? She couldn't worry about that right now. She had to focus on driving. She looked back at the road and nearly slammed the brakes. The same crossing guard and the same group of children. All faceless.

"Oh my god!" Mary said, seeing them, too.

"This whole town is fake," Drusilla breathed. It was like a punch to the gut. Her back squirmed again and her skin began to crawl. Get to the park, she told herself.

Drusilla floored it, nearly running over a faceless little girl in her hurry. No cops tried to stop her, no one even noticed the car zooming past. Drusilla didn't check to see who had a face and who didn't. She didn't want to. Something about this was sickeningly familiar. It made her feel like a fool and she didn't know why. Where did she read about it? Online, maybe? No, that wasn't it.

"There," Michael struggled to say through a fit of coughing.

Drusilla made the turn, and the tires squealed as she yanked the wheel. "Sorry."

"I'm going to hurl," Michael said suddenly.

"We're almost there," Drusilla said.

She pulled up to the spot where the park should have been. Instead was a wild looking glade. The trees were different somehow. Sturdy oaks that curved inwards. Giving the wild plot of land a spherical look. Like a forest in a bubble. Wild flowers and mushrooms bloomed out of season in the wild brush and healthy green vines began their climb up the leaning trunks.

"Do we trust this?" George asked.

"We don't have a choice," Michael groaned and half fell out of the passenger side as he opened the door.

Drusilla rushed out of the car to get to him. She lifted his heavy frame up as Michael struggled to his feet. "What's happening to you?"

"I'm " Michael began.

"You are not fine!" Drusilla cut him off.

Michael waved his hand and bent over to wretch. "I'm throwing up!"

Drusilla pulled Michael onto the grass. He spit up dribbled down his chin. Mary and George screamed, and Drusilla looked back. Michael tried to look, too, but the motion made him fall to his knees. George looked at his carved hands. Drusilla bit back her scream as she looked at the wooden doll that was George. His large painted eyes looked up at Drusilla. Fear on his carved expression. Drusilla's stomach turned.

"What's happening to me?" George cried.

The ground is cursed, Drusilla realized too late. Stupid! "Get off the land!"

Drusilla tried to pull Michael off the cursed land, but she stopped. Michael fell to his knees again, and this time Drusilla could not contain her screams. Michael planted his hands firmly in the grass and vomited blood in a long gush. Something sparkled as Michael choked. The hilt of a sword. He gagged on it and vomited again. Its shining wet blade followed. Michael gasped for air, but the sword was half in, half out. He took the sword with both hands by the hilt and pulled. The rest of the sword came out with a rush of bile. More blood mingling with the vomit.

"Mary, we have to get them out! We have to-"

"Why?" Mary's voice was too calm.

Drusilla felt her heart crumple as she turned to look at her sister. Vines twisted from the ground at Mary's feet. Horror burned Drusilla's brain as the vines wrapped around Mary and lifted her off her feet into a strange throne. Her whole demeanor had changed. George turned his nightmarish, wooden head to regard Mary. The plants that covered her body began to sprout little silver bells and cockleshells.

"Mary, we have to go," Drusilla said again, ignoring the ripple under her skin. "We have to undo the-"

Something came up Drusilla's throat in a rush, and Drusilla vomited a thick torrent of black sludge. She felt her back split, and the pain blurred her vision. Drusilla screamed and it sounded like someone else screamed alongside her. Or maybe through her. This was bad. She had to fight this. She had to push past whatever was-

A baby. Little and curly haired. A blond baby girl. She had to die, Drusilla knew it. She couldn't remember why or where she was. The baby gurgled up at her happily, and a mummer rippled through the great hall of stone. This was an unwelcoming place. She had gone here to hurt the baby. Why hurt the baby? A man spoke, and she looked up to see the king and queen. A ripple of fear crossed the queen's blue eyes as she looked at Drusilla. A rage nearly burned Drusilla alive from the inside out. She owed them pain! She owed them all-

"Drusilla!"

Drusilla blinked up at the prince. Michael. His name was Michael. "What did you call me?"

"Are you okay?" Michael Prince asked again. He helped her to her feet.

Drusilla pushed him to the ground with a tiny giggle. She flexed her knobby fingers. Long dark talons extended and retracted as she did. Her wings fluttered easily, and Drusilla's feet lifted from the ground. It was as easy as walking, no... it was as easy as thought. Her black eyes looked from the prince to the wooden construct, and then to the silly little plant witch. Her eyes finally rested on the sword in the prince's hand. Get rid of the sword. Disarm the prince before- her eyes flicked back to his confused face.

"Drusilla, what are you-"

"Silence," said her echoing voice. She looked around at this feebly held together magic. Nothing compared to what she would have made. Had she been given the chance? "I'll dance your life away."

"Babe, what are you talking about?"

Drusilla smiled nastily, and Michael Prince took a step back. Drusilla gnashed her durable rows of pointed teeth menacingly. George groaned and shed his wooden shell. Mahogany wood gave way to brown flesh. George fell to his knees in a fit of exhaustion. Vines retracted, and Mary was on her feet. She knelt by George's side. How sweet, Drusilla thought darkly. Too bad she hated sweet.

"Figuring things out are we?" Drusilla cackled.

"I have memories, but... but how?" George rambled. "What the hell?"

"I don't know. I have them, too," Michael said. He looked at Drusilla. "Your turn. You have your memories. It's in the past. You can-"

"Oh, I think not, Prince," Drusilla giggled.

"Come on, Drusilla," Mary said with more authority than she once had. "We need to get out of here before the witch that did this finds us-"

"And what do you know of what this witch did to us, Mary.

Little Mary Contrary," Drusilla laughed.

"That's enough," Michael's voice was steel.

Drusilla looked at the prince wearily. He was going to be a problem. Drusilla knew princes were any witch's undoing. Faerie or no. She locked eyes with him. He'd kill her. She just knew it. She had to get away. She had to distract them. She lowered her lashes at him and let him step closer. Just a little closer Prince, she thought darkly, but he was wary. He had her pegged. Princes always did.

"Fine," Drusilla said, more to herself than to him. She looked up at him, and his easy smile made her ill.

She thrust her magic out. Thorns flew from her fingertips. The prince and his friends shielded their faces with their hands. George attempted to turn to wood again, but he was too slow. The thorns bit into flesh, and the magic worked almost at once. Mary fell first. The sleep-like living death was meant for her type, anyway. Then, George. He was half wooden and asleep as much as Mary was. The prince fought the spell. He fought it hard. A small part of her didn't want to see him suffer. It was just a trick of the witch's spell, she told herself. It wasn't real. None of it was.

"Why?" Michael asked. He was still under the spell, too. She could tell it would not last.

"Because I know what must be done," Drusilla said. "The circle will keep you safe."

"What circle?" Michael wheezed drowsily. He was dropping off. "Safe from what?"

Drusilla watched, and the things the witch's spell made her do... the feelings the spell made her feel nagged at her. She should have killed them, but instead, she let them drop off to sleep. "From things like me, Michael."

*

Barnabas Bonnet cracked his crooked back. It popped painfully, and Barnabas cursed under his breath. Quiet echoed through the crooked house. It always made his skin crawl. He moved to the bathroom to drain the main vein and caught a glimpse of himself in the mirror. What a piece of shit he'd turned into. My god. Bald, fat, and divorced. Why? The unanswered question rumbled in his guts, and Barnabas took his pants off. He sat on the cold toilet seat. Standing to pee just made a mess now a days.

When he was finished, he almost remembered to flush. He made his way to the kitchen, opened the liquor cabinet, and poured himself a scotch. Not the good stuff. It had been a very long time since he could afford the good stuff. It had been a long time since a lot of good things came his way. He remembered Aneira and the good times. Before there were problems. Before there were kids... Before Andrew. He missed Aneira. Even now. Even after... all that she did. Well, that's what the scotch was for.

The front door opened, and he hoped upon hope that it was the soft footsteps of Mary. Barnabas had royally fucked up his son, so had his mother, but damnit. Andrew was his son, and Barnabas failed him when he needed him. He shoved Andrew away. He could have gotten him help. Sent him to a place. A place that helped sons get rid of thoughts like that. Evil thoughts planted by his witch of a mother, probably. He downed the rubbish scotch and turned to greet Mary. He had assumed it was Mary since the footsteps were so light that he couldn't even hear them.

"Hi, Princess," Barnabas said in greeting as he turned. He froze. The empty glass locked in his hand. Andrew fluttered there, no... not Andrew. Whatever was left of Barnabas's son was dead in those cold black eyes. Huge purple wings fluttered around the lithe purple skinned thing. The husk of what his child was. "Uh..."

"Hi, Daddy." The voices were high pitched, raspy, and unmistakable. Drusilla.

This thing waved its inky hand, and Barnabas flew crashing into the liquor cabinet. This was a spell. A spell gone wrong. All wrong. Pain raked his twisted back, and he fell with a thud into the splinters of glass and wood. Barnabas tried to move, but an arc of agony ripped through his muscles. The creature's too wide mouth stretched into a hungry smile at his yelp. It hovered over him. Barnabas couldn't move even if he hadn't been so messed up. The cold, slimy hands gripped him by the jaw and forced him to look into the soulless black eyes.

"Perhaps it's time for a little bonding."

Then, before Barnabas could say a word, the monster forced his mouth open too wide. Barnabas tried to scream as he felt his jaw snap. Then, Drusilla reached with its long, spindly arm, down Barnabas's throat. Drusilla sank down elbow deep, and Barnabas gagged on the warm, wet thing. He felt the thing's arm lunge deep inside him. Things in his body began to rip as the arm searched and scratched. Barnabas's body convulsed as his insides were being scrambled by the sharp fingers. Blood oozed from his nostrils and blurred his vision.

"Not much left in you is there, you crooked man?" Drusilla said, then the thing giggled, and Barnabas was unable scream.

*

He was a prince, a selfish one. Until the witch had shown him what he truly was. The curse ravaged Michael for many years. Twisting him. Making him beastly. Anger was his constant. Then, she came and saved him. She was beautiful and she showed him kindness. It was that kindness that let him see through Drusilla's bullshit even now. Michael remembered growing old. His wife was dead and he was alone again. That was the past. He was king no longer. That old man died a long, long time ago. Now, he was trapped again, and Drusilla needed him. Yeah, she had done this to him, but he remembered that moment of confusion. That moment when his past life and the now blurred, and he had to fight to come back.

Drusilla. It was the thought of Drusilla that brought him back. Drusilla. He remembered her. Stuck halfway between the evil faerie she was and the good person she is now. Michael struggled against the sleep. It was a heavy enchantment, but he knew it was an enchantment. He remembered the tale. A sleep-like death. He was in a coma. He had to fight it. Fight hard, Michael thought over and over. It's only magic.

He could stand, but he wasn't awake. Awake in a dream. He wasn't really standing. Awesome. Now what? Michael looked around the dark shadowy forest and hopped for something. He needed a light. Something flared in his hand. His sword. Okay, he thought. Bodies lay at his feet. No, not bodies. People in their own comas. Mary, the vines still winding around her sleeping frame, creating a protective cover over her. George was next to her, the wood thickening over him. Making him look more and more like a doll than a human man. He couldn't help them right now.

A light caught his eye in the distance. Okay, Michael thought, and moved deeper into the woods. Following the light and hoping it was the way out. It seemed right, right? He walked and walked. It felt like forever. This wasn't helping him. Rage bubbled up in him. He needed Drusilla. He wanted her back. He wanted her. He was on the edge of the light now. A circle of oaks. A circle. Drusilla said something about a circle. The circle would keep you safe. Michael remembered. He stepped into the light.
Drusilla sat there on a fallen log. Her purple eyes were lost in the glowing middle of the clearing. It was the light source. He sat down next to her. She seemed to be wearing a gown of light. Was she really dead? Michael was suddenly determined to make the most of whatever this was, if it was his last moments with the woman he loved.

"I'm so sorry," she said. Her tear stained eyes looked up at him. "I never wanted any of this to happen."

"This isn't you fault," Michael said. He took her hands in his, and they were like ice.

"Are you going to kill me?" Drusilla asked.

"Why would I do that?"

"It's how it goes. The prince defeats the witch. The witch defeats the princess, and the princess defeats the prince," Drusilla said. "I think you're going to kill me."

"I'm not going to kill you!" Drusilla flinched at his outburst. He needed to control himself. "I'm sorry. I love you, Drusilla, and yeah, witches hate princes. And that's how it's always been for a stupid amount of time. Things change. That was a whole lifetime ago. I love you in the now."

"Make me believe you," Drusilla said seriously. "Make me

believe that you love me. That you'll never hurt me. Make me believe you, Michael Prince."

"How?" Michael asked.

"You'll think of something," Drusilla said. She kissed him with as much fire and aggression and love that she had to give him. Michael could feel himself fading. "Make me save myself."

*

"Maybe he's dead," Mary's voice echoed in the distance.

"No," George replied. "You were just like this when I woke you."

"Okay," Mary said. "How did you wake up, then? Maybe guys wake up different than girls."

"No, everyone wakes up the same."

"I wasn't awake to kiss you," Mary sounded suddenly angry. "Who were you smooching with?"

"I had a dog once, when I was little," George replied, "but he got old and died."

"So, you made out with your dead dog?" Mary asked. "Did he slip you the tongue?"

Michael tried to move. The grass was wet underneath him, and the chilly winter air wasn't pleasant against his bare arms. Why the hell wasn't he wearing a jacket or something? He wiggled his fingers and toes furiously while George and Mary argued. He couldn't help Drusilla like this. Then suddenly, his eyes snapped open. Mary and George drew back in surprise. Michael sat up.

"Well, how the hell did he wake up on his own? Unless he has a dead dog, too," Mary said.

"Drusilla woke me up," Michael's voice was raspy with sleep. He looked around and it was night. How long had they been out? He felt his chin. Only a light stubble, so only the day. They might not be too late. "We have to hurry."

"Drusilla did this to us," Mary said.

"Yeah, but she's not in her right mind," Michael said. "You know she isn't."

Mary nodded gravely. Michael got up with the help of

George. Then, Michael stretched and picked up the sword. He looked at George. He looked real again. Flesh and blood. As if Michael asked, George lifted his arm and concentrated on it. Wood erupted over his dark skin and then fell away again. Cool, Michael thought. Mary walked over and ran her fingers along the skin of George's arm, and tiny flowers sprouted in her wake.

"That gives a new meaning to getting a woody," she teased, and George rolled his eyes. Mary kissed his cheek. "I think it's really cool."

"Thanks, plant lady," George teased with a smile.

"Okay, we have to get Drusilla back," Mary announced.

"Good plan, let's go," Michael said.

Chapter 13

Darkness enveloped Drusilla inside and out, and it felt good. She stopped to inhale the sweet scent of bleeding in the woods. She followed the pain drenched moans with a flutter of her wings. Landing by the felled tree, Drusilla tucked her wings neatly against her back and bent to see who was caught in the witch's snare. Paul Hunt struggled with the trunk. A splintered branch drove deeper into his leg, and Drusilla's smile was too excited at the sound of Paul's screams.

"Well, well, isn't this awkward, Huntsman?" She reached out a long finger to the sticky, sweet blood from Paul's wounds and savored it on her long tongue.

"Drusilla?" Paul half screamed. "What's wrong with your eyes?"

"Frightened?" Drusilla rasped out. She bent down lower to show off her newly razor sharp teeth, like a shark's mouth.

Paul shrieked and struggled, much to Drusilla's delight. She reached out to him again, and Paul lurched back, tearing his leg open even more in the process. Blood leeched from the leg in earnest. He didn't have long before he bled out. Drusilla could feel the witch's magic whirl around the forest. It was a hungry, terrible thing. Come closer, Drusilla thought. Yes, just like that. A little closer. Thank you.

"You, my dear, have one last role to play in this little

drama," Drusilla whispered into Paul's ear.

"What?" Paul cried.

"Messenger."

Paul's lifeblood began to slow. Drusilla felt the magic charge towards Paul. Drusilla stretched one arm out to buffer away the witch's magic with her own, and with the other... Drusilla reached out for Paul and held fast to his life energies. In one fluid motion, Paul gave out one last scream as Drusilla ripped his magic from him. His flesh shredded and fell away from the bloody bones. Drusilla consumed Paul's essence. It was delicious. Sticky sweet and powerful in Drusilla's new form. The witch's magic halted, considered Drusilla for a moment, and then ran. Now she knew who the witch was.

*

"Oh little girl?" Drusilla sing-songed through the darkened halls of Elderberry High. She made her way past the lockers and stopped. The twisted and scratched face of one locker door glowed red hot. Cold iron? No, Drusilla thought. This building was filled with it. That little torment was behind her now. She studied the spell. A mark of difficulty and it had her name on it in big, fat letters. Drusilla was impressed with the torture device. She began to slow clap. "You thought of everything!"

A sudden rattle echoed through the bleak hallway. Drusilla fluttered off to go see what the fuss was about. The sound led her to the front doors. Michael Prince was struggling with the locked handles through the wire-laced glass. Drusilla landed gracefully in front of her side of the glass. Michael's attention turned to her. Grief hung from him like a corpse. It was beautiful. Maybe she would eat this one last.

"Drusilla, Babe. Let me in," Michael pleaded desperately.

Over his shoulder in the grass, Drusilla could see the silhouettes of George and Mary. This could wreck all. Drusilla knew it. She looked back at Michael. The prince should never have come. She was one damsel he could never save. He was watching her. The pain in his eyes told Drusilla he was thinking along the same lines. The poor thing still loved the illusion. Still believed in it. How fun.

“There is no help for you here,” Drusilla said.

“Babe, open the door. Let me in,” Michael pleaded in his one track way.

“Wake up,” Drusilla said. Her hand pressed against the glass. “Live in the real world, Prince.”

“You think I'm not?” Michael asked. He passed the sword past the window. “I know exactly what's going on.”

Drusilla froze. He wasn't laboring under the spell. She wasn't counting on that nasty little twist. Her mind began working frantically. This was a trick to slay her. Had to be. If she opened the door, he'd cut her down as sure as he claimed to love her. He could do it, too. In a toe-to-toe fight He would win almost every time. Michael's eyes filled with tears and he pressed his hand against hers. The cold glass was keeping them apart. His sadness deepened. Nice touch, Drusilla thought, but she wasn't fooled. Reaching for the magic, Drusilla shot it deep into the ground. Roots developed and heavy vines sprang up through grassy lawn and concrete walkway alike. Michael jumped back as the vines crawled up the glass. Angry thorns scratched the window’s surface.

“Get through that,” Drusilla said, more to herself than to Michael, and she turned her back on him. “Sometimes the old ways are the only ways to work.”

*

“Why is she doing this?” Mary asked. “We all remember who we were and who we are. That doesn't fucking change anything.”

“She's confused,” Michael made his way back to the group.

“If she isn't thinking right, then she can't win in there,” George said.

“Maybe it's a spell,” Mary offered.

“More like she can't deal,” George corrected. “Like maybe who she was can't deal with who she is. Her mind snaps and who she was takes dominance. Like some kind of dissociation identity thing, or something..."

"Maybe it's both," Michael replied. "Maybe all that stuff was enhanced by her innate magic, or -"

"That could happen," Mary confirmed. "Magic is a powerful force, and Drusilla hates change. That could totally happen."

"So she snapped," Michael concluded.

Mary didn't like the sound of that. What if Drusilla was broken beyond repair? She looked at the vine-covered building. Vines were not the smartest choice for Drusilla. She knew exactly how Mary's magic worked. Those vines would be as easy to manipulate as a piece of paper. Really, it was an insult. Mary grabbed the attention of the plant and politely asked her to move aside. The plant denied her. This rubbed Mary the wrong way. First men, and now plants where saying no to her. This was bullshit.

"I'm torching that plant," Mary said.

"What?" George and Michael, together.

"Babe, no," George groaned. "It's just going to try and strangle you."

Mary ignored him. She walked up steps and reached out to the vines. The plant ignited in bubble gum pink fire. Unfortunately, instead of burning to a crisp, the plant began to morph into something else. The vines latched to one other and began to wind together like a huge, thick rope. The magical fire seeped into the thing and bolstered the thing's magic. The plant grew thicker and longer. Unfairly so. Michael gripped his sword with both hands. Mary shot a nasty look at Michael before the creature opened its mouth.

*

The roar reverberated through the school, and Drusilla smiled at her own cunning. Mary would be frustrated enough to set fire to the magic. Way to wake the dragon. She giggled to herself and pushed the lunchroom doors open. Candles burned and dribbled wax on to the wide circle of salt and chalk. The witch stood in the middle, her back to the fairy. Drusilla's plan was coming together perfectly. How nice, she thought, as she let the heavy door close behind her.

"You sicced a Snap Dragon on your own friends," said the witch. "How diabolical of you."

"The kids call it savage. Isn't that just delicious?" Drusilla smiled. Then, she took a few steps closer to the figure. "Little Bo Peep lost her sheep..."

"I ate them." Peep turned to look at Drusilla. The dark skirts of her gown smudged the salt and chalk as they swirled to right themselves. The outfit was crowned by a thick ruff of dark feathers.

"Very clever," Drusilla praised. "Tell me, when I began teaching you magic, did you always plan on stabbing me in the back, or only after I told you my clever little plan?"

"It was clever," Peep said, "but I thought trapping you in your own hellish plan and slowly feasting on all you knew would be a little more clever."

"speaking of which. Witch?" Drusilla giggled. "Where do you have Mrs. Gooseberry squirreled away?"

*

The green leafy monster raised her long neck and spewed a long torrent of pink flame. She lifted her massive front legs and slammed them down with a rumble. Her red berry eyes narrowed, and her massive wings expanded. Michael pushed George's wooden frame back a step and stood between the dragon and his friends. They were pretty fucked, Michael thought. Nice job, Drusilla. If he managed to get everyone out alive, Drusilla would be in the doghouse for so long.

The dragon swung her long neck like a massive flail. Michael bumped his friends back and then swung his sword at the dragon's neck. His sword came back sticky with sap. The thick purple substance ran down the blade like molasses. He tried to flick his blade clean, but to no avail. The dragon roared and her neck swung the other way. Again Michael swung his sword, but the sap slowed his strike. Both he and his blade went flying into the grass.

Hitting the ground felt like being gut punched ten times

over. The dragon loomed over him. Michael looked up to see the large, flat feet coming down and he rolled. The dragon's feet met ground with a thud that reverberated through Michael like a shock wave.

Vines! Long and green, shot from the ground at Mary's command. She stepped between Michael and the dragon. The vines began to sink in and meld with the dragon's flesh. "Michael. Take George and go inside the school."

"Um, or no," George snarled.

"Ha! Good sass, baby," Mary teased. "Really though, you and Michael go get my sister."

"Mary, no-" George began, but Mary cut him off with her lips. The dragon bristled a little.

"I love you. Like, for real love with feelings and shit." Mary kissed him again. "He's going to need your help in there."

"Babe, this is crazy."

"I know that. I also know I can handle a simple Snap Dragon." She gave him a wide smile. "Now, grab Michael and drag his hairy ass into that school. I'll catch up soon."

*

"Well, you almost had it." Drusilla produced a carpetbag from thin air and dropped it on the floor. A snap of Drusilla's fingers and the carpetbag opened.

"If it weren't for that damn Prince," Peep agreed. "I should have known taking Jack would lead to this."

"Princes always get in the way. I told you that," Drusilla said.

"Well, it can't be helped now," Peep said in her teacher's voice. "What nasty trick do you have in that bag?"

"Butterflies." Drusilla's smile turned vicious as she unleashed her construction paper butterflies on Peep.

They flew at her like a swarm of angry bees. Paper wings sliced through flesh and came back bloody. Peep screamed and batted away the swarm as best she could. It was not helpful. Drusilla smiled at the inflamed paper cuts. The swarm fought on, and one by one the wet little things fell, blood-drenched to the floor. It lasted only a few minutes, but by the end, all the paper butterflies were wet on the floor, and the battle had begun.

Peep – who was covered in hundreds of tiny, inch-long paper cuts – gathered her strength. Drusilla let her. Then, Peep unleashed a cascade of magic fire from her hands. The ruby red bursts came crashing towards Drusilla. With a wave of Drusilla's hand, the fire swerved around and crashed into a wall. Her wide mouth turned up in a toothy smile. Her black eyes sparkling like two wet beetles in the rain. She took a step towards Peep. Peep waved her hands in a large circular pattern, and the fire came back around. Drusilla screamed as the fire licked her side. She flapped her wings furiously to get away from the flames.

Drusilla got a face full of black feathers. The things fluttered slowly to the ground. Drusilla looked up to see Peep hold a glowing magenta crystal in her hand. There was where she kept Mrs. Gooseberry. Peep flicked the crystal in her hand. At once, the feathers came to life. Darting around wildly. It was Drusilla's turn the flail about while her wet paper butterfly charms beat their wings furiously, trying to shake off the heavy blood. The quills jabbed sharply into Drusilla's flesh. They ripped and scribbled agony into her skin. Hiding her face with her hands, Drusilla joined in on the wing beating. The gusts she created only helped a little as the sharp, little feathers stuck quill side into her.

Drusilla whipped out her own fire. The purple green magic licked around her, burning the feathers to ash. Through the falling cinders, Drusilla advanced. Peep inclined her head and brought her hand up in a lashing motion. Pain ripped from Drusilla's left shoulder to her right hip. The wound bled in gushes. Peep smiled and brought her hand up for another fey lash spell. Drusilla and her paper butterflies charged. Peep countered the move and lashed fire around them.

Not wanting to lose butterflies, Drusilla pulled them back. She grabbed Peep's fire hand, and they struggled with the fire. Peep waved the crystal in Drusilla's face to throw her off balance. Drusilla socked a quick sucker punch into Peep's side and her hand collided with the metal ribs of Peep's corset. Her knuckles cracked painfully. Peep's stream of fire halted and her newly free hand joined the melee.

Both witches wound up on the ground. Each attempting to roll over top the other for dominance. Peep grabbed a handful of Drusilla's stubby hair and pulled. Drusilla laughed and sank a fist into Peep's jaw. The glowing magenta crystal skittered away. Peep retaliated with a head-butt. She scrambled on top of Drusilla and pulled a tiny dagger from the folds of her gown. She plunged the very sharp tip into Drusilla's soft underbelly. Drusilla screamed.

*

George and Michael ran through the halls. Where could they be? The sound of battle sounded like it was coming from everywhere, and nowhere at once. Michael hooked a left. George followed and skidded to a stop next to Michael. Hundreds of dead students shambled around. Some were fresher than others. The scent nearly made George gag. They were screwed, George thought. Thank you, Drusilla, for flipping out and making us come get you.

"Um... well. I have a sword," Michael said, sounding supremely unconcerned. "Where does this hallway lead, anyway? It all looks the same in the dark."

"The lunchroom," George answered. "Though, let me go check something really quick." George was off. Fading through the halls as fast as he could, and yep. He faded back. "Yep. Every hallway that leads to the lunchroom is overrun."

"Well, shit," Michael sighed. "I guess we could burn the building down."

"The school is literally made of cinder blocks," George sighed. Then, boom! It hit him. "I think I know what to do." George transformed into a wooden doll. "Get that sword handy."

They rushed. George buffered back the undead where he could, and Michael went to work lopping off heads where he could. It was working for a little bit. They were halfway dealt with when it happened. The things started to reform. Michael groaned and began chopping harder and faster. George took a hold of Michael, and they zoomed off. Unfortunately, the undead's magic began to beat against George's power. Each step felt like a mile. George pushed through as hard as he could, but he was just running out of steam. They collapsed. The undead moved in for the kill. George shielded Michael as best he could, but Michael screamed, and the scent of blood drove the creatures mad with hunger.

Thinking fast, George flipped Michael onto his stomach and laid on top. “Crawl!” Michael did. He crawled, and George added a little of his magic to speed up the trip. It wasn't a zoom, but it helped a little. “Okay, we're almost out. When I say go, dump me and make a run for it.”

“Dude, what?”

“Damnit, Prince! Do you want your ladylove or not? I'm made of wood. Once they figure out what happened, you'll be long gone. Okay?”

“Okay,” Michael agreed, “but you aren’t allowed to die on me.”

“You're the one that got bitten by zombies. You're probably dead already.”

“Nah. In the movies it burns or something. These just feel like scratches.”

“I hope so because...” and George rolled off. “Go!”

*

Michael crashed through the lunchroom doors, sword in hand and stopped. Drusilla sat there in the bloody carnage of the witch. Peep’s mangled face was still recognizable. Drusilla was bathing in peeps entrails. Her two large, almond-shaped eyes twinkled at Michael as her very wide, blood-smeared mouth stretched. Michael took a step towards her. Drusilla's smile relaxed into a scowl. Her angular eyebrows met in the middle. She raised her hand, and twiddled her knobby fingers. Wet and bloody, the paper butterflies began to flap their wings as fast as a hummingbird’s.

“It's over, baby,” Michael soothed.

One of the paper butterflies took off quick as a shot. Michael's cheek stung as the paper wing sliced past. Michael gritted his teeth and took another step. Another paper butterflies, another cut, and another step. Michael struggled through the butterflies and took the paper cuts. The pain was incredible, but he pushed forward. The butterflies were dropping, weighed down by fresh blood. Michael looked down as the last paper cutout fell. Their wings began beating faster again. The hum came from all around.

"You should go," Drusilla said.

"Not without you," Michael said.

The butterflies flew! Michael dodged and rolled, but Drusilla was on him, raking at him with her claws. Michael kicked, and Drusilla fell back. She unfurled her bug-like wings and stabilized herself. Michael hopped to his feet and ran at her. Drusilla's foot came up and around in a graceful reverse windmill kick. Michael dodged and lunged with his sword arm. Drusilla leaned back, missing the pommel of the sword in one fluid motion. She grabbed Michael's sword arm with both hands. Michael used his strength to pull her in. His free arm went to her back. The flat of the blade pressed against her throat. Drusilla's wings flapped frantically, but Michael was too heavy. She went limp, panting from the exertion.

"Go on then, Prince. Finish it." Drusilla's voice was raw. She leaned into the blade. Black blood ran down the length of the blade. "Do it."

"I love you. I'm not killing you," Michael said.

"No more tricks!" Drusilla breathed desperately. "What are you waiting for?"

"I'm waiting for you to catch some fucking sense," Michael replied. "You killed the witch. Thank you. Now, can we go home?"

"And where's home?"

"Wherever. Drusilla, baby, come on. We won. Snap out of this."

Drusilla shifted awkwardly. "I am the Witch, and you-"

"Baby, I don't care. I love you. I'm taking you out of this shit hole curse and we're riding off into the sunset like bosses."

Drusilla regarded him skeptically and attempted to claw Michael's face. Michael grabbed her wrist and forced it down by her side. The sword clattered to the ground. Drusilla's retaliation was a swift head-butt. Michael's brain rattled, but Drusilla was unable to break his hold on her. Next, came a knee to his side. Still, Michael held on. Wings buffeted around Michael, but still he was able to hold fast to her. Drusilla's roar was one of frustration. She sank - exhausted again - downward. Michael sank with her. They lay on the floor together, face to face.

"Please," Drusilla's voice shook. "Stop toying with me. I can't... I don't want you."

Sadness threatened to drown Michael's voice. "I don't believe you."

"I don't love you anymore."

"Alright then. You wanna be that way?" Michael pulled Drusilla with him as he sat up. He took one of her clawed hands in his and gently positioned it around his throat. "If you don't love me, then there's no point in living."

"Don't do this," Drusilla whispered.

"It's your choice," Michael whispered. "If you don't love me, then it's an easy win for you."

Drusilla's black eyes faltered and a glimmer of the purple irises showed through. Michael watched and waited. "I love you, Drusilla. I'm not living without you."

"Stop saying that!" But her voice was thicker, lower. Less brassy.

"Okay." Michael rested his forehead against hers. "Then can we rest for a little."

"What?" Drusilla yanked her face away. It was less lavender now and more moon pale. "What are you up to?"

"I'm exhausted, Drusilla," Michael answered honestly. Her purple eyes fluttered back tears. "Just will you let me hold you one last time?"

"Ew, on this dirty floor?" Drusilla bristled. "Are you trying to get sick?"

"Well, I don't have the energy to get up and find us a better place to sleep."

"Ha! Finally," Drusilla laughed. "I've exhausted you for once, and here I thought... oh." Drusilla slipped away from him. Michael watched her crumple. It was just a little bit, but there was a little scrunch of a hurt feelings face in there. Instinctively, Michael made to scoot in, but she held up a stubby hand. The pink patches burned her cheeks. She looked away. "Well, bravo. You got me to drop my defenses." She stood and made her way over to the sword. Lifting it up, she moved casually over to Michael and plopped down beside him. Then, she put the sword in his hand and pressed the blade against her neck again. "You win."

Michael lowered his sword hand and let the sword clatter to the ground. Drusilla's mournful eyes followed the movement. Michael skidded the sword away, and Drusilla's eyes widened. Then, he pulled her in. "Cool. I win. Kiss me-"

An enormous crash resounded through the school. A wall from the outside crumbled, and the roar of a dragon reverberated through the cafeteria. The Snap Dragon came bounding, and Michael had just flung his sword away. What the actual-

"Get some!" Mary roared from atop the dragon. George clung on to Mary for dear life. "Oh! So... it looks like the fights over. Well... I got a dragon now, Bitches!"

Drusilla's eyes were even wider than Michael thought they could be. She sagged in his arms. "Mary tamed the snap dragon."

"It appears that way," Michael murmured in her ear.

"I quit," Drusilla said, sounding exactly like her old self again. "I can't. I'm closing my eyes for whatever amount of time. Do whatever you want. You win. I quit."

"Hey, same team-" Michael began, but she was already snuggling up against him. Her eyes closed. He bent down and kissed her scalp. Drusilla scowled and popped an eye open to peep at him. Michael kissed the eye closed. A smile played on Drusilla's dark, little mouth.

*

Drusilla opened her eyes. A thunk sound had woken her. Her blurry vision fixed on an orange glowing rectangle. Something flitted in its center. Drusilla had to blink a couple of times to realize that she was staring at a gas pump. The orange counter was telling her how much gas was being pumped into the car for how much money. Her body ached, though the passenger seat was comfortable. Drusilla sat up and arched her back. The driver's side door opened and Michael deposited a plastic bag full of goodies. He looked at her and smiled.

"Hey," he said softly. "How are you-"

"No!" Drusilla cried. Michael's face and arms were littered with scabbed over scratches. "What did I do to you? What did I do?"

Michael slipped into the cab and pulled her in. Drusilla sobbed into his neck. Michael held her and made little shushing sounds. Unforgivable, she thought, as Michael rocked her. It was ripping through her. The events of her awaking, and the deaths that followed it. The pain and the darkness she felt. It was intoxicating. It was like watching unspeakable acts in first person while being jacked up on crank. The withdrawal was a bitch.

"Why did you let me do that to you?" Drusilla moaned. "Why didn't you kill me?"

"Because I love you," Michael replied.

"You should have killed me," Drusilla sobbed. "You should have-"

"No!" Michael barked. He pulled her face up. "Drusilla, look at me. I don't give a fuck what happened. I love you."

"I went nuts."

"Shit happens," Michael retorted.

"So, you don't care that I killed?" Drusilla demanded.

"Not a flying fuck do I give," Michael answered.

"I didn't just kill the witch. If I freak out again, or-"

"Then, I'll be there," Michael cut her off and bent in.

"So, should I go?" Mary asked from the back seat. "If not, can you toss back the popcorn? This little soap opera isn't going to watch itself."

Drusilla looked back at her sister. She didn't really want Mary hearing that, but when did anything go right? Drusilla sighed and went back to looking at the gas pump. It stopped with a thud, and Michael went around to pull out. Mary munched happily on her popcorn. Drusilla didn't know what she was going to do. The sickening sweet scent of imitation butter hit Drusilla's nostrils and she gagged. Mary began to hum.

"You're gutting your insides with that crap."

"I like it," Mary answered and munched some more.

"Did I hurt you?" Drusilla asked.

"Oh, please." Mary rolled her eyes. "So you tried to feed me to a dragon..."

"I'm sorry." Drusilla turned to look at her.

"Oh, whatever. I got a new pet out of it." Mary held out her wrist. A thick, green vine spiraled down her forearm.

"You know you can't keep her," Drusilla sighed.

"Oh no, Bitch. Not after what you pulled." Mary's eyes narrowed. "I get to keep her, and you aren't going to say another word about it."

"Mary I-"

"I've named her Tank and she's adorable!" Mary roared. "She's my dragon now. You should have known better than to throw a plant-based dragon at me. You dumb Bitch."

"I didn't know they would turn into that," Drusilla lied.

"Bullshit," Mary called.

The backdoor opened. "Okay, cookies, soda, hot dogs- oh, Drusilla's up. Hey."

"Damnit, George!" Drusilla scolded. "You can't just feed Mary junk food. She's like a gold fish. She'll never stop."

"And a sprout wrap for you." George held out the wrap for Drusilla to take.

"Oh, good. George, give Mary the sprout wrap and take all that crap back," Drusilla ordered.

"No, Babe, give me my food. Drusilla here." Mary grabbed the plastic covered sprout wrap and tossed it at Drusilla. "Eat your damn sprout wrap. You need to shut up for a minute."

Michael hopped back into the driver's seat. A condiment smothered hotdog in his hand. Drusilla watched in horror as Michael devoured the monstrosity in one bite. She looked back out the window. They're all going to live short, chemical-ridden lives, she thought darkly. Her eyes scanned the unknown countryside. Defiantly not within the borders of Elderberry. Well, that was something. Doors shut and seatbelts clicked. Michael started the car, and off they went into the darkness. Everyone munched along happily. Michael's hand slipped into Drusilla's, and hot tears wet her face. By the time dawn hit, George and Mary had fallen asleep in the back.

“Are we going to stop somewhere?” Drusilla whispered. “You have been driving for hours.”

“Soon,” Michael promised.

“Okay.” Drusilla turned back to look at the landscape.

“Thank you for choosing me,” Michael said, as quietly as possible.

“Dork,” Drusilla accused. Then, she paused. She watched her human looking face in the window’s reflection. “I'm going to spend the rest of my life making up for what I've done to you.”

“Or, you could just love me,” Michael replied as they drove past a stretch of skyscrapers.

“Is that New York?” Mary asked in a sleepy voice.

“Yep,” Michael answered. “We'll be there in a few hours.”

“There where?” Drusilla asked.

“Philadelphia,” Michael said with a sly smile.

“What?” Drusilla's eyes narrowed.

“Mary said it was your favorite,” Michael said. “It'll be a few hours if you want to nap some more.”

“Fine.” Drusilla scowled. Then, she stopped. “I do love you, you know.”

“I love you, too.”

Epilogue

The bell rang. All the students began packing up for the day. Drusilla stood and joined in the packing up. Their professor, a large trans-woman with long, red hair and a love of black velvet, began handing out papers to students on their way out. Her Potions professor wasn't the only transgender person at this school. A few of her classmates were trans women as well. It was nice not being the odd one out. Her professor's fluffy black cat watched Drusilla as she finished packing. Drusilla made her way to the door, the cat's lavender eyes never leaving her. Drusilla was even with the desk now. The professor handed out Drusilla's paper. Red ink scrawled over the cover page. Drusilla knew there would be a lot of red marks on all the pages.

"Mrs. Prince."

"Yes, Ms. Moon," Drusilla answered.

"B plus. Not bad."

Drusilla took the paper gratefully. "Thank you."

"Work a little harder and you could pull an A next time," Ms. Moon mentioned. Her cat's eyes narrowed in Drusilla's direction.

"Sure." Drusilla paused. "Do you know-"

"Mrs. Prince, we are doing everything we can to get your friend out of that imprisonment crystal. It's going to take a little time, but we will set her free."

"Okay," Drusilla said.

"See you Tuesday."

Drusilla walked through the halls along with the other girls. She made her way to her wooden locker and opened it with ease. She plopped her books in for the night, touched up her black lipstick in the locker mirror, and shut the door. Mary's musical voice could be heard reverberating through the halls. She and her gaggle of friends came up to Drusilla. All of them chewing on what looked like twigs.

"What do you have in your mouths?" Drusilla scolded.

"Ms. Melissa taught us how to make honey licorice out of honey mead and anise root." Mary held out an extra twig for Drusilla.

Drusilla plucked it from Mary's fingers with her teeth. "How did you do on your paper? I got a B."

"Ms. Moon gave me a D," Mary groaned. "Can you believe that shit?"

"Yes, I can," Drusilla sighed.

"She's the worst," Mary whined. "She's so strict, it's like there are two of you now."

"We *are* both trans," Drusilla replied. "Ready to go home?"

"*Oh* put it back in the deck. That's not what I meant," Mary groaned. "Anyway. Yeah, I'm starving. You cooking?"

"Yes, Mary, I'm cooking. I'm always cooking," Drusilla sighed.

"Can we order pizza?" Mary begged. "Please?"

Drusilla rolled her eyes again and walked past brick and white walls with wood trim. Past portraits of long dead witches and twisted gardens, towards the large wooden door. Mary was hot on Drusilla's heels yowling at her like a hungry cat. Drusilla pulled the heavy metal ring and slipped out into the graffiti ridden alleyway. Mary stepped out after. Drusilla turned and with a wave of her hand, the door melted into the filthy wall. She looked up at the buildings and modern towers that hid the school. It was a neat bit of magic. Drusilla would figure it out someday, but for now, she was content with her B.

"The boys are here," Mary announced.

Drusilla turned to see Hel pull up. George and Michael hopped out in their suits. Mary's butt wiggled in her mustered yellow, and shit brown pleated skirt. She was getting chubby,

Drusilla noticed. Michael's arms wound around Drusilla, and she turned into the Michael's waiting lips. It was so easy to just let herself be happy here. Michael pulled away and smiled down at her.

"How's my college girl doing?" Michael asked.

"Fine. I got B in Potions," Drusilla replied. "How was your day?"

"Awesome. I love being my own boss," Michael answered.

"Agreed," added George. "Much nicer then the bosses we never had to deal with in the past."

"Now, Babe" Michael said, ignoring George's sarcasm "how do you want to celebrate this B?"

"With pizza!" Mary cheered.

"Opportunist," Drusilla accused.

"Pizza sounds good though," George agreed.

"Can we at least make the pizza?" Drusilla offered. "We have so many tomatoes from Mary's garden."

Michael's lips found their way into Drusilla's hair. She leaned into him. "Whatever you want, Darling. It's your B."

ABOUT THE AUTHOR

D. H. Torkavian was born in the dead of winter under the auspicious sign of the quarter moon. Most of her family was woefully unprepared for the baby bundle of transgender realness. Her Mummum was the only one who understood her growing up. At a young age Mummum taught her the finer points of being a proper Norwegian house wife and witchcraft. All of this was done in secret. Her childhood was split between New Jersey and California as her Mummum fell ill.

When Mummum died, D.H. Torkavian was devastated. At the age of 12, D.H. Torkavian began writing to cope with the loss, despite not being able to read or write. Despite this hurdle, D.H. Torkavian pressed on and was eventually published in her high school newspaper and literary magazine. In college she was a top editor and contributor for her college literary magazine, Rewrites. D.H. Torkavian has also been a contributor for The Press of Atlantic City, Heaven Sent Gaming, and The Geek Initiative.

D.H. Torkavian currently holds court in coffee shops in the Pacific North West. She is often found drinking hot chocolate and hoping for rain.

www.ingramcontent.com/pod-product-compliance
Lightning Source LLC
LaVergne TN
LVHW010612100826
845148LV00014B/2927
9781735227306